PRAISE FC

"*Amber Wolf* is enjoyable as a narrative, edifying as history, and inspirational as a story of struggle, survival, and ethnic pride—the David of Lithuania is caught between the twin Goliaths of Russia and Germany. What can a young girl do? You'd be surprised."
—Steve O'Connor, author of *The Witch at Rivermouth* and *The Spy in the City of Books*

"Captivating. *Amber Wolf* is a compelling story of bold resistance in the face of insurmountable odds. Wong skillfully paints a portrait of the hidden and mostly forgotten people who struggled to survive behind the front lines of the cataclysm of World War II."
—Guntis Goncarovs, author of *Telmenu Saimnieks – The Lord of Telmeni* and *Convergence of Valor*

"*Amber Wolf* is a compelling story that captures the brutal truth along with fictitious elements of Lithuania in World War II. Before my parents passed, I listened to countless hours of stories just like this and the reasons why they fled their beloved homeland. Bravo to Ludmelia for never giving up!"
—Daina Irwin, daughter of Lithuanian survivors

"In *Amber Wolf*, Ursula Wong turns an unflinching yet sympathetic eye on a brutal slice of history. Compelling and engrossing, and almost impossible to put down."
—Leigh Perry, author of the *Family Skeleton Series*

"Ursula Wong takes on a heavy subject: the grass roots of World War II—not of large-scale mass destruction, but of hand-to-hand combat, villager against soldier, deep in the forests of Lithuania. Ludmelia Kudirka is a girl who must quickly grow up if she wants to survive and ultimately fight for her people, her land, and her freedom. In *Amber Wolf*, Wong gives us a story complexly woven, yet easy to follow, and impossible to forget."
—Stacey Longo, Pushcart Prize-nominated author of *Ordinary Boy*

"*Amber Wolf* is a trek into territory that, seventy years after the dramatic events enacted there, still remains largely unexplored. Ursula Wong, using new source material and careful research, has crafted a harrowing, heroic, and at times poetic, tale of people caught up in the cataclysms of war."
—David Daniel, author of *The Skelly Man* and *The Marble Kite*

## Other works by Ursula Wong

*Amber Wolf (The Amber War Series Book 1)*

*Amber War (The Amber War Series Book 2)*

*Purple Trees*

*The Baby Who Fell From the Sky*

### With other Authors

*Insanity Tales*

*Insanity Tales II: The Sense of Fear*

*Insanity Tales III: Seasons of Shadow: A Collection of Dark Fiction*

Ursula is available for speaking events and lectures on writing and publishing. For more information, contact her at urslwng@gmail.com and sign up for her popular Reaching Readers newsletter at http://ursulawong.wordpress.com.

# Amber Widow

Ursula Wong

Genretarium Publishing ~ Chelmsford, MA

Copyright © 2018 Ursula Wong

Genretarium Publishing, Chelmsford, MA

Cover Design by Allyson Longueira

Cover Photography Copyright: https://www.123rf.com/profile_edoma14 / 123RF
Stock Photo

Map courtesy pixabay.com

ISBN-10: 1727059441
ISBN-13: 978-1727059441

For more information about the author and her works, go to:

http://ursulawong.wordpress.com

First printing, August, 2018
1 3 5 7 9 10 8 6 4 2

*To Sue.*

The death of one man is a tragedy. The death of millions is a statistic.

*—Joseph Stalin*

# ACKNOWLEDGMENTS

I'd like to thank everyone who graciously supported this project: Dale T. Phillips, Melinda Phillips, Winona W. Wendth, Joyce Derenas, Ester Czekalski, Sally Cragin, Ray Slater, Paula Castner, Claudia Decker, Daina Irwin, Susan Fleet, Ieva Grauslys, Maria Egle Calabrese, and Jonas Studnzia, president of the Lithuanian Patriot's Society. I'd also like to thank the following organizations for their support and kindness: LABAS of Nashua, NH, the South Boston Lithuanian Club, the Corpus Christi Parish in Lawrence, MA, the Charles Zylonis Trust, Maironis Park in Shrewsbury, MA, and the St. Peter Lithuanian Parish in South Boston. I'd also like to thank the New Hampshire Writers' Project, the Seven Bridge Writers' Collaborative, and my dear friends in the Storyside.

I'd like to thank the staff of WMG Publishing, Dean Wesley Smith, Gwyneth Gibby, and especially Allyson Longueira.

I'd like to thank the Radak family for the laughs.

A special thanks to Genretarium Publishing for tremendous support from a small but exquisite staff. Thanks for sticking with me.

Finally, my deepest thanks to my family, Steve and Steph, who tolerate me at my worst when I'm trying to do my best.


Ursula Sinkewicz Wong
August, 2018
Chelmsford, Massachusetts

# PREFACE

Set generally around the year 2020, *Amber Widow* is the third in a series of novels about the relationship between Lithuania and Russia, bringing the history of the first two books to a fictitious next step.

The series starts with *Amber Wolf*, which tells of the early and powerful days of a resistance movement during WWII, when farmers and office workers take up stolen weapons to fight the Soviet army from camps in the woods.

*Amber War*, the second novel in the series, tells of the situation in Lithuania a few years after the war ends. The US is at peace and our soldiers are home. Europe is beginning to rebuild, but partisans in Eastern Europe continue their resistance war against Soviet occupiers. Lithuanian guerilla tactics incite Russian leaders to explore new strategies, including ordering Soviet spies to infiltrate the partisan camps. As living conditions deteriorate, the population begins to accept that the West isn't going to rescue them from Soviet dominance, and the tide turns. People begin leaving the resistance, even though the desire for autonomy from Communist rule remains a strong driving force.

Before the breakup of the Soviet Union, Lithuania declares independence, and immediately makes strides to enter the western world. It joins NATO and the EU for the necessary alliances to help protect its sovereignty.

*Amber Widow* portrays modern-day Lithuania, inspired by the true theft of uranium from the Chernobyl-style Ignalina Nuclear Power Plant in eastern Lithuania during the 1990s. To this day, it remains unclear whether all of the uranium has been recovered. Central to *Amber Widow* is a fictitious Russian coup through which a ruthless new leader increases the military threat level in Eastern Europe. Fearful that war might be imminent, a desperate band of radicals enacts a plan to detonate a nuclear device to force NATO's hand, ensuring their freedom at the expense of a neighboring country's safety.

The word Soviet may have been used less frequently in Lithuania toward the 1990s and after. However, I use the term to refer to the time prior to the breakup of the USSR. As the novel spans decades, I hope this helps ground the reader.

TP508 is a real drug that proved an effective countermeasure to the workers at the Fukushima power plant during the meltdown in 2011. Z-109 is a fictional and powerful predecessor to TP508.

Lithuania has a FedEx office in Vilnius, and excellent internet service.

The Annie program and Sagus Corporation are fictional, but work is moving forward on the Nord Stream 2 pipeline that may eventually pump

Russian gas into the European grid. The nuclear power plant in Belarus, some forty kilometers from the Lithuanian border, is real and under construction.

Baltic Watch is a fictional organization. ARAS, the Lithuanian Police Anti-terrorist Operations Unit, is real.

Names of cities, towns, and people have the same omission of ligatures and diacritics from the Lithuanian language as is the case in the previous novels. This makes the reading experience smoother for American readers while keeping the flavor of the original language. I've italicized those non-English words, whose meaning should be clear from the context.

For those who wish to read more on topics covered in the novel, I've included a biography at the back of the book, along with a list of *Amber Widow* characters. A map provides the general area where the *Amber Widow* story takes place.

# MAP OF THE BALTIC AREA

From the *Nuclear Monitor Issue #400-401*

05/11/1993

"Smuggling of radioactive material escalating"

*In Western Europe the list of Eastern European- and former Soviet-origin nuclear materials includes osmium, niobium, scandium, californium, cobalt, deuterium, cesium, strontium, natural uranium in the form of U308 (yellowcake), milligrams of plutonium in smoke detectors, and pelletized UO2 enriched up to 5% U-235. Most of the [smuggling] cases involve small quantities of materials; a few involve lager amounts. For instance, in Lithuania criminal investigation agencies are now investigating reports that seven metric tons (!) of manufactured fuel from Ignalina [are] missing.*

# CHAPTER 1

## Ignalina Nuclear Power Plant, eastern Lithuania—1990

Boris thought of his mother as he backed his off-road vehicle, a dented Lada, up to the loading platform at INPP. She had a place to live in the apartment block, food, and plenty of heat from the snake of pipes that provided steam all the way from the reactor to town. But she needed medicine, and the only way to get it was on the black market. So Boris needed money. Desperately. And fast.

Train tracks bordered the loading platform where Boris waited, the perfectly straight lines extending from the power plant to the storage facilities and beyond. Outside lights hung to the left and right of his position, providing cones of illumination and areas of shadow for the Lada to blend in, so that anyone passing through the long glass-walled corridor from the administration building to the reactors wouldn't notice. Or so he hoped. He looked over his shoulder. No one was watching from inside, not even Misha, another Russian guard, who should be on break. Boris felt a drop of sweat run down the side of his face, and wiped it away with an unsteady hand.

He watched the oversized loading dock door, glancing back at the brightly lit corridor every few seconds. He couldn't help himself. If another guard caught him, he was to say he had a message for his friend Tomas that his girlfriend was at home waiting and anxious. The men would laugh, and Boris would be told to move along. The worst that would likely happen was a reprimand in the morning by his supervisor, for people working inside weren't to be disturbed. More likely, Boris would be mocked. He was often mocked by the other guards. After all, he had no wife, no prospects, and his best friend was his mother.

He flinched when the door opened to a massive interior space, dark and threatening. Tomas appeared dressed in the white work clothes they all wore inside the facility. Boris got out of the vehicle and followed Tomas back in. The two men came out a moment later, carrying metallic suitcases that contained nuclear waste. They set them side by side in the Lada's trunk. They went inside two more times, for a total of six suitcases. When they were done, they covered them with an old blanket and closed the trunk.

After a brief nod, Tomas went inside. Boris glanced up, noticing the top edge of a door that was opening at the far end of the glass-walled corridor. He considered waiting in the shadows, but couldn't risk being caught, not now. He started the Lada's engine, keeping the headlights off. He drove along the tracks as fast as he dared, crossing them to enter the parking lot containing the cars owned by the night shift workers. His gaze constantly went to the rearview mirror, his stomach in knots. Each moment seemed like forever until finally he was on the avenue leading to town.

He slowed down. At the sign with four smokestacks marking the entrance to *Ignalinos Atomine Elektrine*, he clicked on the headlights. *Four smokestacks, what a joke!* Construction of the third reactor had stopped, and plans for the fourth were scrapped after Chernobyl had blown up. Not that the Soviets cared what happened to the reactors here, but the world was watching.

Boris was sure Ignalina would be shut down soon. He would be out of work, and his mother would be even worse off. She'd be forced into the state-run clinics where cleanliness was a matter of opinion and medicine hard to obtain. He had no choice but to do this. Boris wiped his eyes with the back of a hand. He drove past the power lines and street lamps that brought a shine to the fat steam pipes lying alongside the road in a broad swath of land unnaturally devoid of trees.

He took a left at the four-way intersection and drove through the local town, passing the rows of identical apartment buildings where the workers at the power plant lived, and where Mother lay dying. He feared someone might be watching from the dark windows of the gas station. His speed increased. Twenty kilometers later, Boris was finally in the forest, outside the town of Visaginas. He turned onto the dirt road by the appointed marker, a tree that had been partially felled to form an upside down V.

Two kilometers down the bumpy road, he stopped the vehicle and cut the lights, his hands returning to the steering wheel. He flexed his fingers when they cramped, going back to their vise-like grip when the muscles relaxed. Fifteen minutes later, a light flashed through the trees once, then again. Boris shone his flashlight out the windshield, counted to three, and snapped it off. He got out of the Lada. It might be the Secret Police. It might be a trap. He could be dead in seconds. He stood with his hands in front of his crotch, quelling the urge to run.

Several men approached holding automatic rifles. More were probably hiding in the woods, ready to react if something wasn't right, if any little thing seemed out of place. They had probably been there all along, watching him. Boris's chest felt tight.

The tallest of the men advanced. His shoulders were slumped. A scarf covered his nose and mouth. Boris couldn't make out any features in the dark. It bothered him that he couldn't see the man's eyes.

An urgent whisper in the dark. "You have it?"

"Suitcases in the back," said Boris.

The tall man motioned to the others who opened the back of the vehicle and took out the six suitcases, lying them in a neat row on the ground.

Boris knew that nuclear waste could be used to harm people, but he couldn't let himself give a damn what they did with it. He wouldn't care if they blew up the rest of the world. Just as long as Mother lived. That was all that mattered.

The tall man handed him a wrinkled envelope. Boris put it directly into his pocket, noting the bulk, but not daring to count the money inside. Even if they shorted him, he wasn't going to challenge half a dozen men with guns. He didn't know where these people had gotten the money to pay him. They had probably stolen it. He didn't care.

Boris stared at the man and swallowed hard. "Will you need more?"

"We'll let you know."

Each man picked up a suitcase and walked into the trees. When they were gone, Boris climbed into the vehicle, slowly backing up in the glow from the Lada's taillights. He turned the vehicle around at a spot where the ditch wasn't so deep. At the paved road he stopped, opened the door, and vomited into the gully. After spitting out the sour residue from his mouth, Boris drove home to his mother.

~~

In 1992, Boris and Tomas stole again. This time it was a long, cylindrical rod filled with fresh nuclear fuel that they clamped to the Lada's undercarriage before driving off. Tomas was counting on proceeds from the sale to buy a house for his new bride.

Unfortunately, they didn't realize the fresh fuel was useless to weapons makers, and their attempts to find a buyer went unanswered. Acting on an anonymous tip, Lithuanian authorities found the rod dumped in a river near the border with Poland. Upon interrogation, Boris admitted to the theft, and was sent to prison.

After Boris's mother recovered from her illness, she spent the bulk of her days in the small apartment holding an icon of the Virgin Mother to her breast, praying for her son's timely release.

# CHAPTER 2

## Visaginas, eastern Lithuania—1992

Tilda Partenkas waited across from a row of Soviet-style apartment buildings with concrete walls covered in black decay. Clouds smothered the moon, making the broad avenue look ominously dark. Wearing a trench coat, jeans, and a cap hiding her gray curls, she felt less like a noted nuclear physicist and more like an outdated version of a Cold War spy. *Perhaps I am*, she thought, *although a little old for one.*

Lights in the windows went out for the night like monsters closing their eyes. An old man walked a dog along the other side of the street. *Is he watching me?* The dog raised its hind leg and urinated on a cement message board covered in graffiti. He sat on his haunches as the man lit a cigarette. A few minutes later, the man threw the butt down and they went inside. Tilda relaxed a notch and put her hands in the pockets of her coat.

A dull orange Audi pulled up next to her, and her heart beat faster. The driver stretched across the front seat and rolled down the passenger window. She recognized him as Darius, the man she had met a few days before. He was young, maybe twenty-five, with brown hair, and big eyes. He was extremely thin.

"I'm looking for Dominykas Simkus," he said. "Do you happen to know his apartment number?"

Tilda went to the car, leaning over to look inside the vehicle. Crumpled pages from a newspaper lay on the dashboard. Through the open window, she caught a smell of stale food. She used the passphrase indicating all was well. "He's at another location, but I'm going there now. Let me show you."

Darius unlocked the door. Tilda hesitated only a moment before getting in. The gears made a grinding sound as he shifted. They drove along the deserted boulevard, turning right at the next cross street. The smell of the food was stronger, making her feel sick. She opened the window a crack and took a deep breath. They went slowly toward another row of apartment buildings, driving between two of them onto another wide street. Tilda nervously clutched the door handle, sure the car was going to scrape against the walls, but it didn't. They traveled several kilometers in silence before Darius clicked the headlights on.

"Was anyone watching you?" said Darius. The fingers on his right hand tapped the steering wheel as he drove.

"No." Tilda folded her hands on her lap so Darius wouldn't see them shake. "Isn't the KGB out of the country by now?"

"We're a free and sovereign nation, but old habits are hard to break. There are plenty of Russians living in the area. Most of them work at the nuclear power plant. The KGB is gone, or so they say. It's been replaced by a new organization, the SVR, which is like a Russian CIA. And there are plenty of Russian soldiers here." Darius paused. "The apartment you're using is comfortable?"

"Yes, it's lovely inside. Your friend was kind to let me stay there."

"Are you sure no one was watching you?"

"There was a man with a dog. They went inside, though." Tilda leaned back against the fake leather upholstery, feeling the same fear she had forty-four years ago, when she and Mama had avoided patrols and bribed guards to get out of this country. What did this boy know of the old days and the real dangers? Soldiers could be out there in the dark, waiting to capture or shoot them.

"When you asked about what happened to your father, I checked with some people. The bastards killed him," said Darius.

Tilda turned away and stared out the window.

"When the Soviets realized you and your mother had escaped, they went after him. I'm sorry to tell you they kept Marius in prison for weeks. When he died, they left him outside a church in Utena, on the steps so everyone could see. That's what they're like, which is why we're asking you to help us." Darius's voice sounded strained and unnaturally high. "My father fought them, and they killed him, too."

Tilda dug her fingernails into the palm of her hand, trying to stop herself from trembling. All these years she had suspected the worst, for they had never heard from Papa again after that morning in 1948 when they left Utena. She *knew* he was dead. But Darius's words stabbed her heart for they removed the possibility that Papa had died peacefully in his sleep. For so many years she had longed to feel the gentle touch of Papa's hand on her cheek and hear the sound of his voice.

Darius turned onto a dirt road leading deeper into a forest. Tilda braced against the dashboard and held onto the door handle as the vehicle bounced over ruts. They stopped in front of two large bushes. A tall man came out from the dark and opened the door. Tilda got out.

"I'm from Baltic Watch," he said. "Jonas."

Tilda couldn't see his face, but had the impression from his slumped shoulders and slow movement that he was an older man. His posture reminded her of her late husband. She felt a little more at ease. "I'm not familiar with the group."

"We monitor and report on Soviet military activity that could indicate a pending invasion. We watch everything they do, and tell the people. Our members come from Latvia, Estonia, and Poland. But tonight it's just Darius and me."

While Darius drove the car in between the bushes, Jonas continued. "People know us from Baltic Watch, but they don't know that tonight we put our lives in your hands. My father was a partisan, and he fought side by side with your father against the Soviets. They trusted each other like brothers, and now I'm trusting you."

Tilda tucked her hands into the pockets of her trench coat, holding onto the vial of pills containing Z-109, the crowning accomplishment of both her and her husband's lives. She took a deep breath. The air smelled of pine. *What in hell have I gotten myself into?*

"You knew Papa?" She waited for Jonas to explain, but before he could, Darius joined them.

"I'm ready, Jonas," he said.

Jonas took Tilda's arm and led her through the trees. *These men have eyes like cats,* she thought, passing brushwood and low-hanging branches. Somehow her companions knew just when to duck, and when to hold her arm tighter so she wouldn't fall into a depression or trip over a root.

Eventually they came to a cabin. Dark windows indicated the place was either deserted or its inhabitants were asleep. Darius unlocked a padlock securing the door and went inside first, turning on a halogen lamp hanging from the low ceiling. He let the others in, closed the door, and stood just inside the threshold. He began pacing. Tilda looked around. Fishing poles leaned in a corner. On a table in front of a stone fireplace sat a stout metal container that looked like a squat suitcase, more square than rectangular, and a generous half meter in each dimension.

"Oh my God," said Tilda. She knew immediately what it was, as she had worked at the Three Mile Island Nuclear Generating Station in the United States before meeting her husband.

"We need to know if it's viable," said Jonas.

"This is from the power plant at Ignalina, isn't it?"

"Before the breakup, no one knew what *Glasnost* would mean for their families, just that it would change things. Everyone was willing to take risks. People made a point of looking the other way, making it possible to get away with things like never before. Let's just say the fall of the Soviet Union has been good for us in unexpected ways."

"This is crazy. The Russians must be searching for these."

"Of course. But they blamed the theft on a Russian guard at the power plant who admitted to it. The Russians are confident they'll find all the stolen material in due time, but we excel at hiding things." Jonas grinned. "After the breakup, our Russian friends have become fine entrepreneurs. If we'd waited, we could've just bought what we needed from the black market and saved ourselves all this trouble. You can get anything today, if you have money and know where to go."

Even his voice reminded her of Tilda's husband, gone now five years. Time had a way of passing slowly when you missed someone. Her shoulders were stiff. *Are there more containers like these buried in the woods?* She ran her hands over the metal. "The casing seems to be intact. Did you bring the Geiger counter?"

Jonas opened a gym bag hanging from a peg near the fireplace. He rifled through some clothing and pulled out the device. Tilda took it from him, turned it on, and held the probe to the container. It clicked a few times; nothing dangerous. She put the device down on the table and looked up at Jonas. His clothes were rumpled, as if he had slept in them. He had a kind face. Maybe she could trust him.

"If there were leakage, the Geiger counter would register it. If you're sure this contains nuclear material, it's well-protected and should be viable," said Tilda.

"Good," said Jonas.

"Of course you did what I just did, and saw for yourself. So why did you bring me here?"

Darius stopped pacing.

"I don't know what you're going to do. Take me back to the apartment, please," said Tilda.

"Help Darius build a bomb," said Jonas.

Tilda flinched, her mind racing. "What does he know about building a bomb?"

"He learned from his father."

"Absolutely not. It's too dangerous. Besides, I'm a physicist. What makes you think I know how to build a weapon? Get someone else. I'll have nothing to do with this." Tilda took a step toward the door.

Darius crossed his arms.

"There is no one else who can help us, only you." Jonas gazed down at her. He didn't look threatening, just sad.

"Are you forcing me?" said Tilda.

"You're the only one who can help us."

Tilda looked at the suitcase. "What would you do with it?"

"Nothing. It's just a precaution to keep the Soviets at bay. If they move to occupy our country again, we'll use this as a bargaining chip to keep them out."

"Why don't you just lie to them? They won't know if you have a bomb or not."

"It never ends well when you lie to the Soviets."

Tilda had to agree with that, at least. She shrugged. "Even if I were willing, I don't have the right components."

Jonas pulled a box out from under the table. He opened the lid to a collection of items including blasting caps, dynamite, and coils of wire. "We don't exactly have a Radio Shack at our disposal, but these should do."

9

Tilda shook her head. "This is insane. If they find out you're behind this, it'll be the end of your country," said Tilda.

"*Our* country," said Jonas. "You were born here, too."

"We'll be criminals. Terrorists."

"To our countrymen, we'll be heroes."

Darius cut in. "I told you what they did to your father. We should set it off in Moscow for what they did to him and all the rest."

Jonas gave him an angry look.

Tilda wiped her eyes. "I remember what it was like here after the war. Even now, I have nightmares."

"After WWII when the Soviets made it clear they weren't leaving, the West ignored our pleas for help," said Jonas. "They thought we were lying. *Lying!* We just want to be able to defend ourselves in case the Soviets come back. This is all we can do. We are few, and the Soviets have an almost unlimited number of men. We have no money and they have billions of rubles and the means to build whatever weapons they want. Until we join NATO and the EU, we have no defenses. We have to be ready, because there's only one thing we can be sure of."

"And what's that?"

"One day, the Russians will be back."

Tilda pressed her lips together as she fingered the vial in her pocket. If she were being honest, she had suspected something like this. It all added up: she being a nuclear physicist, the thefts at INPP, the secretive meeting with Darius two days ago. "It's only a precaution?"

"I give you my word no one will die. Will you do it?" Jonas put a hand gently on her shoulder. "Please."

Tilda took out the vial of pills. "This is what I developed with my husband: Z-109. The treatment from this medication keeps people from radiation poisoning. It protects the most vulnerable parts of the body: the brain, internal organs, and the gastrointestinal system. One day, we may develop it into a vaccine, or add it to public water supplies, or even spray it over crops. My life's work has been to keep people safe from the effects of radiation. Now you're asking me to terrorize them with a nuclear weapon that I build with my own hands."

"In a few years, maybe Russia will change, and we won't fear her as we do now. Help us secure the future for our children."

Tilda touched her cheek, almost feeling the whisper of Papa's last kiss. She had been fourteen years old; a mere child. Papa had stayed behind when she and Mama escaped so the Soviets wouldn't suspect they were gone. He had given his life to protect her, and they had tortured him to death.

"I remember how it was." She opened the vial and handed a pill to each of the men. "Take it." She dry-swallowed hers and got to work.

~~

Two days later, Dr. Tilda Partenkas walked into Vilnius's magnificent old Narutis Hotel in the heart of Old Town, carrying a bag in which was hidden the Order of Merit award she'd received an hour ago from the veritable head of state. All joy from her accomplishment in creating the anti-radiation drug was overshadowed by the nuclear device she had made in the woods. Z-109 wasn't available in mass quantities yet, and certainly not in Russia. If Jonas used the bomb, people would suffer the effects of radiation and die horrible deaths. And she would be the woman responsible.

Now, her countrymen waited to congratulate her. She had to bear it, for no one must know what she had done. She wondered what they might say if they did.

She took a deep breath, and entered a large room with mirrors on the dark paneled walls and paintings of old European cities, as elegant as the best hotels in London. The upholstered chairs were occupied by guests beaming their approval. Several tea carts were laden with delicacies, and wait staff stood stiffly, dressed in black, ready to serve.

When Tilda held up a red ribbon attached to a five-pointed cross of gold, she felt like a fraud. The audience erupted in cheers and applause. Some people jumped to their feet and went to honor her for what she had accomplished as a physicist, unaware that her most striking contribution to humanity might very well be the nuclear device she had assembled for Jonas and Baltic Watch.

# CHAPTER 3

## Almost Thirty Years Later
## Presidential Inauguration, Moscow—9 May

Vera Koslova headed for the Kremlin, where she was about to be sworn in as the first female president of the Russian Federation. She patted her prematurely white hair in a nervous habit. Then she put her hand down so as not to disturb the perfect coiffure. She tapped her fingers against the limousine's seat, trying for a measure of calm. She focused on the luxury around her; the soft feel of the seat, the smell of leather and a hint of men's aftershave. The car had been designed years ago for President Putin. Built in Russia, the sleek black car was magnificent, even obscene when compared to the stripped-down Ladas driven by those people who could barely even afford a car. That no luxury had been spared made the limousine seem like a microcosm of the society itself. Either you had everything or nothing. Today, Vera had everything, and she beamed with pride at her accomplishment.

Her husband Michael sat next to her, fidgeting with his shirt collar. "This is too tight. I'll be uncomfortable all day."

Vera tried to ignore him, a habit she hadn't quite perfected over the years of their marriage. At first, she had been attracted to Michael because he was handsome and charming. She'd stayed with him because he was useful. He had the uncanny ability to put people at ease. They confided in him. And he would tell her the secrets he had learned. She had profited a great deal from the gossip he painstakingly recalled from the people he had befriended.

He also played the part of devoted husband better than anyone. The public wanted to see an adoring husband at her side. It made her seem more traditional, even conventional. Perception was everything.

But all too soon she had found Michael boorish and without convictions, other than the antiquated belief that Russian men were superior to all creatures on earth. His opinion always matched that of his last conversation partner, and he knew very little of the world outside Russia. He was vain, taking far too much pleasure from the privileges she had acquired over the years; the private apartment, access to fine restaurants, shopping in special stores, and use of a car. Now even those were trumped by the spoils of her new position.

"President Fedov didn't look sick last time I saw him, but you can never tell with the elderly," said Michael. "I still can't believe he named you his successor, my beloved. But even with what's going on in Novosibirsk, I think you'll do a fine job. After all, there are many experienced men among your advisors, and in the security council. They will help you. You're sure to be effective. But as the first woman President of Russia, you shouldn't take any risks."

That very morning, the riots in Novosibirsk had blossomed from mere anticorruption dissent into cries to oust Vera Koslova, just hours from being sworn in. While local police were containing the situation, someone had detonated a bomb. Fifteen people had died in the blast. Over three hundred were injured. The fleeing crowd had crushed a small child to death. Five hundred people were arrested. Soon to be ex-President Fedov had sent in troops to maintain order.

"I pray President Fedov has a long, contented retirement. He's been my friend and mentor for years. It shouldn't surprise people that he selected me to carry out the rest of his term," said Vera.

In hours, she would be the most powerful woman in the world, but being the target of today's demonstrations had unsettled her to the core. It showed that people in Novosibirsk would rather die than accept her as their president.

"Everyone says Prime Minister Grinsky expected the position," said Michael, tugging at his tie.

"Grinsky's an idiot."

"But he's not the only one who was surprised. After all, the riots . . ."

"Riots are acts of terrorism. I don't care if it's directed at me as a woman taking power, or if people object to my politics. In any case, they were crimes against the state, and I will deal with the perpetrators quickly and harshly."

"Yes, my beloved."

"Even more than that, the families of the dead and wounded are suffering. Imagine what the parents of that poor dead child are experiencing. No one is immune from terrorism, and I won't allow it to tear the country apart."

"You'll find the people who did this." Michael patted his wife's hand.

"Unfortunately, I think many are like you, and not ready to accept a woman as leader. We'll find the criminals behind this, certainly. But right now, I have to deal with public opinion, and that can be a complicated matter."

"I think you'll be a fine leader. Just let the men take care of business; your old friends at the FSB, your inner circle, the military. I'm sure even Grinsky will help. They'll settle things and return our country to a sense of safety. After that, all you have to do is let things go on as usual for two years, until the elections. God willing, it will be a time of peace. Afterward, you and I can take a long vacation."

Vera reached over and took his chin in her hand. "The people need to see a dutiful husband at my side today."

"Of course."

Easing past the brick walls surrounding the Kremlin, the car, surrounded by a phalanx of motorcycles flashing their lights, drove along a street devoid of vehicles and people. The motorcade turned left at Saint Basil's Cathedral, finally coming to a stop at the Grand Kremlin Palace, its white exterior resplendent in the May sun, the troops of the Kremlin Regiment lined up in perfect order to greet her.

Michael got out of the limousine first, offering his hand to help her from the car. The red carpet extended to the edge of the walkway. Vera's feet wouldn't touch pavement. The heels she wore were higher than her usual two-inch pumps. She'd had to practice walking in them to avoid tripping, but they heightened her stature and made her appear more regal. She wore a long dress with white ermine trim around the neck that matched her hair, a sharp divergence from her usual business attire. She wanted to impress.

She stepped out of the car, passing Michael and making her way up the steps and through the massive door, down the long hallway past a line of soldiers in dress uniform. Golden doors opened to an ornate room full of officials, businessmen, generals, scholars, and wives, all standing, all applauding *her*. She followed the red carpet up to a white stage where her predecessor, Fedov, sat. He stood, taking her hand to kiss it, but didn't quite touch his lips to her skin. Using a cane to walk, he stepped up to the microphone on quivering legs, and held onto the sides of the podium to steady himself. Michael assumed his place at the rear of the stage.

Fedov spoke into the microphone, welcoming her to the office of the presidency. He urged her to continue his great accomplishments in diplomacy, the economy, and in making the nation secure. He advised diligence in the continuing fight against terrorism. He spoke of working toward the common good.

Vera had heard the same sentiments expressed many times before. In Russia, it wasn't what you said that was important, it was what you did. Fedov said what was expected, what the audience wanted to hear, but he had actually accomplished very little. His publicized reforms against government corruption had changed nothing, other than increasing the size of his secret foreign bank accounts by millions of rubles—another bit of information Vera had gotten from Michael that was confirmed by her spies.

As she waited for her moment to come, Fedov did the unthinkable. He paused midsentence and looked out over the audience. He raised a trembling hand as if to make a point. But instead of finishing his thought, there in front of thousands of people, he broke down and cried. Amplified by microphones, the sound of his sobs filled the room. Within seconds, reformer Fedov changed from leader of the Russian Federation to doddering old fool. He leaned against the podium as Vera stepped up and put her arm around his shoulders.

She spoke. "We will all miss our dear President Fedov as much as he will miss us. I pray he recovers his strength quickly and regains his health while watching his grandchildren play at his feet."

The applause was astounding.

Fedov looked into her face, his lips curled in unrestrained anger, his face contorted, his cheeks wet. She wanted to slap him. Vera gestured for assistance. The old man was escorted off the stage by a soldier in a gold-trimmed hat.

Moments later, with her hand on the Russian constitution, Vera took her oath, the same one taken by her predecessor, and his predecessor, and the one before. She swore to protect the rights and freedoms of the citizens, to enforce the constitution, independence of the state, territorial integrity, and to serve the Russian Federation faithfully. She thought of Catherine the Great's leadership, and the grand expanse of land that was the Soviet Union as she repeated the words swearing fidelity to her country. As the first woman in modern times to lead Russia, she already had her place in history. She would show these old men what it meant to be great.

Afterward, Vera gave the speech she had committed to memory days ago; six hundred and forty-nine words declaring her vow to elevate the nation to its past success and lead Eurasia into a new era of world influence.

When she finished, the audience applauded and the dignitaries on stage moved to congratulate her. Grinsky, the prime minister, wore an ingenuous smile, as always. She felt a chill when he took her hand.

The ceremony over, Vera walked alone down the red carpet past the crowd standing behind velvet ropes, each step a victory; the first woman ever to have traversed this path in this role, head of the largest nation on earth. She stopped to shake hands with a blind woman who thanked her and reached out clumsily to touch Vera's cheek. Vera felt like she was floating. She accepted a hug from Grinsky's wife, an overweight matron whose singular talent appeared to have been an ability to bear children. The director of the FSB clasped Vera's hand and whispered congratulations into her ear as if he were telling a secret.

The world knew little of Vera, but in time they all would revere her, perhaps even fear her. She felt like a queen.

Swelling from the triumph of the moment and the power that she now held, Vera followed a long corridor to the right, taking plenty of time to shake the hands eagerly reaching out over the velvet restraints. Glancing back at the stage, she noticed Grinsky staring at her, and felt that chill all over again.

# CHAPTER 4

## Vilnius University Hospital, Vilnius, Lithuania—9 May

The doctor listened to Leva Krukas's heart and lungs, and shook his head before adjusting the morphine drip. The high-pitched beat from the heart monitor was the only sound and at that, it was barely audible after the doctor had turned down the volume.

Zuza Bartus sat in a chair on the other side of the bed, her thick brown hair highlighted in golden strands looking limp, just like she felt. As an anti-terrorism agent in ARAS, she'd seen some disturbing scenes, but none had hit her as hard as this. She looked the question she didn't want to ask.

"It'll be sometime tonight," said the doctor. He reached out to touch the shoulder of Otto Krukas, Leva's father, as a gesture of sympathy. But the big man didn't acknowledge it. The doctor went out, leaving them alone.

The shades were drawn, the corners of the room dark, the only lighting from a small lamp near the bed. All that was left to do was hold Leva's hand and wait, hoping that her time remaining was long enough for God to work a miracle, or short enough to ease her suffering.

Through the ravages of breast cancer that had spread to her brain, and the cloud of painkillers intended to make her last moments bearable, Leva Krukas opened her eyes.

Zuza leaned in, gently squeezing her friend's hand. "Otto, she's awake."

Otto went to the other side of the bed and took his daughter's free hand. Leva didn't seem to notice him as she spoke with difficulty. "Zuza, take care of my father."

"Of course, I will," said Zuza.

"I'm right here, baby," said Otto.

Leva kept her gaze on Zuza. "And don't give up. Ever. Don't listen to the others."

"Okay. I promise."

"Tell my father I love him."

"He's right here, sweetie."

Another breath, a blink of her eyes, and as quietly as a butterfly landing on a flower, Leva Krukas was gone.

Neither Zuza nor Otto moved. Neither one ran for help or shouted for the doctor. Instead, they continued to hold Leva's hands, as if that physical contact could tie her to the world of the living.

Zuza was the first to let go. She glanced at Otto, who wasn't bothering to hold back his tears any longer as they streamed down his face. There were no sobs or changes in his expression, just the tears.

It broke Zuza's heart to see him like that. Even though he was her boss at Police Headquarters in Vilnius, more often than not he was like a father with advice, and occasionally a glass of beer after successfully closing a case. But he was mostly aloof. His job was to send her on missions that might cost her her life, and he had to do it without hesitation, but that was the problem. Ever since Leva took a turn for the worse, and they knew cancer would kill her just as it had Leva's mother over ten years ago, he gave Zuza the light work, the easy jobs, the safest jobs, and rarely sent her out on assignment. Most of the time he kept her on the computer, supporting the other agents who were out working in the field and making a difference.

She had joined ARAS to keep her country safe. Her ancestors had fought here decades ago to achieve freedom, and Zuza felt compelled to preserve it. ARAS was more than a job. It was a way to live. It was protecting people who couldn't help themselves, and it was a way to avenge her father's death.

But right now, she couldn't think of that. Nothing mattered except for the person in the hospital room with her now. Her problems would wait for another day. Zuza got up and put an arm around Otto's shoulder, gently guiding him out into the hallway, quietly closing the door behind them.

# CHAPTER 5

## Moscow—11 May

Vera Koslova was in her new office at the Kremlin admiring the warm paneling on the walls and the crest of the double-headed eagle, the flag, the letter-opener and pen set on a tray of marble, the antique samovar handed down from *Babushka*, her grandmother, and the rest. It was hard to believe she was actually here. Babushka would've felt this life strange. She would have missed her kitchen, the garden, and the cow she called Galina. She had saved kopeks all her life to buy the samovar and have something valuable she could proudly hand down to her daughter. Now Vera had it. The samovar had been the crowning achievement of Babushka's life, and Vera liked keeping it close, because it reminded her how strong and determined the women in her family were.

A knock on the door brought Vera back to the present. "Come."

Prime Minister Grinsky walked in. He had well-groomed gray hair and was strong looking, but was at least thirty kilos overweight. *Why do so many Russian men let themselves go?* thought Vera. Grinsky clicked his heels together like a damn Prussian count, an affectation she despised, much like the man himself.

Vera waved him to a facing chair, one deliberately lower than her own, so he would have to look up at her. Like the newly hung portrait of Catherine the Great staring down from the wall, everything was carefully set to remind a visitor of Vera's power.

She took out two small glasses and a bottle of Khortytsa vodka she kept in the bottom drawer. She had grown to like it during a brief undercover stint in Ukraine when she was just starting out at the

KGB in the mid-1980s. The organization was disbanded five years later, when an attempted coup had failed to topple Gorbachev's reformist government. But new organizations had risen like phoenixes from the ashes, and became as feared as their predecessor. Two of the most influential were the Federal Security Service, or FSB, which focused on domestic intelligence, and the SRV—the Foreign Intelligence Service—which focused on the international sphere.

Vera joined the FSB. It gave her the opportunity to observe the worst in human behavior, and gain access to information invaluable to securing the loyalty of those who held the real power. Coupled with Michael's gossip, she knew enough secrets about the oligarchs, government officials, and military officers to affirm their loyalty and ensure her success. Besides, the FSB supported her. That alone was enough to deter any opposition. Father Stalin would have been proud of her.

Grinsky had made no qualms about wanting the presidency. He and Fedov had taken dinner together once a week for the past few months. She was sure Grinsky had been stunned by her appointment. But Russia didn't need Grinsky. He, like all the others, was just a watered-down version of the great Vladimir Vladimirovich Putin. Russia needed someone strong who would bring stability and prosperity to the entire region. Russia needed Vera. But she was sure Grinsky didn't see it that way, for even from across the wide desk, she sensed hostility leaching from his skin.

She poured the vodka and handed him a glass.

"To the most powerful and beautiful woman in the world," said Grinsky.

She took a sip.

Grinsky continued. "And to the tragic victims of the riots in Novosibirsk, including that poor boy who was trampled to death by the mob. It's unfortunate that so many died at a time when we should be celebrating your presidency. If I may say, Madame President, your appointment was a surprise to us all."

Vera's stomach twisted at Grinsky's gall. She was perfectly capable of leading the country. All she needed was a little luck, and Fedov himself had given it to her. Just months ago, Fedov had had a brief affair with an Oxford-educated Russian woman whose best friend had ties to MI6, Great Britain's foreign intelligence agency. It had only been dinner and a bedding at the presidential estate at Cape Idokopas, likely a one-night liaison. Regardless of the casual nature of the tryst, Fedov had ordered the cameras that recorded everything in every room in the estate turned off. Vera'd had the foresight to order a cameraman to turn the recording back on in the bedroom.

Fedov's initial anger quickly wilted when confronted with Vera's pictures. He promised to leave office. A smooth transition to Grinsky was all he wanted, but she pointed out what he had done might be considered treasonous; that not only his life would be ruined, but the lives of his children and all eighteen grandchildren. In the end, he had begged her to save his family.

She had hushed up the affair after receiving assurances that she would become the next president, and agreeing that his reasons for resigning from office would be old age and fatigue. But hiding the information about his affair presented a risk for her, too. It was treasonous to keep something like this a secret, so the man who had recorded Fedov with that woman was a liability. Vera had mentioned this problem to her trusted childhood friend, Nina Ditlova. Nina was like a sister to her; the women would do anything for each other. It was Nina who had contacted Alexy Bok, their man for special assignments. Days later, the cameraman was found frozen to death in a park in Moscow, an obvious victim of petty theft that had left him unconscious and out in the cold all night. How unfortunate for the poor man that Moscow winters were such a bear.

*Scratch one liability.*

Grinsky knew nothing of this. *He couldn't.* And yet, he watched her.

"I think, if I may say so," he said, "that it would be in your interest to announce you will not run for election in two years. It would quell the dissidents, and you could leave office peacefully after making this an historic time for women in Russia."

"And in two years, you would have no competition in your quest for the office of president." Vera smiled. It felt like she was sitting across from a viper.

Grinsky shrugged. "I'm sure there will be *some* competition."

She felt that chill again. "Right now, we have other things to deal with."

Grinsky reached across the desk for the bottle.

Her voice was as cold as a Russian winter. "You feel privileged enough to help yourself to my vodka?"

He flushed, and apologized.

"All you need to do is *ask*, my dear Grinsky." She gave a thin smile and poured another measure.

"The people need to feel secure. We need to show the West our country is unified. I want the pro-Western elements in Ukraine to know we are watching. And I want the Baltic countries to see that Russia is as strong as ever. So I'm reinforcing our military along the borders with Kaliningrad and Ukraine."

Grinsky cleared his throat. "I wonder if that's a good idea, Madame President. Additional military presence changes the status quo. It will make our businessmen nervous, especially those who have financial interests in the Russian Federation, to say nothing of foreign investors doing business here."

"I'm sure your businessmen want things to be as stable as possible. And I want to assure the people they are protected, and the troublemakers can't harm them." Vera picked up the letter opener lying on her desk, it's ornate wooden handle imprinted with an ancient crest. She ran her finger along the shiny edge of the dagger-like blade.

Grinsky's gaze was on the blade as Vera played with it, turning it back and forth. His eyes looked flat, barely human. He spoke. "It would be a disaster for the West to see fresh troops in politically sensitive geographies. NATO might respond with even more sanctions."

"You mean it will be a disaster for the oligarchs."

"They're just businessmen. We help them and they help us. It's been that way for years. After all, we both want what's best for *Rossiya*."

Vera put the letter-opener down.

He continued. "Madame President, you have my complete support. I'll do everything in my power to assist you and the citizens of our great nation."

"That gives me comfort."

Grinsky stood, taking a slow look around the office, as if mourning the loss of his rightful place. He clicked his heels together and walked out the door.

# CHAPTER 6

## Burlington, Massachusetts—11 May

Sitting at the head of the conference table, Vit Partenkas looked out the windows to the trees lining the pathway to Sagus Corporation offices. Covered in stunning white blossoms, the trees reminded him that spring was his favorite time of year.

A tall and muscular man, the work boots, jeans, canvas jacket, and button-down shirt, made him look more like a construction supervisor than owner and CEO of his own company. His pale skin and light hair faded into nondescript features until he opened eyes that sparkled like the sea. To his right sat Max, his second-in-command, a technical guru with a law degree. To Vit's left was a group from the Department of Homeland Security, consisting of a manager and two IT experts. The manager, a Mrs. Brown, acted like she knew more than anyone in the room, and she actually seemed to. Vit didn't know why she had bothered to bring her IT people, as all they'd contributed to the meeting was making a dent in the tray of breakfast croissants on the side table.

She spoke in crisp tones. "My people tell me our validation testing on your Annie program is going very well, and we may be wrapping up in a few weeks, after which we'll be making our final decision. But just so I understand, Annie can be used as both an uber-criminal data investigator, and also as a personal assistant? That seems like an odd mix of capabilities."

Vit smiled as he turned back around. "Annie is the most sophisticated personal assistant known to mankind. Her programs can run on any available device, platform, and operating system, including phones, tablets, laptops, and even on a car's computer. Besides that, Annie has the ability to learn. Because she's my personal assistant, she learns about my habits. However, she could also learn a great deal about anyone on the planet."

"And she can predict behavior and preferences."

Vit nodded. "I asked Annie to get a birthday gift for my mother. Annie selected a diamond tennis bracelet because Ma loves jewelry. Annie ordered it, paid for it, and sent to my mother with a personalized note. My mother loved it. I did nothing, but don't tell Ma."

"What prevents me from stealing your phone and using Annie myself?"

"Regardless of whether Annie is running on a laptop or a phone, she has multilevel biometric security, including body language sensors, daily random password change, and a small collection of duress codes to ensure that I alone control what Annie does. If you were to buy the rights to Annie for Homeland Security, you'd set your own security parameters to prevent theft." Vit pulled out his phone. "Say hello, Annie."

"Hello, Vit." Annie's dulcet voice filled the room.

"I want you to take commands from Mrs. Brown here."

"Vit, you know I can't do that."

"Please."

"Sorry, Vit."

Mrs. Brown leaned forward. "Annie, call my private number. I just got a new cell phone and no one knows my number except my husband."

"Vit, would you like me to do that?" said Annie.

"Sure," said Vit.

Almost immediately, Mrs. Brown's phone rang. She smiled as she pressed a button and the phone stopped ringing.

"I could use Annie to learn about a suspected terrorist," said Mrs. Brown.

Vit nodded. "Absolutely. Annie can find out where a person has been, who they've communicated with, and more."

Max spoke up in his thick German accent. "We talk about data in levels. Annie can search for level one data, which is everything that's publicly available on the internet. This includes online phonebooks containing home addresses, dates of birth, names of family members, and so on. The amount of public information is usually a surprise to people. Level one searches also look for information on social media sites. Annie's efficient facial recognition algorithms determine where a person has been and who they've spoken to, thereby making associations between people who have no obvious connections. It also helps create a timeline of where a person has been both physically and online. Level one also combs the massive public storage systems generally referred to as the cloud, where we can look at digital photo albums, unencrypted video—some from commercial and private security systems, and more."

Vit spoke. "Level two searches look for private data, including identity numbers in Europe and Social Security numbers in the US. That's the level you want for finding bank accounts, financial history, encrypted data, and more."

Max's German accent returned. "What's interesting is that Annie learns. If Vit's mother had hated the diamond bracelet, Annie would figure out why, and send her something completely different next time. With level two data, Annie has already figured out how to read simply-encrypted files, and eventually, she'll be able to read files with stronger security."

Vit spoke again. "Level two is probably what you're interested in at Homeland Security. The legal and privacy aspects of using level two data are something we need to discuss, including what to do with data that should be encrypted by law, but isn't for whatever reason. Normally, Annie doesn't even access level two data."

Mrs. Brown turned to Vit. "But she could."

Vit nodded. "Because the version of Annie I run on my phone and laptop is a prototype configured to show maximum capability, Annie could access level two data on my command. But she could be easily configured to access level two data only when the appropriate authorization, such as a warrant, is in place."

Mrs. Brown cracked a smile. "If things progress as I expect them to, I think our attorneys at Homeland Security will need a meeting with Max here by the end of the month to discuss next steps."

After some additional discussion and handshakes all around, Max escorted the IT folks out, but Vit asked Mrs. Brown to stay behind.

"I need to make something absolutely clear," he said, closing the door.

Mrs. Brown watched him for a moment before returning to her seat. She gestured to a chair, and Vit sat, too. "What's on your mind?" she said.

"Homeland Security does extensive background checks on all its employees. But I vetted all my people here at Sagus before hiring them. They're loyal, trustworthy, and honest. You can't find better people."

"I know. We already checked them out, including you. We like to know who we're doing business with. But you want me to offer all of them jobs." Mrs. Brown shrugged. "I can't promise anything, but I certainly can consider it."

"I won't sell unless I know my people will be taken care of."

"I would think they'd be pleased with the financial compensation."

"That's not enough. Every person here put all they had into making Annie the best program possible. I have to make sure they can continue working on her if they want. Besides, they're the only ones who have the true sense of her potential. If you can't guarantee them jobs, it's a deal-breaker."

"And will you be part of the deal?"

Vit shook his head. "That would be like watching someone else raise my child. No one knows except Max, and I'd like to keep it that way for a while."

"That'll be our loss, Vit. As to the others, I'll see what I can do."

Mrs. Brown stood and they shook hands before Vit led her to the cramped lobby where the others waited. The visitors left.

Upon returning to the conference room with Max, Vit's other employees, a small mix of IT, computer security, and database experts were there. Yellow balloons bumped up against the ceiling. Max popped the cork on a bottle of champagne as everyone cheered. As the wine bubbled out, Max poured the overflow into plastic glasses. A chocolate cake with the words, *At Last*, sat on the side table.

Vit laughed. "Guys. Isn't it too early to celebrate?"

Max spoke. "Why not, Vit? It looks like Homeland Security is on target to buy us out, and we're all going to have enough money to take a nice long vacation. We should seize the moment, as you Americans say."

"We'll have to wait it out for the next few weeks while Homeland Security finishes their evaluation, but I agree. It's looking good. Damn good." Vit broke out in a grin as he held up his glass. "To Sagus, the best five-person company on the planet."

"To Annie," said the others.

It had taken Vit quite some time to realize how valuable his idea had been, and even now, he doubted this was all actually happening.

It had been a simple and logical concept: an algorithm that learned from its mistakes. All he had done was use databases already publicly available, master simple security, and figure how to make the algorithm become smarter and faster.

He knew his employees would be upset when he announced he was leaving, and he didn't want it to cloud any personal decisions anyone would make. He also didn't want his employees asking him about his new role at Homeland Security, because he didn't want to lie. It might be best if he stayed out of the office as much as possible until Homeland Security made its final decision. He'd have to think of a good reason to be away, because his people could sniff out a ruse as easily as they could brew a cup of coffee.

He sipped the champagne, hoping the others would eventually forgive him for leaving.

If things worked out as planned, he'd exit the company with a large check, and his own personal version of Annie running on his phone, although he was certain Homeland Security would insist he disable level two searches, but that was all right. He couldn't imagine why he'd want to use them anyway.

# CHAPTER 7

## Moscow—13 May

Vera watched the security monitors from a room down the hallway as the elite advisors of her new inner circle entered the conference room in the Kremlin. All were Fedov's friends, except for a few of her own people. They included a group of businessmen representing key industries: oil and gas, mining, military machinery, agriculture, broadcasting and news outlets, a smattering of generals, speaker of the Duma, her bootlicking secretary Smirnov, Grinsky, and an economist from Saint Petersburg State University, among others. Nina Ditlova's was the only welcome face in the bunch, and the only woman in the room. As newly appointed special assistant to the president, Nina had a far more important role than any of them, but they didn't know it yet.

Most of the men in the room were old. All had survived difficult times politically, socially, and even personally, along with divorces or strings of affairs that satisfied their lust while freeing them of some of their wealth. It showed in their overweight bodies, poor posture, faces lined with wrinkles, and most of all, in their expressions. No one looked happy, but everyone wore something that showed success; a diamond signet ring, a suit from the finest tailors in Great Britain, shoes from Italy, a tie from Paris, a big Swiss watch.

If the riots and the bombing in Novosibirsk had been caused by the old guard, it was sure to be someone in that room. That the instigators had not yet been found was bad. She needed answers. She needed to know whether the citizens of Russia were truly against her, whether an opponent was trying to bring her down, or both. No one in the room would dare question her right to be there, for she was too powerful. There was a huge difference in wanting Vera gone and taking actions to remove her from office.

The men moved around the room, reacting to the new layout with guffaws. The round table Fedov had preferred was replaced with a long rectangular one. Vera's was the largest chair at the head of the table. The place across from her at the opposite end held no seat. All the other chairs were lined up along the sides, like good soldiers.

Vera had changed the table because she didn't want any of them to feel they had an equal say in matters. She had no need to hear opinions before making up her mind, even on the most complex issues. She knew what she wanted, and always had. That was another thing she had grown to detest about Fedov. He was slow to make up his mind in all matters, except one. He always knew which woman he wanted to bed next. His knock invariably came to the door of a guest room in one of his many dachas across Russia. No woman could refuse him and live a good life. He had come to Vera's door too many times, despite her efforts to avoid being his guest. Those invitations, too, were impossible to decline. But in the end, it made Vera's photos of Fedov with that woman who had ties to MI6 all the sweeter.

The only benefit from Fedov's slow and lumbering mind was that it had provided her time to observe and garner unique insight into the political process in Russia as she watched him climb the ladder to become one of the most trusted confidants of the president, before gaining the office himself. It had taken Vera years to follow his path and identify the dominoes, but when the time came, she had toppled them all.

Now Vera had her own ideas about who to take into her inner circle, and ultimately, it wouldn't be everyone in the room. She would pare it down to a trusted few. In the meanwhile, she wanted them to squirm, claw, and compete with each other to try to gain her favor. She looked forward to a good show, and based on the grumblings, it had already begun.

Grinsky put his hand on the back of the chair at the head of the table—*her* chair. He glanced up at the tiny camera, as if he knew she was watching. He chose the seat next to hers and sat down.

Vera shivered. She was becoming accustomed to feeling cold whenever Grinsky was around. No doubt he and Fedov had discussed the next term's elections. But she, Vera Koslova, had ripped the presidency from Fedov. He hadn't wanted to leave. She had forced his retirement. He was angry. Grinsky was angry. And yet, she didn't believe that either man, alone or together, would revert to underhanded tactics such as orchestrating a riot to sway the people and eventually take the presidency from her. It was simply too risky to challenge a former director of the FSB.

Next to Grinsky sat Yuri Rozoff, an oligarch who had made his billions selling Russian gas to countries that had no choice but to buy it at inflated prices. By far the best-dressed man in the room, Rozoff wore a suit made by one of the finest tailors in London. His shirts were hand-made in Hong Kong, and embroidered with a dazzling R on the pocket. His shoes were from Italy. Despite all the personal trappings, Rozoff looked worried. He leaned toward Grinsky. "Business as usual?" Rozoff had a hand up in front of his face and spoke so softly, Vera could barely hear.

"Don't worry, I've already spoken to her," said Grinsky. He gave Rozoff an assuring nod.

Vera was glad to have witnessed the interaction, for every little bit of information was important. She went down the hallway to the meeting room. When she strode in, they all rose. Nina was the only one smiling.

Smirnov pulled out her chair. Vera sat. Smirnov proceeded to run the meeting according to the precise instructions she had given him earlier that day. He showed great eagerness, obviously impressed with himself that at his age he had a vital role. But he just did whatever she told him to do. He, like the rest, merely assumed he was important. Vera made a mental note to have him arrange lunch with Nina over the next few days. Then Vera might threaten to fire him, just to see how he reacted.

The oligarchs looked bored, shifting in their chairs, so Vera closed the file in front of her, folded her hands, and spoke. "Terrorism has reached mother Russia. Our citizens of the great continents of Asia and Europe aren't safe. As the investigation into the cause of these riots continues, I'm making some changes to protect our people."

Everyone was looking directly at her, except for Grinsky.

Vera continued. "We can't keep with the status quo. It makes us vulnerable, as we were during the riots at my inauguration. Instead, we'll do everything possible to protect our citizens and our high value assets. I'm sending in additional troops to secure our interests in Kaliningrad. I'm asking the military to guard our oil interests in the Caucuses and along the Baltic Sea. Additional troops have been ordered to protect our resources in Crimea. I'm also securing the border we share with Ukraine."

Grinsky was staring at her now. Vera ignored the knot in her stomach as she nodded at Smirnov, and asked for the next item on the agenda.

# CHAPTER 8

## Kaunas, Lithuania—17 May

Darius enjoyed the cool breeze wafting over him through the open window in his cluttered apartment near the reservoir. It felt like his heart was going to rupture from the swell of pride at what he was about to accomplish, and the undercurrent of expectation and danger. Ignas, his dear father, would have been happy and proud. Darius took his evening dose of medication from the container on the kitchen counter and swallowed it with a sip of water; two doses every day, one in the morning and one in the evening, to control his arrhythmia, the unusually rapid heartbeat he'd suffered with since he was thirty-three years old.

The bomb Darius had made with Tilda's help almost thirty years ago would finally finish Ignas's work, for Darius was going to use it. Jonas, the man who had practically raised him, was too weak to, even though he'd had many opportunities. Years ago, the apartment bombings in Moscow and Volgodonsk, the Russian annexation of Crimea, the crash of Malaysia Airlines flight MH17 had all provided reasons. But instead of bringing Russia to her knees with their nuclear weapon, Jonas had waited. Darius was tired of waiting. He was tired of Jonas's meaningless words. He needed to act, especially now that Vera Koslova was leading Russia.

Already she had moved her troops along the border with Ukraine, possibly in reaction to the protests at her inauguration, although the news had been downplayed, no doubt the result of Russian censorship. He could hardly believe Russia would condone a woman as leader, especially *this* woman, whose finishing school had been Lubyanka prison, and whose best subject had been interrogating enemies of the state before ordering them to be killed.

When she sent more troops into Kaliningrad, an oblast that shared a border with Lithuania, Darius was certain she was preparing to invade the Baltic countries. His first reaction was panic. But Darius's thoughts fell quickly into place, and a plan emerged. It was simple, beautiful—even brilliant.

All Darius needed now was for someone to know and affirm his ideas. He needed someone to understand how much he was willing to risk for his country. He needed Jonas. After hearing what he wanted to do, Jonas would no longer question Darius's judgement. And once Darius's plan had been put in place, Ignas's death at the hand of the Russians would finally be avenged.

The alcove next to the kitchen in Darius's apartment was where he kept his electronics equipment, although tools and devices he was working on covered most surfaces, like the spare laptop with a broken CD reader on the coffee table, and the drone he was trying to fix on the lamp stand. He used the alcove area to make the how-to videos he sold to support himself and pay for his apartment in this beautiful old stone building on the Nemunas River.

Darius switched on the heavy-duty lights in front of the bench that was normally laden with wiring, components, and tools. This evening all the debris was piled to one side, the rest of the workbench covered with his nation's flag of yellow, green and red stripes. He clicked a mouse, activating the application on his laptop that recorded his actions. He went behind the bench and took a deep breath, looking down at the script he'd prepared that day.

For the first seconds, he stared into the laptop's camera, knowing it would catch every nuance of his expression and every sound. Darius prepared to convey a sense of dedication and sincerity. With Vera Koslova's image stuck firmly in his mind, he spoke. At first, he stayed on script, but before long his passion overtook his carefully prepared speech. His voice grew higher and the words came faster. He made a broad gesture with his hand and pointed his index finger at the camera.

"Vera Koslova, the world is watching you, and we are not fooled." He felt his face grow hot. He hit the bench with a fist. "You are as much a threat to Baltic safety as Stalin was. You're as much a threat to world safety as Hitler was. Lithuania's leaders sit around and wait for diplomacy to work in the time of crisis but diplomacy doesn't work. Nothing will work against you, Vera Koslova, except bullets and bombs. NATO must take action, or else *we* will have to. We at Baltic Watch have no doubt that the rebel separatists will force a Russian invasion of Ukraine. Why else would you send troops to the area, unless to join with your supporters and take over the country? Once Ukraine falls, the Baltic countries will be next. Why else are you fortifying Russian troops in Kaliningrad, unless to invade? You're intent on expanding Russia's borders, as the Soviets were. You want Russia to become the next Soviet Union. NATO will—NATO *must*—protect us with troops, because we know from history, once Russian tanks move, they don't stop!"

Darius went on with stronger and harsher words, even threats. When he was done, he shut down the laptop and turned off the lights. He collapsed into the upholstered chair near the window, glad it was over. He didn't need to review the video. Edits would not be necessary, for he knew it was perfect. He felt it in his soul. The logic and passion of the old Baltic Watch was back, and it was all captured in that video. He was the new generation. Jonas would hand the reigns of Baltic Watch to him tonight after seeing it, Darius was sure. People would want to join them again, and he, Darius, would be their leader. He felt his body pulse with expectation and his heart murmur with excitement.

He was going to ask Jonas to post it, and actually press the keyboard key that would release the video to the world. Darius would show him which key, and together they would do it. Afterward, they'd drive to the cabin and unearth the bomb he had made thirty years ago with Tilda Partenkas. Jonas would be mad that Darius had moved it, but Darius would explain that Baltic Watch needed new blood, and Jonas would agree. He'd even let Jonas watch him examine the bomb and determine the parts needed for a new detonator, no doubt degraded after so many years buried in the earth. Together, they'd make a plan to get it to the Russian Embassy in Kiev.

Darius was on the verge of greatness, and it was time to show Jonas what he had in mind for the future. He stood, gathered up his laptop, and headed for the door.

# CHAPTER 9

## Utena, Lithuania—17 May

Jonas Volkis sat at the front window of his small yellow house with the faded green door. Years ago, his dear wife had painted it that color, even though Jonas hated green. Now he couldn't bear to change it. Inside, the cramped living room held a table and chairs, an upholstered chair by the window where Jonas sat, and a large bookcase overrun with books on everything from history to politics to science fiction. Her meticulous housekeeping had long ago given way to Jonas's preoccupation with his country and with Darius's future, leaving messy piles of notes and open books on every available surface. A stack of newspapers easily reaching a meter high lay to the left of the front door, next to a purple ceramic umbrella stand. A shorter stack of magazines lay under the window.

The picture of his wife, God rest her soul, hung next to the door and above the monitor controlling the home security system Darius had built. She had gone to heaven a year after their marriage began, long before Baltic Watch, even before Darius had come to live with him. With her picture hanging next to the door, Jonas could see her every time he came into or left the house, and each time wonder how her gentle ways might have changed his life had she lived.

"Jonas, are you home?"

The sound of a woman's voice startled him, but he recognized it. "Come in, Elena."

A small woman about Jonas's age, with white hair, wearing brown pants, a blue shirt, and pink sneakers came into the living room carrying a plate of potato dumplings. "When are you going to weed your garden? I hate looking at it every time I'm in my back yard. I made dumplings and thought you might like some. Have you eaten today?"

"With you as my neighbor, I eat too much."

"A woman who likes to cook likes a man who enjoys food."

Jonas went to the table and moved aside the mess of papers. He sat. Elena set the plate of homemade dumplings down in front of him, and placed a knife and fork next to the plate.

"I miss Ignas," said Jonas.

"Darius's father? You're thinking about him today? When you think about the dead, it's a sign that something bad is going to happen."

"I was remembering back in '62. I was just fourteen. I sneaked out of the house and went with Ignas on a mission. My first ever. Ignas was remarkable that night, distracting the guards with his wolf calls. They were so drunk I was surprised they could even walk. Drunk Soviets carrying machine guns. It was crazy. It's a miracle we survived. We broke into a depot and took some dynamite. It was a night I'll remember for the rest of my life. Ignas used the material to blow up a transformer in Vilnius to keep the Soviets in the dark."

"I know you were one of them. So was my husband. So was Ignas. But you're the only one living. Stop talking about the past and think about today."

"Ignas lived in the woods for too many years. You remember my parents, Jurgis and Raminta? They lived in the woods, too, during the war, but they had the good sense to get out. They were partisans, Brothers of the Forest, people unafraid to fight the Soviets occupying their country. They worked with Amber Wolf; Ludmelia Kudirka."

"I remember the stories about her."

"My parents used to talk about her. There's one story I remember in particular. It was during the war. The Soviets had set up headquarters somewhere in central Lithuania. Those days, they arrested anyone with a political opinion and brought them in for questioning, capturing most during early-morning raids. The partisans wanted to do something about it. One night, Ludmelia put on a dress, combed their hair, and waited in an alleyway off the main street. Of course, she wasn't alone. My father and another partisan, Dana Ravas, were with her. A military truck came down the road and Ludmelia walked out, pretending to be drunk. The truck stopped and the guards got out, surrounding her. They told her to get inside the truck, obviously wanting a little fun before carting her off to prison.

"Ludmelia climbed in the back with one of the guards while the others waited their turn. Ludmelia took care of her companion with a knife. While the man bled to death, she stuck her head out of the back, laughing, and said he was so excited, he couldn't even wait until his pants were off. While one of the guards moved to take his place, my father and Dana shot them all. Ludmelia and the partisans disappeared into the streets, and there were no raids that night. But of course, the next few weeks were a horror of Soviet retribution."

"That's the kind of thing the partisans did in those days. Eat your dumplings."

"After the war, Jurgis and Raminta thought if they could just hang on until the West came to help them fight the Soviets, that they would win, and the Communists would leave for good. But help never came. Years passed, and tens of thousands of partisans were killed. My parents left the cause, and a year later, I was born. But Ignas wouldn't give up. People thought he was crazy for living the way he did, but his parents were partisans, and that was the only life he knew. He never went to school. He could barely read. But he was a first-rate survivalist. After his parents were captured and killed by the Soviets, he lived alone in the woods for years, until an illness drove him out to seek help. He found a family who nursed him back to health. He married the daughter, and Darius came along. But she left him when Darius was very young. It destroyed Ignas, so he went back to the woods. He left the boy with me and ran solo missions against the Soviets. He came out occasionally to see his son. Eventually, the Russians caught him and locked him up."

"It's a sad story. But everyone here has a sad story to tell."

"They put Ignas in that prison they called a psychiatric hospital until he died in the 1980s. All those years, I fooled Darius into believing he was alive. I put shell casings and bullets on his bureau every so often and he thought they were from his father. I never told him the truth. I didn't want him to know both of his parents had abandoned him. Ignas could've stopped waging that damned one-man war long ago. He could have come home to raise his son. But no, he had to keep taking potshots at the Russians until they caught him."

"Tsk. Ignas was a wild one. He never listened to reason."

"Darius worshiped Ignas—I think he still does. It's funny, but I understand why. When I was young, I wanted to be like Ignas, too, and give my life to a cause. But I wasn't good at fighting like he was, so I started Baltic Watch to fight the Soviets with news and political commentary. For years, I had to do it anonymously, because if they knew I was behind Baltic Watch, they would've killed me." Jonas wiped his eyes with the back of a gnarled hand. "I tried to teach Darius good sense. But he never learned to consider the consequences of his actions. Ignas branded the boy, and I couldn't do anything about it."

"Of course, you couldn't. People don't change. You took care of Darius and gave him a home. What more could you have done?" She nudged the plate toward him.

Jonas picked up the knife and fork, but as he gestured with the knife to emphasize the point he was about to make, it slipped out of his hand and fell to the floor.

"My mother used to say when you drop a knife, it means you're going to have a male visitor." Elena bent down to pick it up. She wiped it on her shirt and put it back on the table next to Jonas's plate.

Jonas glanced at the dusty floor and moved the knife away. "I thought Darius would behave with common sense in a time of crisis. Most men do, or at least try to. When Putin invaded Crimea, Darius wanted to do something horrible. I managed to stop him. I love Darius, and I want to trust him. But I can't wait any longer, not with my poor health and Vera Koslova in office. I'm going to give Darius one last chance tonight."

"One last chance for what?"

"To show me he has learned responsibility and temperance."

"If I had a euro for every time I heard Darius arguing with you, I'd be a rich woman. Give him a hundred more chances if you want. Hope for the best but expect the worst. He's just not the man you want him to be. He's fifty years old, and at his calmest, he simmers like hot water in the kettle."

"I owe him. And I owe it to Baltic Watch to give Darius one more opportunity, because there's no one else to take over for me." Jonas put the fork down.

"And if he doesn't pass your test, what're you going to do? You can't teach a cow to climb a tree."

Jonas pushed away the uneaten plate of food. "I'll do what I have to."

"Now you're upset and won't eat. I'll tell you what Darius should do. He should marry my daughter. She would straighten him out. They would make a good match."

"Darius is too old for your daughter."

"She's thirty. When I was her age, I was already married, had a baby, and every day I went to work at the collective farm, the *kolkhoz*."

"They don't raise people like you anymore, Elena."

"Is Darius coming over tonight?"

"I called and asked him to."

"That's your male visitor. Knives never lie. Don't let him keep you up too late. You're looking tired lately. You need your rest." Elena picked up the plate of dumplings and put it in the refrigerator in Jonas's kitchen before leaving through the back door.

# CHAPTER 10

## Moscow—17 May

The recording studio at Ostankino Television Technical Center in Moscow was more modern than Nina Ditlova had expected. She thought there would be black walls and gray drapes, but the red and orange lights in the ceiling made the floor glow, giving a feeling of youthful energy. Nina was escorted by a young man with squeaky shoes to an upholstered chair on a circular stage. An identical chair was across from her, and in between, a coffee table made from a light wood. Cameras on moveable stands were on both sides and two directly in front. An audience, already seated, occupied row upon row of the stadium style seating.

A woman wearing red pants and an artist's apron containing brushes, small bottles, and containers of hairspray, came up and fussed around Nina's face with her implements before hurrying away. The young man who had escorted Nina to the chair placed a microphone on the lapel of her suit.

Ona Chekov, Channel One Russia's special events reporter, walked briskly across the stage as she waved and called out to the audience. "Hello, everyone!" She wore a tight dress that emphasized her substantial curves, and a pink jacket buttoned at the waist. She had straight dark hair that fell to her shoulders. She offered Nina her hand. "I'm glad to finally meet you, Presidential Special Assistant Ditlova. When we start filming, just look at me. Ignore everything else. That's your camera," said Ona, pointing front left. Nina looked across to a man standing by one of the cameras, who gave her a casual salute.

The woman in the apron rushed to Ona, who tilted her face upward to the powder brush. More lights flashed on. The woman ran offstage. A man counted down from three. The studio became silent.

Ona spoke. "We're proud to have with us today the woman who is serving as special assistant to President Vera Yaroslavna Koslova. Welcome, Nina Ditlova."

Nina smiled at the camera, waiting for the applause to die down. "I'm pleased to be here representing my dear childhood friend Vera Koslova, and ushering in a fresh wave of Russian women in politics. We're proud to build on the extraordinary legacy of women like Valentina Matviyenko and the many others who gave their energy and lives to creating a better Russia."

"What is your role as special assistant to the president?" said Ona.

"It's a new role. I will be helping President Koslova in any capacity necessary. I'll travel for her when it's impossible for her to attend meetings abroad. I'll speak on her behalf when she's tending to important affairs of state. I'll advise her on public opinion. I'll be a liaison to Russian media on all major issues, and other tasks that will evolve as the role expands."

"I think many were surprised President Fedov resigned so suddenly and that he appointed a woman to finish his term in office."

"We can rely on President Fedov's good judgement in naming the best successor possible in Vera Koslova. She's talented, accomplished, and will do an extraordinary job."

Ona glanced up from her notes and leaned forward. "I understand your grandfather was Ivan Ditlov, the brilliant political advisor to President Putin. Tell us all. Was your grandfather instrumental in helping you get to this point in your career?"

"My grandfather was a great man, and I miss him terribly. Being close to an influential person didn't hurt me in any way, but I grew up far away, in Tomsk."

*Nina remembered the morning Mama had sat in a chair in front of Grandfather's massive desk in his apartment in Moscow, her arm bandaged, bruises on her face, crying. Papa had sat in a chair next to her with his arms crossed.*

*Grandfather, the great Ivan Ditlov, had turned to Mama and spoken. "You will stay with your husband. The Russian people think I control my family; I will not have them thinking otherwise. Do you understand me?" Grandfather landed a fist on the wood. Little Nina jumped at the noise.*

*"Yes," said Mama. Her voice sounded high and squeaky like a chipmunk's would, if a chipmunk could speak.*

*Grandfather turned to Papa. "If you harm your wife again in any way, it will be the end of your career. I will personally see to it that the only work you get is digging ditches."*

*Papa nodded.*

*"If either of you break your word, I'll take Nina away from you both."*

*Upon hearing her name, Nina went around the desk to her grandfather. He looked down at her as she pulled on his sleeve. "I don't want to live here. I want to live with Mama," she said, kicking him in the leg. As she ran to her mother, Nina thought she heard him chuckle.*

Ona held up the tip of her pencil, as if to emphasize a point. "You and your parents lived in Tomsk?"

"My mother and I lived with Vera Koslova and her mother. Our mothers were educators who felt compelled to bring good education to children living in remote parts of Russia. Our fathers had responsibilities in Moscow and weren't able to come with us, but they supported us fully."

*"Why are you already dressed, Mama?" Nina had said, rubbing the sleep from her eyes. Mama's cheek was bruised and her lips red and swollen.*

*After a quick breakfast, Nina got dressed, too. Their mismatched suitcases were lined up at the door.*

*"Are you taking me to Grandfather's house to live?" said Nina.*

*"Oh no, Princessa. I'm not leaving you with anyone. You're with me until the day I die."*

*They carried the suitcases as they walked to the apartment where Nina's friend Vera lived with her parents. The women talked while the girls played in the kitchen. Vera's mother came in, made a phone call, and spoke into the receiver. "She wants to stay with us."*

*In a moment, she said, "I know he'll look here, but not until tonight, and you could protect her. We both could. She has no one else."*

*Seconds later, she continued. "What's she to do? What about your brother's apartment? Please. Just for a few days until she finds a place to live."*

*A moment passed. "All right. I'm making your favorite dish—borsch."*

*Vera's mother hung up the phone, and Mama wiped her eyes with her hands.*

*Vera's mother spoke. "He has the means but refuses to help. I don't understand. Why wouldn't he help?"*

*Nina licked her lips. Borsch was one of her favorite dishes, too.*

*Mama spoke. "Men stick together. It's always been that way. Especially here in Russia."*

*"I don't want Vera learning that her sense of kindness and compassion requires a man's approval. I don't want her growing up thinking that she needs a man to define who she is."*

*"He's your family. The father of your child. What can you do?"*

*"Vera's my family more than he is. Besides, I've only known him for ten years, but I've known you all my life. Doesn't that make us family too?" Vera's mother went into the bedroom. When she came out carrying even more suitcases, she seemed changed, somehow stronger and more resolved. "Vera and I are going with you."*

"How long have you known Vera Koslova?" said Ona.

"All my life. We grew up together."

*The girls packed up their toys and all four of them left together, Vera's mother holding an old silver samovar in her arms as they went out the door. They walked to the train station, stopping a few times to set the clumsy suitcases down and rest. Vera's mother bought tickets. Nina had no idea where they were going as she held onto Vera's hand. All she knew was that they would be together.*

*"They may find out where we've gone, but I doubt that either man will go that far just to take us back home," said Vera's mother.*

*Nina watched as Mama spoke. "They may send people to force us back."*

*"Let's pray they don't. And that Nina's grandfather leaves us alone. I know he loves Nina, and you, too."*

*"My father-in-law has the power to do almost anything. I hope you're right. I hope he thinks about what's best for his grandchild."*

*A week later, somewhere in the massive expanse of Asia, Vera and Nina settled into the new home their mothers shared, restarting their lives as sisters.*

"Are you close to your father?" said Ona, taking a sip from the cup on the coffee table in front of them.

"I'm sorry to say my father died in a tragic accident many years ago. I miss him terribly."

*"Nina, Papa's dead." Mama looked tired as always.*

*"I don't care." Nina tucked a strand of long hair behind her ear and turned back to her studies. Mama just stood there. Nina put down her pencil. "All right! What happened?"*

*"He was hit by a car in Krasny Oktyabr."*

*"Where Moscow has its best bars."*

*"How would you know that?"*

*"I read a lot."*

Ona spoke. "I understand you and Vera Koslova went through KGB training together."

"Yes, we did. Soon after our training, we moved to the FSB. Vera Koslova did particularly well. As you know, she rose to the director position."

"You did well, too."

"Yes, I was honored to serve several years under her as deputy director."

Ona looked into a camera. "And now for the question our viewers have been waiting for. How will a woman president change Russia?"

"I think many things will get better. Vera Koslova is committed to peace and security and will do whatever is necessary to protect Russian citizens. She is progressive. For example, she's committed to finishing Nord Stream 2, the pipeline under the Baltic Sea that will bring Russian gas into the European market. That she supports emissaries like myself speaking on her behalf directly to your audience is proof she believes in the power of transparency and honesty."

The audience applauded.

Ona spoke. "Are you saying Vera Koslova will reform the media?"

"Change takes time, but good things are coming to Russia."

# CHAPTER 11

## Vilnius, Lithuania—17 May

Zuza pressed her foot down on the gas pedal. The Toyota responded, the speedometer climbing to eighty kilometers per hour, easy enough on the motorway. Few cars were out. Zuza clicked on the headlights, brightening the two-lane road. A trailer truck passed by in the opposite direction. Her car trembled in the blast of wind. The image from earlier today of Leva's face in the casket stayed with her as the trees and the open fields became a blur of brown and green in the fading light. It hadn't even looked like Leva; the face was too thin and wearing makeup. Leva never wore makeup, not even on dates, but Leva hadn't had much time for dating. She hadn't married or had children. She never had a career, just a job at the State Data Protection Inspectorate responding to credit fraud. She might have had a career there if she had lived.

She glanced at the speedometer: ninety kilometers per hour. Leva was already sick when they'd met a year ago. Zuza had just finished ARAS training, her boyfriend David was out of her life, and it felt like she was starting all over again. Otto Krukas, a man with a heart as soft as curd cheese, had hired her into an office of men, all ARAS agents. They were good men, most with families. They loved their country just like she did, and they loved what they were doing. But a few had difficulty accepting a woman agent. There were female police officers, but this was different. This was an elite organization that hunted terrorists, enemy agents, and the leaders of organized crime.

Rokas Klem, Otto's number two, hadn't even acknowledged her that first morning.

A hundred kilometers per hour. Zuza had been wearing her new suit—a black jacket and slacks—that day. Her shoulder holster was so new she could smell the leather. The men had all shaken her hand, but the comradery she expected wasn't there. As everyone got back to work, the light banter that followed simply did not include her.

Around midmorning, Leva breezed in with coffee and a *sakotis*, a traditional cake. It started with Leva asking a few questions and expressing surprise upon hearing that Zuza had gone to college in California, where she had majored in international affairs. One of the men asked Zuza if she knew how to surf, and Zuza told a story about her board being overturned by a baby seal one morning. Leva's intervention had saved Zuza that day. It made Zuza approachable, and gave her the boost she needed. After that, Leva and Zuza fell into a comfortable and close friendship.

A hundred and ten kilometers per hour. Two months later, Leva had gone in for another MRI. Afterward, she and Leva had met at a café in Vilnius, one of the many quiet night spots that people loved in Old Town. A man in a suit sat at the next table, reading from his mobile phone. *He's cute*, mouthed Zuza. Leva managed a feeble smile as the waiter brought plates of pork steak and French-fried potatoes. As they ate, Leva broke the news.

The words, *I've got less than a year left and there's nothing they can do*, created a thunderstorm in Zuza's head that spread to her heart, and finally her stomach. She ran into the ladies' room and vomited into the toilet. Memories of her father blown to bits, the closed casket, the numbness that had morphed into anger far too soon to be healthy, all came back, knowing that her friend would also be taken from her.

Eventually, Zuza straightened and flushed away the bile. When she went to wash her face and rinse her mouth, Leva was there. They hugged. Both cried. An older woman came in, said *Oh!* and promptly left. The two women laughed.

Zuza helped Leva through the next months of doctor visits, treatment that had little chance of working, and hospitalizations. Zuza marveled that Leva hadn't wanted to travel or sleep with every man available or deaden her nerves with alcohol and drugs. Leva just wanted to stay with Otto and Zuza, have a quiet dinner and a glass of good Lithuanian beer while listening to music from her favorite show tunes. Ieva liked *Mamma Mia!* the best. The tunes stayed in Zuza's head for days.

A hundred and twenty kilometers per hour. Zuza tightened her grip on the wheel. While glad for the chance to say goodbye to her dear friend, and immensely grateful to be included in Ieva's life during those last few months, the memory of the wake made Zuza go even further back into her past. The speedometer continued inching upward as she remembered the pain of her father's death.

Based in Lithuania, the company Zuza's father had worked for sold lasers, and he'd developed one of their best-selling products. When Zuza was just a girl, he had the opportunity to relocate from Vilnius to New York City, and later to LA to start new offices. The family went with him. Sometimes he was gruff and quick to anger, but Zuza knew he loved her more than anyone. He was interested in everything she did, and encouraged Zuza to extend herself. At twelve, she won a New York state regional swimming competition. At sixteen, she won a state title in California for her backstroke.

Living in the US had changed her life, but what had changed it even more was the phone call Zuza had gotten three months after graduating from college. She was staying at her parents' house in Pasadena, wondering what she was going to do with her life. It was the morning of July 8. Her parents were in London on a business trip. Her mother was on the phone. She said that her father had been killed in a bombing. Terrorists. He had been blown apart. All that was left of him were little bits, but there were so many little bits of so many people all mixed together, it would take months to separate them.

The shock of her father's death erased all of her anxiety about the future, and replaced it with a purpose that determined the direction of her life. Within two months, she was working at Europol in Holland. Years later, when the opportunity came up with ARAS in Lithuania, Zuza jumped at it.

A hundred and forty kilometers per hour. A trailer truck raced past in the opposite direction. The Toyota fishtailed. Zuza hard-turned the steering wheel to avoid going into the ditch. She snapped out of the past and back to the present. She slowed down and got off the motorway, driving to the nearest town. She passed a lighted patch of green grass near a church, and parked under a fir tree. Zuza put her forehead against the steering wheel and cried.

# CHAPTER 12

## Kaunas, Lithuania—17 May

Darius shuddered as his Volkswagen Passat went past another marker for the A6 leading from Kaunas to Utena, the laptop computer with the video he had made earlier that day on the seat beside him. He was on the way to greatness. The car behind him honked. Looking down at his speedometer, he realized he was going far below the speed limit. He pressed down on the gas pedal and the Volkswagen sped up as the car behind tried to pass, just barely switching lanes in time to avoid another car speeding down the road in the opposite direction. Darius winced. He didn't like driving, and lately, found it particularly difficult. His heart condition seemed to be getting worse, and he was taking more medication to control his arrhythmia. Sometimes the drugs didn't work, or at least it felt that way. When stressed like he was now, he was a hazard on the road, but it was vital he deliver the video to Jonas.

If Darius's plan worked, and he was sure it would, the Russians would never come back. The freedom Ignas and so many others had died for would be ensured, and the new generations would be safe. At long last, truly safe.

As he drove, Darius thought back to his teenage years and the last time he had seen his father. It had been a beautiful summer's morning. They were fishing with Jonas along the Merkys River in southern Lithuania. When it got hot, they had settled down on a patch of grass under some trees for a lunch of sandwiches and beer. Darius had wolfed down his food and had stretched out under a shade tree, pretending to be asleep as he listened to Jonas and his father talk. That day, Ignas seemed to be free from the undercurrent of agitation that usually accompanied him, a trait Darius had inherited.

Ignas had come out of the woods for a few days of rest. He wouldn't spend the night at Jonas's house, claiming the Soviets were watching it, so whenever he visited, they stayed in the remote cabin that Jonas's father had built after the war. Very few people knew about it, and certainly not the Soviets, for they would have come long ago.

Ignas took a bite of sandwich and chewed carefully, showing his missing left upper incisor. Darius remembered the day his father had yanked it out in front of him with a pair of pliers. Ignas had done the extraction himself, because he thought dentists or doctors of any kind were watched by the Soviets. The memory made Darius cringe.

"I don't know why you live this way," Jonas said. "I love Darius like a son, and he can stay with me forever. But he needs his real father. Don't you think he wonders why you live like a hermit out in the woods instead of staying at home with him?"

"If the Soviets ever found me, they'd kill me. They know who I am, what I look like, what I've done."

"I don't think they do. They probably think you're dead." Jonas took a sip of beer. "You've fought the Soviets your entire life. I wouldn't be surprised if you were the last partisan alive. It's time for you to have some peace."

"I won't stop fighting. I won't accept that they're here for good."

Darius wanted to run into his father's arms, but instead, held his breath and listened.

"Ignas, they've been here for decades. What can one man do?" said Jonas.

"I want you to promise me something."

Jonas leaned his beer against the fishing bag.

"Take care of my son," said Ignas.

"Of course."

"No matter what. Keep him safe."

"You know I will."

"I've already taught him what I could."

"Why would you teach a child how to use guns and explosives? What's wrong with you?" Jonas shook his head.

"He's old enough, and I taught him how to survive. He may need to know those things one day. But it may not be enough. I want him to know books and history, to go to school. If he has the chance, I want him to make something of his life. Don't let him waste it."

Three days later, Ignas left. Darius anxiously waited for the next visit, as always, but weeks passed, and still no Ignas. One morning, Darius found a spent shell casing on the bureau in his room and knew Ignas had been there. Every week, he searched for more signs his father had visited, rummaging through his clothing and books as if he were looking for a prized birthday gift. Every so often, he would find something, and Darius felt that his father was close. Those insignificant pieces of debris became Darius's treasures. But after that fishing trip, there had been no more time together. As the years passed, the treasures stopped coming. Darius became convinced the KGB had either sent his father to Siberia or had killed him. He asked Jonas to find out what had happened. Jonas went off for a week. When he came back, he shrugged. No words; just a shrug. Darius begged Jonas to tell what he had learned, but the old man remained silent and wouldn't be moved.

This made Darius resentful. They often squabbled, usually about nothing. Darius immersed himself in the electronics that he loved, studying everything he could, and even went to university. All the nights when he came home late, Jonas had a meal ready. Darius always found money in his pocket for food and books.

When Darius was nineteen, he received word that his father was dead. It came through a distant cousin who worked as an attendant in the state psychiatric hospital in Kaunas, where dissidents were controlled by massive doses of sedatives. He had recognized Ignas's body as it was being covered for burial in an unmarked grave. The ember of Darius's hatred for the Russians burst into flame with the news. He promised himself to take up his father's gauntlet and do whatever was necessary to expel the Russians.

Even angrier with Jonas at his father's death, Darius quit university. He spent most of his time arguing with Jonas, drinking in Lukas's Bar, and experimenting with electronics in Jonas's shed.

Then came the day that Jonas told him of a plan to use nuclear waste and with Tilda Partenkas's help, build a dirty bomb. Jonas needed Darius's knowledge of explosives, but it meant that Jonas trusted him and saw him as an equal. Darius didn't believe Jonas intended to use the bomb as mere leverage against the Russians. Darius thought Jonas would annihilate them and finally avenge Ignas's death. Darius became a new man; focused, cooperative, hanging on Jonas's every word. But time passed and Jonas changed. He became quieter and even more pensive. Jonas didn't do anything with the spectacular weapon and the inaction grated Darius's nerves.

Darius spent all his time in the shed studying electronics books and experimenting, as he grew more impatient, restless, and angry. With the invention of the internet, he saw a way to make the money he needed to move out and be free of the old man. Darius started with an instructional video that explained how to make a GPS device. He sold it online and made more than he had expected. His next video showed how to make a baby monitor. From there, it was short-wave radios, computers, even home security systems. Home hobbyists paid a fee to watch each video and get online help from Darius. When his videos finally brought a stream of real income, the young man bought his own place in Kaunas, almost two hours away by car.

The day Darius moved out, Jonas sat by the window looking sullen as Darius came out of his bedroom with boxes that he loaded into his car, a secondhand vehicle he had bought from a tailor in the town of Joniskis, near the Latvian border. His last load consisted of clothing still on the hangers.

"You are the son I never had, so why do you hate me?" said Jonas.

"You don't trust me. You never have." A shirt fell to the floor. As Darius bent down to pick it up, another one dropped. "You knew about my father, didn't you?"

"You were too young to handle it. You still can't."

"You knew he was locked up in that crazy house, and you did nothing. You couldn't even tell me. Your friends say you're brave. I say you're a coward."

Jonas flinched. "If I had told you, you would have gone there and demanded he be released. The guards would either have beaten you or locked you up."

"I deserved to know! Did you ever even try to help him?"

"I visited every chance I could. Most of the time, they wouldn't let me see him. When they allowed us a moment together, he begged me not to tell you anything. He wanted you to get on with your life, because he had wasted his. Eventually, he was too far gone on the drugs they gave him to say even that."

"At least he tried to do what he thought was right for his country. You never did anything." Darius fought back tears as he stormed out, feeling righteous in his anger. Later that night, alone in his new apartment, he wanted to talk some more, but Jonas wasn't there. Darius picked up the phone and dialed the first three digits of Jonas's number before pride made him hang up the phone.

A few days later, Darius got up feeling unusually weak. His heart was racing. He thought it was nerves from his fight with Jonas. He stayed in bed all day, but didn't feel better. The next morning, Darius phoned Jonas, saying he wasn't well. Although Jonas was already miserable with arthritis in his back that made it painful to move, let alone lift anything, he went to Kaunas and brought Darius to the hospital. There, Darius was diagnosed with a heart condition that would manifest itself from time to time as an uncontrollably rapid heart rate.

It was there in the hospital that Darius admitted to himself that the old man had been right. Had Darius known about Ignas, he would have gone to the psychiatric hospital and demanded his father be freed. The guards would have locked him up.

His mother had abandoned him, and his father had gone into the woods to fight. Jonas had been the one true constant in his life.

~~

With the wind coming in from the Volkswagen's open windows, Darius glanced at the passenger seat and the laptop that held the video he had just made. He was intent on doing several things tonight: save his country, get back at the Russians, and finally make Jonas proud of him.

# CHAPTER 13

## Utena, Lithuania—17 May

Jonas folded the newspaper and put it beside him on the worn floor of the old house. He took off his reading glasses and carefully laid them on the windowsill before rubbing his eyes. He stared at his reflection in the window pane. His teeth were bad, and he needed a haircut. His suit jacket was covered in lint, dandruff, and a few white hairs. Each day, it was harder to move, and more tiresome to live. The days when he thought he could influence his country's path were long gone; another lesson Darius had failed to learn. If Darius ever used Tilda's bomb, Russia would raise her hammer and destroy them all. Lithuania would disappear in a river of blood. Thank God he had disbursed the other five containers and Darius didn't know where they were or who had taken them.

Besides, the Russians had never invaded. Jonas had no reason to use the bomb, for he had built it to protect his country, not the damned world.

Jonas knew the end wasn't far off, but he had one more urgent task to accomplish. He had to convince Darius to disassemble the bomb and make the parts unusable. They would bury the nuclear material where no one would find it. When that was done, Jonas would know Darius had learned temperance and good judgement. Jonas could die in peace with Darius at the head of Baltic Watch.

Jonas put his hands together and prayed to God to give Darius the wisdom to see that disassembling the bomb was the only sane thing to do. But the conversation with Elena haunted him. She had called

Darius a hothead with poor reasoning, and judgement clouded by his hatred of the Russians. If Darius didn't agree to destroy the bomb, there was only one thing Jonas could do.

He winced in pain as he rose from his chair and went to the closet in the bedroom. He reached for the box on the shelf and extracted his father's pistol, a Mauser, deadly for its relatively small size. Jurgis had stolen it from a German soldier before the Nazis had fled the country in 1944 like frightened rats. He thought of Jurgis and Raminta and all the love they had given him while growing up, the same kind of love he had tried to give Darius. Now, if Darius refused to help him destroy the bomb, Jonas had to make sure the younger man never used it. And there was only one way to do it with certainty. He brought the gun to his lips and kissed the cool barrel. Jonas hoped he had the nerve to do what needed to be done, if it came to that.

A knock at the back door startled him, and he almost dropped the weapon. He put it in the pocket of his jacket and went to the kitchen door.

~~

"What took so long to get here? I called you hours ago. I told you it was important," said Jonas, glancing out at Darius's car. The evening had faded into a burgundy sky.

"I was busy." Darius pushed past him to the refrigerator and took out two bottles of beer. He was impatient to show Jonas the video and finally have his approval for something that was vital to them all. But Jonas seemed unusually agitated.

Darius handed one of the bottles to Jonas. Both men went into the living room and sat at the table. Darius opened his laptop and turned it on. "I want to show you something." He moved the display screen toward Jonas and played the video he had just made, all the while observing the older man. As the video played, Jonas appeared to be angry, then surprised, and finally, deep in thought. Jonas had to be pleased, for Darius had never felt so proud. In just a few words, he had described the path his country must take to survive Vera Koslova. His ideas were brilliant. Simply brilliant.

When it ended, Jonas sat back looking stunned, his face sheet white.

"What did you think of the video?" said Darius.

"What in hell are you thinking?"

Darius looked up in surprise.

"You can't use that bomb. If you do, they'll hunt you down like a wild dog. And you can't show anyone that video. It will change how the world sees us. We'll no longer be a group who speaks rationally and openly about political issues. You've threatened NATO, for Christ's sake! You're just like your father. You have fire in your veins and rocks in your head."

Darius felt his heart rate quicken. *It wasn't supposed to happen like this.* "Other groups are saying the same thing. Listen to all those political reporting channels you like so much on TV. You're overreacting."

"Even if we wanted to do something, we couldn't. Antiterrorist groups all over the world are watching. We're not terrorists, but your video makes us seem like we could be. If you use that bomb, we definitely *will* be terrorists."

Darius nervously shuffled his feet under the table. "Why? Just because I said Russia is planning to invade and NATO has to protect us? That we'll force them to protect us if we must? Besides, *you* got us the nuclear material in the first place. It was *you* who had Tilda Partenkas build that bomb. It was *you* who said we needed it. I just want to finish what you had planned decades ago. Vera Koslova is going to send Russian troops here, as sure as I'm sitting next to you."

"If we use that bomb, it'll create a stigma our country won't survive."

Darius crossed his arms. "Terrorizing Russians doesn't count. Besides, you don't know what you're talking about. It's not a nuclear bomb. It's a bomb that releases nuclear material. That's all. It's no more or less harmful than any bomb of that size. And no one will know it was us."

"But it does matter. People think dirty bombs and nuclear bombs are the same thing. Listen to me. We'll dig it up and destroy it together. NATO will take care of us. The EU will stand by us. We'll be safe. We don't need the bomb."

"NATO won't send troops here unless provoked by drastic action. If the Russians cross the border, NATO will just impose sanctions like before, and we'll be stuck living under the Russians again. Crimea proved that sanctions against the Russians aren't enough. Wake up! Our youth are leaving the country. There are no jobs here. Our men whose best years were wasted under the Communists are drinking themselves to death. We have to turn things around. We have to give people pride in their country. If we use the weapon in Kiev to blow up the Russian Embassy and blame it on the rebels, the separatists, it will bring the area to the brink of war. Vera Koslova will have no choice but to occupy Ukraine to protect the Russians living there. NATO and the EU will send troops to the Baltics to prevent escalation and establish a line that the Russians won't dare cross." Darius leaned forward, his elbows on the table, his body stiff with conviction, expecting Jonas to absorb his brilliance.

"So that's why you talked about going to Kiev in Lukas's Bar. And you didn't have the sense to keep it to yourself."

"I want us to plan the details together. I want you to be a part of it. I want you to be with me. Think of what having NATO troops here will do for us. They'll need bars and restaurants. Hotels for when their families come to visit. Shops and clothing. Our economy will boom. Our children will come back home to live and raise their families." Darius waited for the older man to react, feeling like he had while waiting for his father to come back home. Darius searched Jonas's expression for the slightest hint of approval, and saw nothing but grief.

Darius pulled his hand back and reached for the laptop. *It was time.* Darius pressed the enter key, sending his video out into the internet. *It's done.* The video would soon be available to anyone in the world who wanted to see it.

Jonas's eyes looked wild as he pulled the gun from his pocket. He pointed it at Darius, his hands shaking.

"You're too late. You're always too late," said Darius.

"You have to be stopped."

Darius got to his feet. *Jonas didn't love me after all.* "Pull the trigger, old man!"

Jonas used his other hand to steady the gun as he let loose a sob.

Darius heaved the table upward, launching it onto Jonas's lap. The old man dropped the gun. Darius rushed to Jonas, now lying on the floor, the expression on the older man's face transforming from love, to surprise, to fear. Darius bent down and put his hands around Jonas's neck, squeezing. *I have to. Jonas will betray me if he lives.* The dying man tried to push him away, but Darius held fast. Jonas hit him in the head with his fists, but the blows were too weak to have any effect. *No one else can save the country.* Darius squeezed harder. Jonas hit him again. Anger seeped from Darius's hands as he squeezed and squeezed until Jonas lay still, and then he squeezed some more.

# CHAPTER 14

## Utena, Lithuania—17 May

In Jonas's messy living room, Darius sat back on his haunches beside the body and wiped the sweat from his face with his sleeve, feeling like an observer to the scene. Darius could tell Jonas was dead by the absolute stillness of his body, nothing more now than a shell. That Darius had actually killed someone with his bare hands made him feel sick. He looked away, but the clear picture of Jonas's dead face remained in Darius's mind. His heart raced. He reached into the pocket of his jacket for his medication. It wasn't there. He pictured it on his kitchen counter. Darius felt weak. He sat in his chair, next to the mess of papers and the body, and told himself to be calm.

He had to cover this up, for there was vital work to finish. He got a blanket from the bedroom and rolled Jonas onto it, covering him, trying not to look at his face. Darius turned out the lights. If any neighbors were watching, they would think Jonas had gone to bed. Darius went outside to his car and moved it as close as he could to the back door, keeping the headlights off. He dragged Jonas through the living room and kitchen, out the back door. With some effort, he managed to get Jonas into the trunk.

Darius went back inside. He put the gun in his pocket, righted the table, and mopped up the spilled beer with a dishrag and threw it into the sink. He put the empty bottles in his pockets, and picked up the papers scattered over the floor, along with Jonas's mobile phone. The papers were wet from the beer, but they would dry. He turned off the phone. He found a small overnight bag in the bedroom and tossed in some clothing. He took it into the bathroom and added Jonas's medication from the cabinet over the sink, plus the phone and beer bottles. He went outside and put the bag into the trunk next to the body. He tossed in a spade leaning against the house, shivering as he closed the lid.

Darius locked the doors to the house before getting into his car. Keeping the headlights off, he drove toward the motorway, trying to push out the vision of Jonas's body lying in the back.

The traffic was light, but even so, Darius had to swerve to avoid a collision with a Transimeksa delivery truck. He turned onto 102 and headed northeast, driving precisely at the speed limit, minding the speed cameras, and constantly looking for police cars in his rearview mirror. Driving took every bit of control he had. He turned onto 111, heading to the general area of the Ignalina power plant. He turned off on the road to Visaginas, following the same path he had in 1992 when Tilda Partenkas was in the car sitting beside him, nervously wringing her hands. He could almost see her, almost smell her perfume.

The road became progressively worse; narrowing, finally changing to dirt. At the meadow, Darius stopped the car and got out. He knew he was alone, but couldn't help glancing over his shoulder. He opened the trunk, reaching in for the spade and emergency flashlight. He shivered when his arm accidentally touched the body.

He walked toward the trees, peering into the recesses of black, imagining someone was there. He paused at every sound and tripped like a blind man, his heart racing, sweat pouring down his forehead. He stopped and squatted, taking deep breaths. He finally noticed the formation of trees he was looking for, just to his left, the lone elm in front. He swept the light over the terrain. It took only seconds for him to get to the spot where he and Jonas had originally buried the bomb, but Darius had outwitted him. Instead of digging there, Darius stood at the elm tree and faced west. He counted out ten paces, turned to the right, and counted out ten more paces, skirting a bush in the path. Darius put his spade in the ground in front of his big toe and dug in the lamplight. He listened to the sharp rasp of dirt against the shovel, and the thump as it fell to the ground.

With each shovelful of dirt, Darius remembered being here before, also in the middle of the night, working with the same resolve and determination, feeling a similar fear. It had been just after Russia's annexation of Crimea. Jonas had refused to publish Darius's scathing article about Putin and Russian aggression in the Baltic Watch newsletter. Jonas had called the article immature, a rant, and unbalanced. Darius had bristled at the words, fuming with anger. They had fought. Darius had stormed out. After posting the article to the internet despite Jonas's condemnation, Darius headed directly for the forest near Visaginas, where they had buried the bomb in 1992. Slowly and carefully, Darius had dug it up, knowing full well the instability of aging dynamite and the danger in what he was doing. He carefully removed the dynamite and placed it in a shallow grave some distance away. He reburied the suitcase of nuclear material, putting it in a different location, one that Jonas didn't know, one he would never find. As Darius felt the pain of betraying Jonas, he also felt the power of knowing *he* was in control. Darius would make the decision when to use the weapon, not Jonas. All Darius had to do now was wait for the right time, and it had come with Vera Koslova.

Darius tried not to remember Jonas's body in the trunk of the car as he dug, but the face frozen in fear stayed with him. He pushed the spade into the dirt, each shovelful bringing back a memory; Jonas sitting quietly in his chair reading a book, pausing every so often to tell Darius something interesting. It felt like a giant hand was squeezing Darius's heart.

He encountered resistance that didn't feel like dirt. He fell to his knees, pushing the soil away with his hands. He pulled up a container holding a treasure that would change the world. Darius carefully picked up the nuclear suitcase, brushed off a clump of dirt clinging to it, and set it aside.

He continued to dig, widening the hole, eventually pulling out a package wrapped in black plastic. Several times, Darius had bought plastic explosive from the sisters Rina and Simona, acquaintances who worked in a car theft ring and had the right connections for most of the material Darius needed to rework the bomb. He had gone to university with their mother, and decades later, when he found out what Rina and Simona did for a living, he got in touch through a mutual friend. Besides cars, the women could also get specialty items for their friends; big plasma screens, drones, sixty megapixel resolution cameras, and more. Darius had ordered explosives from them a few times, practicing with it out in the woods where he blew up trees to see first-hand how effective it was. He had buried the rest in a black plastic bag out in the forest.

Darius carried the items back to the car and placed them on the ground. Next, he turned to Jonas. Darius had no choice but to put his arms around the corpse. He tugged and pulled. In the end, Jonas fell to the ground in a heap. Darius put the explosives and the suitcase in the trunk, then straightened out the blanket under the body. Taking two corners in his hands, he dragged Jonas to the hole. As Darius dug to expand it even more, he thought how poetic it was that Jonas would be buried in the spot where the bomb had been hidden.

A blister formed on Darius's palm and burst. Dirt made it sting. He increased the size of the hole until it was wide and long enough for a body. He dug deeper. He tired and had to rest. He dug again. He wished he had some water to drink. It was a blessing he was too tired to think. When he could do no more, he rolled Jonas into the hole, along with the small bag of clothing and the beer bottles. Darius covered Jonas with the edges of the blanket, then covered everything with loose dirt. He tamped down the soil with his feet and scattered the remaining dirt. Using the flashlight to guide his way, he gathered leaves and pine needles into his arms, tossing them over the disturbed earth. He carried over a long narrow tree branch and threw it over the leaves. In didn't look at all like a grave in the glow of the flashlight.

He went back to the car. He sat behind the wheel in the dark, thinking of Jonas. The tears came all at once, and Darius howled like a wolf pup who had lost its mother. Sometime later, he recovered enough to drive, albeit slowly, his head throbbing. As he looked over his left shoulder before getting onto the motorway, he sensed something on the seat next to him.

"You're not going to leave me out there, are you?" said Jonas. His neck was badly bruised.

Darius yelped like a scared dog, veering off the road, barely avoiding a rock. Next time he looked, Jonas wasn't there. Darius drove home to Kaunas, avoiding even a wayward glance at the passenger seat. When he got to his apartment, he went inside and bolted the door shut.

# CHAPTER 15

## Kaunas, Lithuania—18 May

Inside his apartment, Darius was weak with exhaustion and grief. He showered away the dirt, and put on an old pair of sweat-pants and a T-shirt. He slathered ointment on his blistered hands, drank several glasses of water, and fell into bed. He spent restless hours trying not to think of Jonas, while picturing the old man's last expressions. Darius did anything he could to divert his mind from that look of fear; adding large numbers in his head, remembering old friends and their names. In the hours just before dawn, he was too tired for mental tricks, and remembered how Jonas had taken care of him and loved him, and he cried again.

When Darius got up, the sun was high in the sky. He felt weary, lost, and more despondent than ever before. He fortified himself with coffee and tried to eat some bread, but couldn't, finally tossing the torn bits into the garbage in frustration. He remembered his dirty clothes from last night, lying on the bathroom floor. He wadded them into a ball and threw them into the garbage. He carried the bag of trash downstairs and tossed it into the bin behind the building.

Back in his apartment, he went to the desk in his bedroom where he'd left the bomb. He knew he had some of the components needed to rework it, but not all. *Jonas was supposed to have helped me.* He considered what he needed, and worried that he had forgotten something. After opening the safe in his closet and taking out a few hundred euros from the cash he usually kept there for purchases, Darius made a frantic visit to the electronics store, hoping they would have the right items. He easily found the untraceable burner phones and some additional wiring, chiding himself for worrying so much.

When he returned to his apartment, he carried everything he needed to the desk in the bedroom and placed it next to the bomb. He stepped back and looked at the items, an odd mix of new components and that dirt-encrusted suitcase. Some of the soil had dried and fallen to the surface, revealing minor corrosion. But Darius didn't care. It was his crown jewel, his treasure, what he had risked his life to obtain, and what he would risk his life to use. Exhausted, he lay down and closed his eyes. Jonas appeared, standing next to the bed, blood dripping from his neck. Darius woke up screaming. He gave up on the notion of rest, choosing instead to sit in bed watching the suitcase, Jonas's old Mauser on the nightstand next to him.

Early the next morning, Darius had the fleeting notion of giving it all up to the police and facing the consequences. But he couldn't. No one on earth could do what he was about to. No one on earth could save his country in one sure stroke of genius. It all hinged on his composure, for ultimately, no one could suspect he was behind the bomb. He would make it look like someone else had been inspired by his video, and had taken on the job of killing Russians in Ukraine by defiling the country with poisonous radiation. He congratulated himself, knowing he was the only one. The calm that followed brought the promise of progress.

He considered going online to see how many times his video had been viewed, but decided against it. It was a distraction. Instead, he settled down at the desk and got to work on the bomb.

# CHAPTER 16

## Moscow—18 May

Nina took a breath as she stood outside the door to Vera Koslova's office. She smoothed her skirt, anxious to see her friend for tea, but knowing they would discuss any matters Vera had in mind. She felt uncomfortable in the new suit, as it was tighter than what she was accustomed to. But the days of shapeless gray dresses, plastic belts, and sensible shoes were gone. The navy pinstripe jacket against the light blue shirt and Givenchy ascot contrasted nicely with her rosy complexion. The black heels felt a bit strange, but she would get used to them. She was among the wave of modern women in Russia who looked as good as their counterparts in New York and London, and who were as influential as any politician in the West.

Nina knocked. Vera Koslova herself opened the door. Dressed in a slate-gray suit, she was a glorious vision of the New Russia. Nina stepped inside. The women looked at each other for a moment before hugging. When they broke their embrace, Nina wiped a tear from her cheek.

"I can't believe it," said Nina. "You're the most powerful person in all of Russia. I never dreamed you'd come this far. I'm proud of you."

"I wish our mothers could be here to celebrate with us." Vera took Nina's hand and guided her through the office to a room few others visited. It resembled a living room with ornate wallpaper, bookcases, and a blue satin couch. Babushka's samovar sat on a coffee table, the hot tea steaming. Vera poured some into glasses set in silver filigree, before adding a cube of sugar to each. She handed a glass to Nina.

"To our fathers," said Vera. "May the devil find them both enchanting company and keep them close for eternity."

"While our mothers enjoy the view from heaven."

Vera offered her the plate of tea cakes. "How do you like your new office?"

Nina laughed. "I never imagined having one so large and elegant, and my own staff of secretaries."

"You'll need them. We have a lot of work to do. By the way, your interview on Channel One Russia was excellent. All those preparations paid off."

"Just as you predicted." Nina took a tea cake, remembering the nights she and Vera had spent reviewing the questions they had scripted for the TV show, and looking for just the right nuance in the answers.

Vera put her cup down. "I want to talk to you about the riots in Novosibirsk. I don't want the people to think there's a faction so violently against me that they resort to extremism. I couldn't prevent the news from getting out, and all Fedov did before leaving office was to secure the area. But perhaps we can turn the situation to our advantage. I want the people to think that the unrest was the result of an outside threat. I want you to position it as an act of terrorism."

"Influence from the West, trying to sway the people against you?"

"That would work. But make it more than the meddling in the US that Vladimir Vladimirovich was accused of, God rest his soul. I want this to be positioned as a deliberate and organized plan to oust me from power. After all, *someone* has to be blamed."

"The Americans will deny it, of course. There will be some retaliation."

"It's not a matter for NATO or the UN, so it will be our word against theirs."

"I'll have some experts write up news articles and political analysis."

"Start slow and be subtle. Have the articles come from outside Russia. Raise concerns and state suspicions. Give our people the impression that the US is embarking on a cyber warfare campaign to sway Russian public opinion. Speculate on what they might be planning. Our people are smart enough to come to the conclusions we want, especially when it involves the US government that they already see as corrupt and superficial."

"Excellent."

"Once our people believe this, they'll see military buildup as a necessary precautionary step, not that we fear invasion, but to make a show of power. I want the people to stop talking about me as an ex-KGB agent. I want them to see me as a leader willing to expose the truth and protect our country."

"I have no doubt that you will." Nina smiled.

Vera leaned toward her. "I guarantee, if we do this properly and plant the right seeds, our people will be proud. They'll think we stopped the Western devil from asserting influence over us, and that we're acting as a great nation once again."

"Do you have specific media channels in mind or just the usual TV, radio, the press, and of course the internet?"

"Let's start with the internet. Tomorrow, I'm doing a one-woman TV show, where people call in with their problems. Vladimir Vladimirovich did it to improve his standing, and there's no reason why it wouldn't work for me, too. It'll be a big step toward everyone thinking of me as mother to all of Russia. But during the disinformation campaign, we need to find the people responsible for the protests, and make sure they're dealt with. Quietly. All updates come to me. What have you found so far?"

"Several people in the crowd were carrying explosives."

"Do you know who they were?"

"The bodies were vaporized, along with bystanders. Eventually, forensics may identify them, but it's a long shot."

"All suicides?"

Nina nodded.

"Any information on the type of explosive they used?" said Vera.

"We were able to determine the explosive was synthetic and manufactured in the US."

"Anyone can get that here on the black market."

"The detonator however, may have been made in Russia."

"A conspiracy against me." Vera dropped another cube of sugar into her partially filled glass of tea and stirred it with a tiny silver spoon.

Nina continued. "The riots could've been organized by a political group, although we don't know for certain yet. It could be a warning from Fedov's people telling you not to get too comfortable, and paving the way for Grinsky to become our next president. It could be something else altogether."

"I need to know everything you find. I want you to oversee the investigation yourself. Orlov has it now?"

"Yes, it went to him as new Deputy Director."

"Keep the investigation confined to as few people as possible. In fact, I'll have a chat with Orlov myself. I want to know the person responsible for those riots."

"Yes, Madame President. I'll do my best to get to the bottom of it."

At that, the women stood. Vera kissed Nina's cheeks before escorting her to the door.

"Have you ever thought that we were luckier than most?" said Nina.

"We're smarter and more accomplished."

"At certain points, we were chosen over men who were just as capable and certainly better connected than we were, and of course, they were men. Have you ever thought that someone was helping us?"

Vera shrugged. "You think it was your grandfather? Ivan Ditlov was certainly important enough to influence our careers. But your mother thought he was going to take you away from her if he ever found you."

"But he never came after us. He left us alone even though he certainly had the means to find out where we were."

"So why would you think he was helping us?"

"Age? Regret?"

"I don't know if anything was ever handed to me, and if it was, I don't care. What matters is what I do with the opportunities I have. And if there are no opportunities, I create them."

"Until our deaths," said Nina.

# CHAPTER 17

## Lahey Hospital, Burlington, Massachusetts—18 May

The nurse at the reception counter looked up from her computer as Vit Partenkas came down the hallway. She smiled as he dodged to the side to avoid a technician with a harried look on his face hurrying down the corridor, pushing a portable X-ray machine.

Vit approached the nurse. "The sun's barely up and you good doctors and nurses are already hard at work."

"Security calls us when you arrive, and we rush out of the break room and try to look busy."

"How is she doing today?"

"She didn't sleep well last night. She wanted us to call you, but it was too early and you haven't missed a morning yet."

"Did she say what it was about?"

The nurse shook her head, her gaze going to her computer screen.

Vit reached into his pocket, pulling out a baseball wrapped in red ribbon and handing it to the nurse. "For your son."

"You didn't have to do that."

"It's autographed. J.D. Martinez, designated hitter for the Red Sox. Tell him I said happy birthday." Waving his goodbye, Vit made his way over the gleaming gray linoleum to room 1732 and gently pushed the door open. "Morning, Tilda."

His grandmother was in bed, staring at the TV. Her eyes were red. Her skin was pale. Her body almost disappeared under the rumpled blanket. The channel was set to one of the national cable outlets. A panel of political commentators and a retired Army general was discussing Vera Koslova, the new president of Russia, and the recent troop maneuvers along the border with Ukraine. Tilda held up her index finger, her gaze on the screen as it flashed a news bulletin.

"We just received confirmation that Russia is moving additional troops into Kaliningrad, taking the reinforcements they sent last week to an even higher level of readiness," said an attractive young reporter. Her hair and scarf were blowing in the breeze, the white froth of the surface waves on the Baltic Sea visible behind her.

Tilda turned the sound down. "Close the door and come in."

Vit wasn't sure what it was going to be today; ramblings about the old country, or more likely, venomous comments about Soviets who didn't exist anymore. As he pulled up a chair, Vit lamented how her brilliant mind had slowly deteriorated from the effects of the drug she and her husband had created to save people from radiation poisoning. He had died of a heart condition, unrelated to the drug, long before the disastrous side effects had been noticed. The medication they had invented had proved deadly over time, and Tilda was the prime case study, having taken the suggested dosage over the recommended period of time. Muscles deteriorated, and for some like Tilda, that included the brain. Years ago, she had been heralded as the genius of her time. She'd helped create a drug that was far more effective than potassium iodide at protecting the body from the effects of radiation poisoning. Now, she was considered a complete failure. The news commentators called her a "walking, talking corpse." He remembered how hurt she had been upon first hearing this, but sometimes her damaged mind was too far gone to remember, and for things like that, it was a blessing. Other times, with great effort, she was lucid, but those occasions were rare.

Her only redemption was that her research had inspired scientists to continue searching, eventually creating TP508, a drug that had proved an effective countermeasure to radiation exposure for the workers at the Fukushima power plant after the meltdown in 2011. Unfortunately, she probably didn't even remember that one positive outcome of her work.

Now Tilda had good days, but mostly bad ones. As he sat down, Vit prepared himself for a bad day.

"Remember when I went to Vilnius in 1992 to accept the Order of Merit award?" Tilda leaned over her bed to the nightstand and opened a box with a red ribbon attached to a five-pointed gold cross. Vit smiled, remembering that she took it with her wherever she went. It looked like she was straining to speak. "Had it not been for that night in Visaginas, this award would've been the crowning glory of my life."

"You deserved it." Vit had no idea what she had been doing in Visaginas, and assumed it was just another town in Lithuania. He knew little about the country, and barely remembered the language Tilda had tried to teach him when he was little. He had no particular interest in the country or its dialect.

"I figured out how to protect people from radiation, especially those who worked and lived around nuclear power plants. It was too late for Three Mile Island and Chernobyl. It helped the people at Fukushima, although only indirectly. Ignalina is almost gone, thank God. The EU forced it to be dismantled because they feared another disaster like Chernobyl, even though it will take another twenty years to finish the work. But what I did was good for the world, wasn't it, Vit?"

"Of course, *Bobute*." She was unusually lucid today and Vit breathed a little easier.

"Before I left Tufts for my award ceremony, I got a letter from a group called Baltic Watch, saying they had information about my father, your great-grandfather. At the time, I didn't even know what Baltic Watch was. But I learned they're a watchdog group, keeping an eye on the Russians and offering political analysis. In 1992 there were members from Latvia, Estonia, Poland, and two from Lithuania. Most have died off, though, and only the Lithuanians are left. Their leader is Jonas Volkis. Darius Artis is the other. He contacted me." Tilda looked feverish as she pointed at the cup of water on her nightstand. Vit brought it to Tilda and held it while she took a sip through the straw. He was surprised she was talking so well.

Tilda continued. "After your great-grandmother and I fled the old country in 1948, I never heard from Papa again. Not knowing what happened to him was the worst thing I ever had to deal with, aside from burying my husband. Darius, Jonas's second-in-command, told me the horrible things the Russians did to your great-grandfather. It's hard to remember, but I have to. You have to hear this." She touched her fingertips to her forehead.

"How could those people know what happened to my great-grandfather?"

"Darius said his father had seen the Soviets torture Papa for weeks. *Weeks!* He saw it with his own eyes. Why do you doubt me?" Tilda leaned back against the pillows. She looked in pain.

"Did Baltic Watch ask you for any money?"

"Money? Is that what you think?" She managed a dry laugh. "They wanted far more than money. Jonas asked me to help him make the future generations safe. And of course, I wanted to, I was so angry about what they did to Papa. I had thought about it before, crazy as it was, but the complications of getting the right materials, building a device, hiding it, and most importantly of all, deciding when to use it, were insurmountable."

"What are you talking about?" Vit's heart sank. *She's speaking nonsense again.*

"Jonas had taken care of all of that. He wouldn't tell me how they got the nuclear material. I assumed they had stolen it from Ignalina. He said there was so much confusion around the time of the Soviet breakup that people got away with things. All I had to do was help Darius assemble the parts. Together, at Jonas's cabin, we made a dirty bomb. But Jonas promised me on his life he would never use it. He told me it was a bargaining chip. I trusted him."

Tilda's eyes were wild. "Jonas reminded me of my husband. I thought my pill would eventually make the bomb useless, and that we only needed to protect the homeland for few years until we joined NATO and the EU. With my pills, I was going to protect the world. But my medicine's no good, is it Vit?"

Vit took her hand, hoping the nurse would come in with Tilda's meds.

"I was so angry at the Russians for what they had done to Papa that I helped willingly, despite my reservations. Jonas was level-headed, and I thought if anyone could make a good decision, it was him. I worried about Darius, though. He was young and passionate; too passionate. But I thought it was all right as long as Jonas was there. So, I did what they asked of me. Afterward, I went to Vilnius, collected my medal, and went back home to Boston.

"For decades, it was peaceful. I got worried when Russia took the Crimean Peninsula, but nothing happened. I knew Jonas was keeping his promise to never use it. In the years that followed, I almost forgot about what I had done, what I had built. But I still call Ignalina the Amber Widow, because it may yet be the cause of many deaths." Tilda fingered the amber wedding ring she still wore, its stones a symbol of Lithuania.

She touched the TV. A screen popped up running a video of a man, probably over fifty, white hair at the temples, waving his hands spasmodically, speaking in a high, squeaky voice. He was talking about Vera Koslova, claiming she was a threat to a secure world, criticizing the Baltic countries for passive diplomacy, and demanding that NATO take action or *else*.

After the video ended, Tilda continued. "That's Darius. He's speaking for Baltic Watch now. It means Jonas isn't the head of the organization anymore. I don't even know if he's alive. I think Darius knows where the bomb is. You have to find him and stop him from using it."

As she gazed into his eyes, Vit could see the glimmer of awareness fade into tears. "Promise me you'll go to the old country," she said. "Find Jonas Volkis and make sure he's okay. Make sure no one uses that bomb. And don't mention this to anyone, especially your mother." She lay back looking even more exhausted than before. She closed her eyes. Within minutes, her deep and rhythmic breathing told Vit she was asleep.

He sat back, watching her, amazed at the fantastic story she had told him, and equally surprised that she seemed to believe it. She was clearly relieved to have finally shared this burden.

As he stood and headed toward the door, Tilda opened her eyes. "Vit? You're here. I've been expecting you. Come sit down."

# CHAPTER 18

## VGTRK All Russia State Broadcasting Studio, Moscow—18 May

Vera squinted into the lights surrounding the makeup mirror. The brightness bothered her, but she could stand it. She could stand anything. The cosmetician gently pulled away the tissue paper protecting Vera's collar, declaring her beautiful. Vera nodded, allowing herself a moment to admire her strong features. She had the slim face and straight shoulders of a woman thirty years her junior.

She went down a poorly lit hallway to a small stage. The seats in the audience were empty, except for Michael and a few others whom she knew. None of the general public was allowed inside; they would have to watch on TV.

She sat behind a desk, a replica of the one in her office and the only furniture there except for a Russian flag behind it and to the right where it could be clearly seen, and a narrow table holding Babushka's samovar. She turned toward the cameras and lights that were even brighter than the ones in the dressing room.

"Madame President, shall we begin?" The stage manager was a mousy-looking fellow, but she could tell from his tone of voice that he commanded respect. She cleared her throat and nodded, ready to resume the time-honored tradition of the president of Russia directly addressing the people of the motherland.

She began with a brief greeting, claiming they were investigating new leads in the riots and resulting deaths, and that the military was improving overall security. She concluded her preliminary comments with the observation that any indication of meddling by foreign powers would be dealt with severely.

"Who is our first caller?" said Vera.

A girl responded, her high voice clear over the overhead speakers. "*Tetka* Vera. Daddy said the gas meters aren't working right in our town and everyone is getting bills they can't pay, so they shut off the heat. Daddy comes home from working all day and goes out in the night to cut wood for the fire for us and Babushka who's old and doesn't have any heat, either. It's very cold, Tetka Vera, and my brother Yuri is sick. Can you help us?"

"What is your name, child?"

"Eugenia."

"Eugenia, tell your father that no one will have to pay their fuel bills in your town for the rest of the year, and Tetka Vera will make sure that the gas is turned on."

"I love you, Tetka Vera."

"I love you too, Eugenia. Next caller, please."

This time, a man with a shaking voice explained that ever since the Tsai Kai alumina refinery had closed production in Kemerovo, the company wasn't paying the back salaries. "We have no money. We have no jobs. We're starving. And they owe us for months of back wages."

"Have you spoken to the local authorities?"

"They say there is nothing they can do. Tsai Kai has to remain profitable, and it costs too much to ship from our little town. My children are hungry, Madame President. All we're asking for is the money they owe us. Please help us. No one else will." His sobs came clearly over the speakers.

"I will see to it that you get your wages. In addition to this, I want to invite you and your family to Moscow, to stay with me as my guests. Let me take care of you for a week, as you have taken care of Mother Russia with years of faithful service in providing materials important to our military and the security of our people."

"God bless you, Vera Yaroslavna. God bless you."

Vera smiled that the man had used her middle name, as it was considered a form of endearment. The next caller referred to her as Vera Yaroslavna, as did the next one, and the one after that. Four hours and thirty-two minutes later, Vera brought the TV show to a close. The spotlights clicked off, making the room immediately cooler. Vera sat back. She was exhausted, but it had been a great night. She had come off as strong, compassionate, and caring. She had turned the country away from thoughts of terrorism and internal unrest, to the issues of food and heat. It was what she had needed to do. She was sure her popularity rating was about to soar.

The mousy-looking man removed the microphone from Vera's lapel as Nina came in from stage left. Following her was Orlov. Tall and gaunt, he looked like he hadn't had a good night's sleep in a decade, a situation that wasn't likely to change with his new position. With Nina moving on to become Vera's assistant, he had been appointed to Nina's former position, deputy director of the FSB. It meant longer and more intense hours than ever before. Vera smiled upon seeing him; it had been a long time.

"Were you able to catch some of the show?" Vera waited for Orlov to give his opinion. Even if she had failed miserably, which she had not, he would say it had gone beautifully.

Orlov stepped up to her and kissed her hand. "You were magnificent, as always."

His touch felt like a caress. Vera had forgotten how much she'd enjoyed him.

Michael ran up the steps to the stage. "Vera, you were wonderful. That little girl Eugenia calling you Tetka brought tears to my eyes."

Orlov let go of Vera's hand.

Vera waved Michael off. "We have business to discuss. I'll see you tonight at home."

Michael shrugged and went slowly back down the steps. Vera shook her head as she watched him leave. Then Nina and Orlov followed Vera to the dressing room, where she poured out three glasses of Khortytsa. Her guests sat on the couch covered with red velvet and ornate wood trim in the style Vera preferred. She settled into the matching upholstered chair across from them and thought about the mole in the shape of a crescent on Orlov's back.

He made a toast to her success and good health; they drank. Vera poured out more vodka and sat back watching her guests. That Nina had come with a trusted associate from the FSB meant this was more than a congratulatory visit. Something serious was going on that might require Vera's personal attention.

Nina ignored her drink. "There's something you need to be aware of. Baltic Watch just released a video."

Vera set the glass down, recalling the network of dissidents from countries that bordered the Baltic Sea. They had constantly fed their countrymen analysis of Russian affairs that was alarmingly close to the truth. She hadn't been involved directly with them as her scope was domestic intelligence, but she remembered some of the treatises with disdain. "I thought they were all dead."

"Not quite," said Nina as Orlov went to the TV and inserted a flash drive into the slot on the side. Darius's video played.

After it finished, Vera spoke. "So?"

Nina took a minute. "He's making a plea to NATO to send in troops to the Baltics. They've made such requests before. Of course, NATO has never responded. On the other hand, he may be planning something to force NATO into taking action."

The success of the day faded as Vera spoke. "We haven't heard from Baltic Watch in years. Why are you even showing me this? I have far more important things to deal with."

"The only ones left are this man Darius Artis and Jonas Volkis, who founded the organization," said Nina. "There have been no new members in years. They're far less influential than in the 1990s. But people remember them, especially Jonas."

"Damn those Lithuanians. They're always up to no good. We should've taken care of them when we had the chance." Vera tossed back her drink and set the empty glass down on the coffee table with a bang. She recalled their defiance after WWII, constantly provoking the Red Army troops with ambushes, cut telegraph and telephone lines, and assassinations. In the late 1980s, they had the gall to declare independence from the Soviet Union, even before the breakup occurred, kicking the Russians in the teeth during a time of confusion and adjustment. She knew she'd hear from them again as her new Baltic pipeline, Nord Stream 2, neared completion. The Lithuanians had already given Fedov many sleepless nights protesting the nuclear power plant being built in Belarus. She expected more protests about that, too. Whenever those people were involved, it was always bad news.

Nina continued. "At his strongest, Jonas Volkis wrote stunning pieces warning people that the Soviet Union was not gone, but had just taken on a new name. People didn't believe him at first, but grew to. He was the one who exposed the true impact of the high prices Lithuanian were paying for Russian gas, although we don't know how he got his information. He never proclaimed overt action against Russia at any time, so we tolerated him. Besides, our people in Lithuania watched him constantly, and he seemed harmless. After a few years of inactivity, we stopped watching him altogether. The problem with this video is that Jonas Volkis isn't speaking. Darius Artis is, and he's completely different. He's a known radical. His piece against the Crimean situation advocated specific action against Russia. It didn't come from Baltic Watch, but Darius wrote it and put it on the internet. I think his video begs for attention, and you need to be aware."

"All right," said Vera. "Send someone in to find out what's really going on. Don't use any of our people, though. We don't know what's involved, and we don't know how bad it is. Send in somebody who can handle a delicate situation. I don't want anything traced back to us."

"I'll get Bok," said Nina.

"Have him find Jonas Volkis and that other fellow. If they're up to something, have Bok take care of it." Vera's stomach tightened. When she had been in the FSB, she had used Bok for *chernaya rabota*—black work. A short stubby man, he specialized in two types of missions: when information was needed quickly, as he had a way of getting people to talk, and when a person needed to disappear, for he was good at that, too. Unfortunately, his methods were repellent to even the most experienced among his associates. He was used when quick results were needed, most recently to convince a file clerk in the Turkish government to reveal a top-secret armament deal with the US. After her meeting with Bok, the poor woman appeared to have slipped on her bathroom floor and was found dead from a broken neck.

Vera had never been alone in a room with Alexy Bok, and never wanted to be.

# CHAPTER 19

## Police Headquarters, Vilnius, Lithuania—18 May

Zuza Bartus drove to the back entrance of the massive yellow brick building on Saltoniskis Street where she worked. The cloudy day suited her mood. To her right, three fellow agents from Otto Krukas's team stood next to a black van, one of them pulling a thin man in an orange hoodie out of the vehicle. All the agents were dressed in Kevlar vests with the letters ARAS written on the back, identifying them as members of the anti-terrorist branch of the Lithuanian Police. *She* should be with them. It was her team, too. But Rokas Klem had left her out of the operation. Deliberately. She guessed it was the call that had come in during Leva Krukas's memorial service. Rokas had taken it, and had summoned all agents in Otto's small team, to go with him, except for her.

As she passed them, the agents waiting in the driveway acknowledged her with a nod, except for Rokas, who ignored her as usual. She continued to the back of the building and parked. On her way inside, she stopped at the blue booth outside the entrance.

"*Laba diena,*" Zuza said to the uniformed officer sitting in front of a console and communications equipment inside. She handed him a plastic container containing two potato dumplings. "I saved these for you from Leva's reception after the service."

"How's Otto?"

Zuza shrugged. "He just lost his daughter. How would you expect him to be?"

The man nodded as he took the container. "You're making me fat, Zuza."

She turned at a scuffle behind her and stepped back as the ARAS agents rushed past her. Two agents grasped the man in the orange hoodie by his arms, practically lifting him up the steps. This time, Rokas caught her gaze with a look of disgust that said she didn't belong. She felt her back stiffen as the agents hustled the hooded man into the building.

The officer in the booth went on. "It'll get better. Rokas is old-fashioned. He thinks women should be home taking care of babies, not out looking for terrorists. Just give him some time." A radio crackled on the bench in front of him and he put headphones on before speaking into a microphone.

"I'm not sure time will make any difference," said Zuza, making her way up the steps. She swiped her keycard into the lock. It clicked and she opened the door. Just a year in and still considered a rookie, she was regretting having taken the job with ARAS. She thought of her father, who was the reason why she had joined in the first place, wondering what advice he would give her.

Zuza thought back to when she was eleven, getting ready to swim in her first competitive meet. *The air smelled of chlorine. Voices from the crowd sounded even louder in the cavernous room holding the Olympic sized pool. All the girls who had qualified for the heat were bigger than Zuza. Minutes before the race began, in her swimsuit and goggles, she had run to her father sitting in the bleachers.*

*"I can't do this, Papa."*

*He smiled. "Of course, you can. Just pretend you're swimming for me."*

*Zuza had placed second.*

If he were alive to advise her on ARAS, he would probably say *Don't leave because it's hard.* Besides, Leva's last wish before dying was to ask Zuza to stick with it. Zuza had to, at least for a while longer.

Zuza went down a long corridor, past several rooms, finally opening the door to the area occupied by Otto and his team. The large room had several desks haphazardly situated throughout the space, and old filing cabinets along the walls. Every surface was messy. No one was inside, as they were all probably with the prisoner in the hoodie. Otto hadn't yet returned from the memorial service. She took off her suit jacket and draped it over the back of her chair before clicking on her computer. She dabbed her eyes with a tissue. *I'm one big, tough anti-terrorism agent, aren't I,* she thought, blowing her nose.

The private funeral had taken place yesterday, just for family and a few friends as Leva had wanted. Today's memorial service was for everyone beyond the immediate family who wanted to pay their respects, and the church was overflowing with people. Zuza had attended both events and cried both times. So had Otto. It had broken her heart to see the big man in pain.

After Rokas and the other agents had gone, she was left behind at the service with Otto, who didn't seem aware of anything, let alone his agents leaving without her once again. She was one of them, dammit!

She knew from the officer in the blue booth that Rokas had objected to Otto hiring a female agent. Rokas had even threatened to quit because of it. Zuza didn't believe the story at first, but in retrospect realized that Rokas's impression of what women could do was deeply ingrained. There might be a reason for it, but Zuza couldn't imagine what it was. The rest of the team looked up to both Rokas and Otto, so to keep the peace, they treated her with ambivalence when he was around, and warmly when Rokas was gone. It wasn't as it should be. Now, Otto protecting her from missions that held the slightest hint of danger only made things worse.

Zuza needed to talk to Otto. She hadn't taken this job to sit behind a desk. He was unnecessarily protecting her, and she had to make him stop. When the time came to confront him, she would have to choose her words carefully, for she didn't want to accuse him of treating her like the daughter he had just lost.

The door to the squad room slammed shut. Otto walked in, phone to his ear, his black suit jacket hanging from his thick shoulders, slouching the same way he had at the service. He had lost weight these last months.

"Zuza, a word, please." He opened the door to his office and went inside.

In the seconds it took for Zuza to join him, Otto had propped his reading glasses on his bald head and settled in behind his messy desk, looking more annoyed than usual. The picture of his wife and Leva lay faceup on top an open file. He'd obviously been looking at them the last time he was here, and was probably still thinking about them.

"It was a nice service. Leva would have loved it." Zuza eased into the worn leather chair across from his desk. She recognized Otto's mood. He was onto something. When he got like that, he was like a dog with a meaty bone. She knew he wouldn't stop, and she had better just do her job.

He looked at her. "What do you know about Baltic Watch?"

"It's a small multinational group of Eastern European radicals who think Russia is going to overrun the Baltics and Poland one day. When Lithuania joined the EU in 2004, we investigated the group. I wasn't working here at the time, but I read the report when I joined up. After that initial inquiry, there's been nothing. They haven't done anything in years, and we believe their statements, given by their leader Jonas Volkis, are concerns raised by an intellectual. He seems more interested in political debate than activism. Membership has died off over the years, except for Jonas and his next-in-line, Darius Artis. They appear to be harmless, although Darius posted a rogue article after the invasion of Crimea. He advocated action, but didn't do anything." One of her jobs was to know everything possible about politically oriented groups in the country. Zuza crossed her legs, already predicting Otto was going to send her on another easy assignment.

"That's what they said about Hezbollah," he mumbled.

"What's going on?"

"One of the people on the cyber team just notified me that Baltic Watch posted a video to the internet." Otto turned his computer screen toward her. Darius Artis was speaking, warning that Vera Koslova was about to expand Russia's borders and demanding NATO send troops to Eastern Europe, ending the diatribe with an empty prediction that the rebel separatists in Ukraine were colluding with the Russians who were preparing to foster an invasion.

"Darius Artis isn't a happy boy. When was it posted?" said Zuza.

"Yesterday."

"Maybe he's spewing drivel. He's never taken any action before."

"I got a feeling that this time, he may do something." Otto shrugged.

"Ukraine has been divided between pro-West and pro-Russian factions for years. The fighting isn't as intense as it was in 2014 during the Maidan revolution, but it's still going on. It only makes sense that someone would predict an invasion. But they've predicted it before. And it's only happened in Crimea. Just because Baltic Watch says something is going to happen doesn't make it true, although their stance in the video appears to be far more aggressive than before."

"But that's not what's interesting about this." Otto put his elbows on his desk and leaned forward, watching her. *Another lesson,* she thought. He often withheld his thoughts, making her look at the information anew, testing whether they would both come to the same conclusions. Sometimes it annoyed her, but she had to admit, Otto was making her think like an agent. The problem was that she wanted to actually *be* an agent. In all aspects of the job.

She got to her feet and walked to the window. It came to her in seconds. "It's not what they're saying, but the person saying it."

Otto nodded.

Zuza ran her fingers through hair. "This is about Darius Artis, isn't it? He's a relative unknown, but we have information on him because of his father, Ignas. We believe Ignas was locked up in a mental institution by the KGB and died there. That's how they used to take care of dissidents." She knew any questions Otto couldn't answer would fall to her shoulders, but it was their game. This sparing of ideas usually got each one further along the path to the truth.

"So, Darius has reason to be angry."

"Almost everyone in Lithuania has reason to be angry. Jonas Volkis was a friend of Ignas's and stepped in as Darius's surrogate father. He practically raised Darius. The father spent most of his time in the woods, planning missions against the Soviets well into the 1960s." Zuza went back to her seat.

"And the mother?"

"A family no-show. She hooked up with a Swedish sailor and escaped the country when Darius was a boy. As far as we know, she had little, if anything, to do with him."

"What do we know about Darius's political views?"

"Very little. We assume he and Jonas share the same ideals. Jonas has always spoken for Baltic Watch. Until now, that is."

"Where does Darius live?"

"Kaunas."

"Based on his father's action, Darius has a legacy to maintain." Otto loosened his tie. "Go to Kaunas and find out what's going on with Baltic Watch. Find Darius Artis and ask him why he's speaking for the group all of a sudden. Then talk to Jonas."

"Why don't we just let the local police bring them both in?"

"They may, eventually. But I want to know what's behind this video first."

"All right. I'll go to Kaunas tonight so I can get an early start."

Zuza glanced through the open door at the room full of empty desks. The other agents were still out, probably with that guy in the orange hoodie. The last thing she needed was a few days of vacation in the country interviewing old men. She needed a *real* assignment, but she had a job to do first. She'd talk with Otto when she got back to Vilnius.

# CHAPTER 20

## Lahey Hospital, Burlington, Massachusetts—18 May

Vit waited in his car at the red light near the Route 128 interchange, thinking through the conversation he had just had with Tilda, and not knowing what to make of her bizarre confession about having made a nuclear bomb back in the 1990s. He maneuvered the vehicle onto the highway and settled into one of the traveling lanes, relieved that traffic was moving along well.

Vit linked into the car's audio-visual system with the words, "Good morning, Annie."

"Hello, Vit." Her voice sounded like honey.

"Damn," said Vit, hitting his brakes as the traffic came to its typical slow crawl during morning rush hour.

"128 is slow all the way to 93. You'll make better time if you get off at Route 3A," said Annie.

"You're the boss."

Annie was learning about him faster than he had ever expected. She knew Vit's friends and family, and how to communicate with them. She knew that Gina, his ex-girlfriend, had preferred text messages, while his mother preferred phone calls and flowers. Annie made hotel reservations, and had dinner delivered from Vit's favorite restaurants. Furthermore, she knew he liked bolognaise better than cream sauce, and baseball better than football.

Recently, he had been thinking out loud about what to get his mother with the windfall he would get from selling Sagus. He hadn't expected Annie to chime in, but she did. She said his mother wanted a condo in Boca Raton, Florida. He had asked how she had come to that conclusion. Annie broke it down based on his mother's age, financial situation, buying preferences, social circle, travel history, recent texts to her friends, and more.

"Annie, give me a timeline for Dr. Tilda Partenkas, 1990 to 1995. With photographs." Vit settled back into the plush leather seat, his gaze on the road.

Pictures flashed on the dashboard's video screen of Tilda at her husband's funeral in 1990. Vit remembered being there, dressed in his first suit and wearing a light blue tie. It had also been his first funeral. He had been old enough to know what death was and had had a hard time hiding his tears. He had loved his grandfather, whom he called *Senelis*. Vit remembered the wonderful bedtime stories from Lithuania about the hedgehog who guided a lost soldier out of the woods and was rewarded with his daughter to marry, and the old man who married a witch who turned his sons into ravens. Vit had always suspected that his imagination and independent spirit had come from Senelis, traits that had given him the courage to start his own company.

Other photographs of Tilda came up on the screen, including one of her speaking at a conference, and another taken while receiving an award posthumously for Senelis. Next came a photograph of Tilda being handed Lithuania's Order of Merit award by the veritable head of state, Vytautas Landsbergis, before he won the national election. It was the same medal she had shown him less than an hour ago.

"Annie, where and when was that picture taken?"

"Vilnius, Lithuania, October 12, 1992."

Vit watched the cars weave in and out of lanes as he considered what to do about Tilda's bizarre story, and whether to go to Lithuania. He could talk to his mother, but decided against it. While pregnant with Vit, she had divorced Vit's father, even changing her name back to Partenkas and giving Vit that name, too. Ma was tough enough to raise him single-handedly, but she could get emotional. If he told her Tilda's story, she would go to the hospital and confront the poor woman. If Tilda remembered what she had asked Vit to do, she would know he had betrayed her. If Tilda didn't remember, the conversation was sure to unhinge her, and that was the last thing Vit wanted.

He could visit the South Boston Lithuanian Club, a bar and restaurant staffed by beautiful and pleasantly sassy waitresses serving traditional food. It was a great place to watch a Patriot's football game, connect with old friends, or even have a party, but there was no one in whom he could confide about something so sensitive.

He thought of Gina, picturing her shiny dark hair and bedroom eyes. They had broken up a few months ago. She was a captain in the US Army, supporting military training at Fort Devens, about thirty-five miles northwest of Boston. He was sure she would inform the authorities immediately, and this would harm Tilda's reputation even more. Gina wasn't cold, but her time in Afghanistan made her react without temperance to any threat, even one imagined by an old lady.

Vit could just as well inform the authorities himself, but why waste their time with a fantasy produced by Tilda's deteriorating mind? The FBI, CIA, Interpol, Europol and even other organizations might investigate, putting his deal with Homeland Security in jeopardy, and he didn't want to do that unnecessarily.

Vit had made a promise to Tilda, and he prided himself on being a man who kept his word. He had to go to Lithuania because he had told her he would. Besides, this was the excuse he needed to be away from the office so he could keep his secret about leaving Sagus to himself a while longer.

"Annie, call Max and tell him I have to go out of town for a few days on family business. He can call if anything critical comes up."

"Certainly, Vit."

Max was always happy to take the reins of the small company. It was also good experience for him to occasionally be completely in charge.

"Contact my mother and tell her I'm going away on business. Tell her I'll call when I get back."

"All right," said Annie.

Vit turned on the car's blinkers and looked over his shoulder to make sure the lane was clear before moving to the right and the exit Annie had recommended.

"And get me a ticket to Vilnius, first available flight, open return."

"I'd be happy to."

Now that his decision was made, Vit didn't feel at all relieved. He had no idea what he was going do once he got to Lithuania, other than try to find Darius and Jonas. If he couldn't find them, he could at least visit Visaginas in search of the cabin Tilda had mentioned, stuck in the middle of the woods in a country he knew nothing about. He had no interest in seeing Lithuania. He had been born in the US.

*This* was his country, not some old, forlorn place on the other side of the world.

"I booked your flight, Vit. You're leaving tonight." It occurred to him that if Annie were a real woman, he might go for her. He made a mental note never to admit that to *anyone*.

He considered phoning Jonas to tell him that he was coming, but he was going to Lithuania anyway. Surely, an old man wouldn't venture far from home. Besides, Vit didn't want to give Jonas a chance to refuse to see him.

Vit's phone rang. Glancing at the screen, he recognized his mother's number. He accepted the call.

"Hi, Ma."

"So, you don't have time to visit your mother, but you have time to go traipsing all over the world. Where are you going this time?"

He had no choice but to tell her. "Lithuania."

"I thought you said you were busy."

"I am."

"So why are you going?"

"Business."

"Your grandmother asked you to go, didn't she?"

"What difference does it make?"

"You tell me nothing. Don't do anything she says. Her mind's not there anymore."

"If she asks me to do something for her, I'm not going to say no."

"Suit yourself. You always do. Call me when you get to Vilnius. And I want to hear from you, not that damn machine."

"Annie's my personal assistant. You've got to get used to her." Vit rolled his eyes.

"We'll see," she said.

"Bye, Ma."

# CHAPTER 21

## Moscow—18 May

In a magnificent estate just outside Moscow, Orlov sat with his back against a cascade of pink satin pillows buffeting the headboard, reveling in his good luck. First, he had gotten the appointment to Deputy Director of the FSB, and already had begun to enjoy some of the perks: use of a car and driver, and access to a private dining room in the Kremlin, where only the best food was served. He was privy to more information and attended more meetings with important people. It felt like his career had soared.

The second stroke of luck was that the magnificent Vera Koslov was next to him in bed. She had aged little after all these years, her white hair the only indicator of passing time. It had been obsidian when they were FSB agents together in Paris, posing as art restorers working on Russian icons at the Petit Palais. The museum's well-connected curator had gotten them into parties at the French Embassy, where they were treated as minor celebrities, and where they worked an asset whose spouse was well-placed in the government and privy to useful information.

Orlov and Vera had first made love in a cheap hotel in the 10th arrondissement. He couldn't remember the name of the place.

Once, long ago, he had considered asking her to marry him, but he had waited too long. Michael came along, and she married him instead. Orlov never understood why. Vera was committed to Russia, whereas Michael was devoted to a life of ease and pampering, evidenced by the fact that even tonight, he was off exploring one of the many dachas Vera had at her disposal. Orlov wondered if it was love that kept Vera and Michael together, but stranger things had happened.

Their marriage had put a halt to the liaisons Orlov had relished, angering him at first. But there was nothing he could do. He had never married. Every night that he would've been in bed with his wife, he would have been thinking about Vera. It wasn't good to pine away in useless might-have-beens.

Over the years, he often relived their moments together while watching Vera rise through the ranks at the KGB, and later through the FSB. When Fedov had appointed her president, Orlov had been utterly shocked. It was as if God himself were guiding her career.

Vera's invitation to the presidential home at Novo-Ogarevo near Moscow had also come as a surprise. But when the president of the Russian Federation wanted something, anything, no one denied the request. He had been summoned for a dinner meeting. Not knowing the subject, he had come with files about everything that could possibly interest her. He had never before been inside the magnificent residence and the six-meter walls surrounding it. They were served a meal of chicken *tabaka* by a servant in a black suit. Vera had asked him questions about many topics including his theory about what was behind the riots at Novosibirsk.

After the meal, she wiped her mouth with a napkin, stood up, and walked into the hallway, crooking a finger to indicate he should follow. He picked up his attaché case, and went with her up a grand staircase, past a small Picasso, and into a lavish room with pink satin pillows on the bed.

His heart beat faster, and even more so when he saw she was undressing. In a moment, she was in his arms and it felt like they were in Paris again.

Afterward, Orlov leaned toward her on the bed. "I can hardly believe that I'm here with the president of Russia." The look in her eyes chilled him completely, and reminded him how deliciously brutal she could be in bed.

She asked to see the files he had brought. He got out of bed, opened the attaché case, and handed her several. Vera chose one and began to read. He glanced at it. It was about the Nord Stream 2 pipeline planned to cross the Baltic from Ust-Luga in the Leningrad region to the Greifswald area in Germany, where it would pump Russian gas into the EU grid and make more money for them all.

Orlov watched her concentrate on the file's contents. He knew he shouldn't bother her, that he should wait until she had finished reading, but he couldn't help himself. His heart raced as he touched her arm. "Vera? Little rabbit?"

"What, again? Your car will be here soon. You need to get ready."

The sheet trembled over Orlov's shoulders.

Vera closed the file.

Orlov watched her as he drew back the covers revealing his hairy midsection.

Vera placed her glasses and the file on the nightstand as Orlov closed his eyes and gripped the side of the bed with his hand. God how he had missed her!

# CHAPTER 22

## Hotel Metropolis, Kaunas, Lithuania—19 May

On her way down to breakfast, Zuza stopped to look at the crests in the stained-glass windows on the landing of the hotel's grand staircase. They were stunning, and reminded her of the grade school lessons about the 13th century Lithuanian leader named Mindaugas, and the start of the Grand Duchy. Eventually, Lithuania extended from the Baltic Sea all the way to the Black Sea, encompassing today's Ukraine, Belarus, parts of Poland and Russia, and more. Decades later, to preserve this great expanse of land and fight off constant raids from Russia and soldiers of the Teutonic Order, Lithuania and Poland had formed a Commonwealth, cemented by the marriage of thirteen-year-old Jadwiga of Poland to Jogaila, a Lithuanian knight. *It must have been wonderful living back then when Lithuania was great*, thought Zuza. But she shook her head, knowing how much she'd miss her car and central heating.

After filling a plate of *silke*, herring, from the buffet in the hotel's restaurant, Zuza selected a corner table. She admired the grandeur in the soft paneled walls and large windows as she ate. But the linens were worn, and no one was in the room except for a lone woman standing in the doorway. She was barely five feet tall. Based on the gray hair and wrinkles, Zuza guessed she was close to eighty. She was pretty, except for the scar running down the side of her face.

Their gazes met. Zuza looked down, a little embarrassed at having gawked at the woman's face. She opened the file she had brought with addresses, phone numbers, financial reports for both Jonas and Darius, and medical summaries for both men, pretending to read. A drop of brine from the herring fell onto one of the sheets. She cleaned it off with a napkin.

The woman approached Zuza's table and spoke. "I hate eating alone. Do you mind if I join you?"

Her mouth full of food, Zuza nodded as she closed the file. The woman introduced herself as Urte Gatus. They shook hands. Zuza tried not to stare at the scar.

"I don't mind if you look at it," said Urte. "It's my badge of endurance. I don't like to remember what happened, but I don't want people to forget. I'm just an old woman, happy to sit here quietly with you, but I'll tell you the story if you want."

"I'd like to hear it." Zuza knew what was coming, and wasn't looking forward to a heart-wrenching story, but the old woman deserved some respect. She put her fork down.

Urte took a deep breath. "I was four when the Soviets sent my mother and me to a camp in Irkutsk. It was 1948. Even now when I wake up in the middle of the night, sometimes I wonder if they're coming for me again. We had so little food in the camp, I looked like a child until well into my teens, but eventually, nature took hold. When I was sixteen, a cook from Gadansk tried to rape me. I fought back, and he went at my face with a paring knife. My mother had to sew the skin back together with a needle she kept hidden in the hem of her shirt and thread she took from her coat. Whenever I look at my face, I remember what I survived."

"I'm sorry you had to go through that. How did you get out?"

"In 1961, Khrushchev freed thousands of us. But my mother was already dead. It makes me sad to know she went to God thinking I was going to spend my life in the camps.

"When I came back to Lithuania, I thought conditions were wonderful. And they were, compared to how I'd been living. Now, we're a free society, and scars from the occupation are disappearing." She touched the wound on her face.

Without a word, the waiter brought over a pot of tea and a plate of eggs. Urte put a piece of egg on a slice of bread and continued. "I can't eat from the buffet. There's so much food there, I can't help but think how much easier it would've been if we'd had a fraction of that food in the camps. I come here often and the waiter knows me. He brings me just enough to eat so there's never any waste." Urte took a bite and slowly chewed. "How old are you, dear?"

"In my thirties."

"So young and beautiful. Many your age are leaving the country for better jobs, and a better life for their children. I can't blame them. I had wanted to leave, too, when the borders opened up in 1990. But I couldn't join those who left for work or because they feared the Soviets would be back, because this is my home." Urte put her fork down and gazed out the windows. "If we could have avoided those fifty years of stunted growth under the Soviets, we'd have more people living here, more jobs, and a better economy. Things would be easier and happier. There wouldn't be the feeling that the country is slowly fading away."

Zuza touched the older woman's hand. "We survived the Soviets, so we can survive anything. Lithuanians living abroad send money home, and come to visit. They help us keep the language and culture alive. Other cultures may fade away, but not ours. And as long as people like you keep telling their stories, the country will stay strong."

Urte smiled. "Even though I thought conditions here were good when I came home, I was very sad. I felt like the Soviets had stolen my youth as well as my mother's life. And I could never get them back. We didn't deserve to be treated that way. All we had done was to be born here, and for that, we were punished. When I came home, I had no one, but everyone in town treated me like a member of their family. No one said, 'Urte, you were wonderful to have survived.' Nothing like that. They just included me in everything and made sure I was all right. No one asked about the camps, but they listened when I wanted to talk. I felt like I was part of their histories, even though I had just met most of them."

Urte took a bite of egg. "It's still like that for me, and I know others who had a similar experience coming back to strangers who took them into their families. Even with all the problems we have as a country, I love it here because of the people."

After finishing her meal, Zuza kissed Urte on both cheeks and said goodbye. She went upstairs for her overnight bag, pausing one more time at the stained-glass window. As the sunlight played against the vibrant reds, blues and yellows in the glass, Zuza wondered what made any country great. Lithuania hadn't changed the world with a new invention or political system, and the Grand Duchy was relatively short-lived. But like the people in many of the small countries all over Eastern Europe, Lithuanians had honed the defiance necessary to maintain its unique cultural identity even after hundreds of years of occupations and Russification. People like Urte made the country great; those with the courage to keep their stories alive regardless of how much it hurt to tell them.

After checking out of the hotel, Zuza made her way to the rear of the building and the fenced-in car lot with a security camera and key-card access to the gate. Cars were valuable, and many people made their living stealing them and selling them to people in bordering countries, an unfortunate consequence of the tight economy.

She drove to the Kaunas police station, as Otto insisted his agents meet with local law enforcement whenever they went outside of Vilnius on business. Zuza was anxious to get the formality out of the way so she could actually start doing her job.

Officer Paulius Juras of the Kaunas Police met her in the lobby of the station. He had nice eyes, and gently squeezed her fingers just before letting go their handshake. She followed him up to his office on the second floor. He was probably ten years older than her, and had a deep voice. He was pure muscle, his hair was cut short, and he smelled clean, like he'd just stepped out of the shower. A gym bag sat on the floor in the corner next to the coat rack. He wasn't wearing a wedding ring.

His office was nothing special except for the long, narrow windows covered by bars. They provided natural light but limited opportunity to look out, or for others to look in. The two exchanged some polite conversation before Paulius leaned forward and asked, "What's ARAS doing in Kaunas?"

Zuza told him about Darius's video from Baltic Watch.

Paulius settled back in his chair, clearly relieved. "I haven't seen it, but is that all? Baltic Watch is irrelevant. We haven't heard anything significant from them in years. But you people don't take chances these days, do you? Everything is investigated, no matter how insignificant. Here in Kaunas, we're too busy to spend time on minor matters."

Zuza watched him as her face cleared of expression, something she had perfected with her father when he'd taught her how to play poker. She had expected friendly rivalry with Paulius as they represented different organizations, but this was a jab.

"You won't find anything significant, at least not here," said Paulius.

"I appreciate your confidence, but I'll be looking into Baltic Watch anyway."

Paulius shrugged and handed her his card. "If you actually find anything, call me."

She smiled politely and put his card into the side pocket of her phone case. He escorted her to the front door. As he extended his hand, Paulius spoke. "And if you need anything, I'd be happy to help."

After a handshake where she squeezed *his* fingers, she was on her way.

She got into her car and drove along the embankment of the Nemunas River, and past Old Town City toward Darius's apartment near the reservoir. The old three-story stone walkup had a large flower garden filled with purple and yellow pansies in the back by the parking area. She left her car there and went inside as a big, red, hot air balloon drifted quietly into the clouds. Its shape reminded Zuza of the Easter eggs she had decorated with her father as a child. They had dipped brushes into melted beeswax and had drawn patterns on boiled eggs before dipping them into a dye made of beet juice that stained the shell red except for the area under the wax. Zuza's designs were always messy, but her father's eggs were spectacular. Then she remembered he was gone, and the red brought back thoughts of blood and his death. She wanted to scream, but all she could do was her job. She opened the door and went inside the building.

The wide marble steps were magnificent, but Darius could afford to live here. According to his records, he made enough money from his online video business to buy an apartment in this beautifully restored building, and have plenty left over. He wasn't married, and didn't seem to have expensive hobbies. Over the past few years, there had been spikes in his withdrawals, up to a thousand euros at a time, but it was nothing unusual.

Darius's apartment was on the top floor. Zuza was glad for the chance to expend some energy, and walked briskly up the three flights. Darius answered on her second knock, looking like he'd had a rough night. His eyes were swollen and red, his skin sallow. He was wearing dark sweatpants and a T-shirt. His face was thin, his cheeks wrinkled. He had gray stubble on his chin.

Zuza showed her badge. Darius leaned toward it, and then stepped back, inviting her in with a flourish of his hand. The area under his fingernails was dirty. *That's odd for a person who works with electronics all day,* she thought.

The living room was small, and every surface was covered with either tools, a laptop, or electrical components, most of which she didn't even recognize. In the alcove near the kitchen, one end of a large bench held video equipment and even more components. A Lithuanian flag covered the rest. The door to the bedroom was closed. He asked if she'd like to sit down. She refused his offer of coffee. She asked if he had seen Jonas recently.

"Yes, he told me he was going away for a while." Darius crossed his legs as he settled into a chair across from Zuza. He looked at the door.

"Are you expecting someone?"

"No. I just have a lot to do today. Why are you asking about Jonas?"

"We want to talk to him about Baltic Watch."

"You can ask me anything. I know as much as Jonas. Even more on some topics." Darius scratched his nose.

Zuza looked closely at him. "Are you feeling all right?"

"I didn't sleep well."

"That's too bad. When's the last time you saw Jonas?"

"Night before last."

"Do you know where he went?"

"He said he was going somewhere to clear his head."

"Did he say where?"

"No."

"Why wouldn't he tell you where he was going?"

Darius shrugged. "He likes to get away every so often, and go somewhere quiet. He used to go to Puvociai and fish along the Merkys River. He was a wonderful fisherman. But he's old now and can't fish very well. He often goes back to Puvociai though, because I think he likes the memories. It's where I'd look if I wanted to find him."

"That's just south of Alytus?"

"That's right. There are just a few houses and only one road that loops around the village. Maybe fifty people live there, if that many. He usually stays in the first house after you turn off the motorway. Fishermen park their vans there. I don't know the name of the owner. Jonas isn't going to walk very far with that arthritis, so you'll probably find him sitting on a bench outside writing in his notebook or talking to the fishermen."

Zuza typed on her phone as Darius continued. "He's worried about Vera Koslova. We all are. He wants to plan a response from Baltic Watch."

"Doesn't your video already capture his response to the new Russian president?"

"We have a huge responsibility to tell people the truth."

Zuza raised an eyebrow. "Are you saying that Jonas doesn't speak the truth anymore? Is that why you did the video instead of him?"

"Oh no. Jonas wanted me to speak. He's not getting any younger, and it's time people got used to hearing from the next generation at Baltic Watch. Of course, he approved the script." Darius turned his feet toward the door. "Jonas raised me. I'm like a son to him." He brushed a tear from his cheek.

"Jonas condones your threats?"

"I made no threats. I said we have to take steps to ensure our survival. We can't trust the Russians. Everyone should know that already." Darius's chest swelled as he took in a deep breath.

"And what steps are you going to take?"

"Jonas and I have discussed several options, but there's nothing definitive yet. When he gets back, we'll discuss his ideas." Darius shifted his weight in the chair.

Zuza made a note on her mobile phone before responding. "Why aren't you with him while he's planning this strategy?"

"He thinks better alone. When he gets back, we'll compare notes and decide what to do."

"Have you tried reaching him by phone?"

"No, but I have no need to contact him, and usually don't. When he goes away like this, he often turns his phone off so he won't be disturbed."

"So that's why he's not answering. If he gets in touch with you, please let me know." Zuza handed him her card.

Darius took it, placing it on top of a disassembled laptop computer. "I didn't know that women were ARAS agents."

Zuza looked straight at him as she silently counted to three. "We're rare, but not extinct."

A few minutes later, Zuza left the apartment. Darius closed the door behind her, clicking the lock. Zuza waited in the hallway for a moment. Darius's nervousness was a little too close to the surface. He looked exhausted. Maybe it was his medical condition, or perhaps something else. She resolved to return here after finding Jonas. But in the meantime, she was looking forward to the trip to Puvociai. She'd never been there, but heard it was lovely. She glanced at her watch. If things went well, and Jonas was where Darius said he'd be, she might even be back in Vilnius tonight, typing up her report for another routine assignment.

# CHAPTER 23

## Kaunas, Lithuania—19 May

After Zuza Bartus left his apartment, Darius thought about her visit. All along, he assumed someone might find him and ask him about the video, and she had. But he hadn't expected the police, let alone an ARAS agent, to visit so *soon*. She couldn't know that Jonas was dead. If she suspected him of anything, she would've taken him to headquarters. That he was standing in his own kitchen made him feel smug that he had fooled her. He was about to fool the entire world. His heart raced. He took a dose of the medication he kept on the counter.

*But, what if she keeps looking for Jonas?* He pictured the inside of Jonas's house. Darius had taken Jonas's medications, straightened up the living room, wiped up the beer. What else was there?

The security system! Darius hadn't turned it on. In a moment of panic, Darius grabbed his keys, intending to drive back to Jonas's house and activate it. He stopped himself. *No!* Jonas was a forgetful old man who often left without turning on the system. Darius put the keys back down on the counter next to his mobile. He picked up the phone and turned it off. He couldn't be disturbed. Besides, the one person who called him regularly was dead.

Any forgotten detail could be a disaster, but he had focused all his energy on the bomb and what he was about to do. He hadn't planned to hurt Jonas. Jonas was supposed to have helped him! He remembered the car. *How could Jonas be gone if his car is home?* Darius couldn't go to Utena and simply drive it off into the woods in broad daylight. He could wait until dark. But he'd have to park his car somewhere close and walk back to it. Someone might see him. *What if the ARAS agent has already been to Jonas's house?*

Darius went to the sink and splashed water in his face. A friend could have picked Jonas up. When ARAS asked for the friend's name, Darius could say he didn't know all of Jonas's friends. If he could talk to Arkady, Jonas's Russian friend who spent most of his time drinking at Lukas's Bar, it might work. Darius could confuse Arkady into corroborating the lie. *It might work. Oh God, what if it doesn't?*

Acid churned in his stomach. He couldn't stay in the apartment. If that agent came back, it would be with even more questions he didn't want to answer. If she looked in the bedroom, she was sure to notice the detonator and other items, let alone the casing over the nuclear material. That would be the end of him and his plan. It would be the end of them all.

*Great deeds require great effort.* He went into the bedroom and the desk cluttered with tools and wiring, and the bomb that awaited a necessary rework after having been buried for so long. Darius ran his hand over the container. Although covered in dirt, it was smooth and appeared to be intact, although a bottom corner felt jagged and rough, potentially indicating a tiny breach. *Another fine example of Russian manufacturing; built not to last.* But he didn't care. He had other things to worry about. He brushed the dirt off his hands. All he had to do now was finish wiring in the new components, adding explosive, replacing the detonator, and he'd be able to start the next phase of his plan.

He went into his closet and opened the small safe. He took out the envelope containing eight hundred euros and shoved it into his pocket.

He gently placed everything he might need to finish the job into an oversized bag: wires, wrenches, monitors, the two mobile phones for remote detonation, and the rest.

He went back to the closet and reached up to the stop shelf, taking down his dark green, wheeled suitcase with zippered pockets in the front. He put it on the bedroom floor, and opened the lid. As gently as a mother with a newborn, he picked up the nuclear waste container, and laid it inside the green suitcase. It fit with room to spare at the top. He used the garment straps to secure the container, and zippered it shut.

He hoped he had enough strength left for everything he had to do. As he prepared to leave his apartment, he had the odd sensation that this was the last time he would ever be here. His gaze went to the kitchen, with the red teakettle on the stove, and the workbench where he had spent so many hours toiling over his videos. He scanned the living room where he had spent many nights relaxing while watching basketball games on TV. Jonas was in the gray upholstered recliner, waving goodbye.

Darius stepped into the hallway, wheeled out the suitcase, and closed the door, the bag of equipment heavy on his shoulder. He went down the steps, carefully lifting the green suitcase so as not to disturb its precious contents, hoping for enough strength and fortitude to drive all the way to Utena. He shivered when he opened the trunk, picturing Jonas inside.

He wasn't there, thank God. Darius put in the bag and suitcase before getting in behind the steering wheel. His hands hurt as he gripped it. He tried not to speed. It was hard staying on the road and driving like nothing was wrong. But he had to do it, because he couldn't afford to be stopped by police. If they found the materials in the trunk, it would be over. All would be lost.

He went slowly, driving like an old man. A car raced up behind him and honked before passing him on the left. He tried to focus, his eyes stinging, his arms tired, his ears ringing. He realized he had forgotten to take the container of medication that calmed his heart. He had to go all the way back to his apartment from the other side of Kaunas.

He parked the car in its usual spot, and trudged up the stairs. Once inside, he found the medication where it always was on the counter. He took another dose, and realized he was still wearing the sweatpants and T-shirt he had put on last night. He went into the bedroom and changed into jeans and a clean shirt. Because he would be gone for several days, Darius put a change of clothing, a comb, a razor, and a toothbrush into a small overnight bag. He put the medication into his pocket, slung the strap over his shoulder, and headed out the door again.

The rest of the trip was uneventful, but took a long time. Finally in Utena, Darius went to a boutique hotel, not far from Lukas's Bar. The manager, an older man with messy hair, was sitting behind the front desk reading a newspaper when Darius came in asking for a room. The manager glanced down at Darius's bags. "How many nights will you be staying?"

"Just one." Darius handed the man enough cash to cover the cost of the room.

"Are you alone?"

Darius tried to smile. "I'm leaving my wife. If a younger woman with brown hair comes looking for me, tell her you haven't seen me."

"A young woman is always a problem for an older man." The manager winked his understanding and gave Darius the key.

In a room with good locks on the door and Danish-style furnishings, Darius continued his work. The job was agonizingly slow, for he had to wait for his hands to stop shaking. It helped to believe Zuza Bartus wouldn't find him there, and he hoped Jonas wouldn't either. Darius made some progress, although he would need tomorrow to finish the job. It would be enough time. He was sure of it.

He had one more critical task, finding a way to get through the border to Ukraine and his ultimate destination: the Russian embassy in Kiev. But he had a plan for that, too.

~~

Wearing a well-made suit tailored to fit his square frame, Alexy Bok climbed the three flights of stairs in the apartment building where Darius Artis lived. Bok's first name was from his mother's side, and shared with his great-grandfather who had served in the Red Army. In the 1930s, Great-grandfather had shot his commanding officer in the head on command from Father Stalin himself. The family still talked about it. Bok also shared his great-grandfather's appreciation for a life in the military, having spent two decades teaching new recruits a variety of topics, including explosives handling and hand-to-hand combat, before taking on special assignments for Vera Koslova, starting when she had been Director of the FSB.

In addition to the suit, the black computer bag hanging from his shoulder made Bok look like any businessman who might be selling insurance or calling on a client. Upon reaching the third floor, Bok paused, listening. He heard nothing, but it didn't necessarily mean everyone was out.

Bok did what he always did, beginning by checking for security cameras in the hallway and motion sensors that might trigger them, although some new systems had sound detection, too. He was as quiet as possible as he looked for the miniature cameras that almost disappeared when hidden in a dark corner near a ceiling. He found nothing.

He went to number 10C, the one that belonged to Darius Artis. He checked the door, looking for wiring that might indicate an alarm, and the mat, looking for a pressure plate, for once he had almost been blown up by one. He and another Russian agent were entering a house in Bulgaria. Bok's companion had stepped on a door mat and *boom*, he was gone. Bok had survived, barely, by pure luck. He had assured himself he would never succumb to a pressure plate again. Few people used them anymore, but he checked for them anyway. He was alive because he was thorough.

He knocked and waited. There was no answer.

Working quickly, he reached into his pocket for a zippered pouch and extracted a small tension wrench and a pick. He put the case back into his pocket and inserted the tension wrench in the bottom of the keyhole. He manipulated the pick until he felt the lock release.

Upon entering the apartment, he put his computer bag on the floor as he called out, "Maintenance. Is anyone home?"

As he listened for an answer, Bok went directly to the security system's panel mounted on the wall near the door. It was flashing red. He managed to disable it in fourteen seconds. People familiar with the Darius Artis video on home security systems could've figured out how, as Darius was very thorough in explaining the details. As a precaution, Bok went to the cabinet under the sink and unplugged the power supply, another detail covered in the instructional video, along with suggestions on where to hide one.

After a quick look in the bedroom and bath, assuring himself that he was alone, Bok proceeded to search the apartment. He began in the kitchen, going in a circle around the room, examining all cabinets, the inside, underside, and back of drawers, contents of the refrigerator and stove. He examined the mess of tools lying out on the counter, and the chests containing more tools in the front closet. He repeated the process in the living room and alcove, checking under tables and chairs, and the oversized workbench with components piled to one side. The other side of the bench was covered with the yellow, green and red tricolor of the Lithuanian flag. He picked it up and looked underneath before replacing it. A drone with its propellers removed lay on a lamp table. A laptop computer that had been taken apart covered the coffee table. The motherboard and disk assembly were intact, but the CD reader had been extracted.

A set of tiny tools lay to the side. He picked up a business card lying on the chassis, noting in particular the ARAS organization and that it was a woman's name, Zuza Bartus. He put the card in the inside pocket of his jacket. Lastly, he went into the bedroom where he checked the nightstand, the unmade bed, and the closet. The small electronic safe inside was open and empty except for a few personal papers. Bok went to the metal desk. Shards of wire were scattered around the floor, what he'd expect from a man who made his living working with electronics. However, on the surface of the desk, among a variety of tools, lay some dirt.

Bok went to his bag and took out a device smaller than an old-fashioned handheld calculator, a CRM-100 radiation detector that he had bought on Amazon during his last trip to London. It replaced the bulkier and less sophisticated Geiger counter he usually carried on jobs like this one. Few people used nuclear material anymore, because it was hard to get and there were detection devices in every large city. He wasn't sure Kaunas had them, though. He had found some nuclear material years ago in a basement in Istanbul, along with parts to make a bomb. Bok had been there looking for a member of the Ukrainian far-right nationalist group known as the Right Sector. Along with the nuclear material, Bok had found a Geiger counter which went into the red zone when he turned it on in that dank basement. Bok had taken it with him when he left. He had used it many times, but it had rarely detected radiation. Recently, Bok had replaced it with the CRM-100, a smaller device capable of detecting trace amounts of alpha, beta, gamma and X-rays.

He returned to the bedroom, turned on the device, and swept it over the desk, the dirt, and floor. He was alive because he was thorough. The warning beep told him of low-level contamination from something that emitted gamma radiation. While it could be from many sources, one possibility was nuclear waste.

Bok left the room immediately. He turned the device off and returned it to the bag, which he slung over his shoulder. He left the apartment, smiling as he closed the door behind him. He didn't bother to lock it again. He went down the steps, a lilt to his gait. If Darius returned, he'd suspect someone had been inside, but would wonder if he had just forgotten to lock the door. It would make him nervous.

Bok liked making people nervous.

# CHAPTER 24

## Vilnius, Lithuania—19 May

The morning after his unsettling conversation with his grandmother, Vit stepped off the plane at Vilnius airport, having barely made the connection through Helsinki. Lithuania didn't require a visa for US citizens, so once Annie had bought his tickets, all he had to do was pack and get to Logan Airport in Boston. He hadn't slept on either leg of the trip, all the time wondering what he had gotten himself into.

The place was busy with other passengers making their way through passport control and the baggage carousels. It didn't have the dazzle of O'Hare or Atlanta International, but it was only a fraction of the size. As he made his way into the main terminal, the lofty modern ceiling drew his gaze upward and reminded him of the sky. He remembered Tilda's story about Lithuanian airmen Steponas Darius and Stasys Girenas, who had attempted a transatlantic flight in 1933. They had taken off from Brooklyn, New York and had flown for almost thirty hours before the plane crashed in Europe, some three hours from their final destination of Kaunas. While the flight had ended in tragedy, it brought the newly independent nation international notoriety and pride from having such brave men. *Too bad some people have to die to become heroes*, thought Vit. He asked an information desk attendant about the flight and was told the broken aircraft was in the Vytautas the Great War Museum, in Kaunas. Vit told Annie to remind him to go there if he had the time.

He made his way to one of the US-based companies in the rental car area. Minutes later, he was in a Mercedes C-class, enjoying the feel of the car, and settling into the job of driving.

As he left the airport grounds, the sun was bright, but the scenery dismal and the buildings dilapidated, just as he'd expected. But lovely old structures with rounded windows and ornate roof lines came into view, deflecting attention away from the Soviet era monstrosities next to them.

He was drawn in, and curious to see more, so Vit headed toward Vilnius. The Neris River divided the charming Old City from the commercial area that had an odd mix of pre-Soviet, Soviet, and modern buildings. On the hill overlooking it all was Gediminas Tower. Vit had read about it in a magazine on the plane. It was originally part of a castle constructed in the fifteenth century during the period of the Grand Duchy, when Lithuania was one of the largest countries in Europe.

He found Vilnius clean and alluring, and wanted to explore, but needed to be on his way to Utena where he hoped to find Jonas Volkis. In front of the sparkling white bell tower on the grounds of Vilnius Cathedral, Vit turned the car around and followed Annie's instructions to the E272, heading east.

He'd had her book a room for him at a hotel in Utena, and asked her to find Jonas's mobile phone number, using level two data if necessary. He knew he shouldn't, but was glad he could. He wasn't going to do any harm, and wasn't going to sell the information. Besides, it was all for Tilda.

Annie had accessed level two data only a few times before during testing. She had performed spectacularly well, her algorithms getting through rudimentary password protections and basic file encryption far more easily than he had expected.

Seconds later, Annie spoke. "Calling Jonas's phone now." It went to voicemail.

Vit wasn't worried. An older man like Jonas might opt for peace and turn off his phone once in a while.

Vit continued driving, enjoying the scenery. He was surprised at all the land under cultivation. Even in the late afternoon, tractors were out pulling plows. Everything was beautifully groomed, with no area wasted.

He made it to Utena, and found Jonas's house along a quiet road outside town across from a field of wild grasses. Vit parked the rental on the side of the road and walked across to the house, a one-story structure painted a muted yellow, with a green door. He knocked and listened. Nothing. He tried the knob. It was locked. He went around to the back. A car was there. He assumed it belonged to Jonas, but instructed Annie to double-check. It was Jonas's. Vit knocked on the back door; again nothing. He looked in through the kitchen window. Jonas didn't appear to be a very good housekeeper. Clearly, no one was home, but if his car was here, where was Jonas?

Tired and frustrated, Vit didn't know what to do next. He looked out past the birch trees and the small garden that desperately needed weeding. A house abutted the property to the back. Vit went over and knocked on what he assumed to be the kitchen door. A small woman in pants and shirt, with white hair and a straight back answered. She gave him a cold stare. After a few halting words in Lithuanian, Vit stopped and shrugged. But he had a perfect translator in his pocket. "Annie, would you translate this to Lithuanian? My name is Vit Partenkas, I'm Lithuanian, and looking for Jonas Volkis."

Annie said the words in perfectly accented Lithuanian. The woman looked impressed as she nodded and told him she spoke English. When Vit said he was Tilda Partenkas's grandson, she smiled.

"Dr. Partenkas is a great woman. How is she?" said Elena, after introducing herself.

"Not so good right now."

"Tsk. Any relative of Tilda Partenkas is welcome here." She opened the door wide and gestured him inside. He followed her into a kitchen that, although sparsely outfitted, looked fresh and clean. It held a counter with lower cabinets, a sink, a stove, and a small refrigerator. A white curtain swayed in the partially open window that provided an obstructed view of Jonas's backyard, due to the birch trees.

The woman motioned Vit to a chair at the table. She poured him a glass of *gira*, saying she had made it herself. He took a sip. It tasted like fermented bread. He cringed at the bitterness. On his second sip, she asked what he did for a living.

"I own a company."

"Oh. Businessman. Very good."

He didn't think her well versed in technology, so he explained that it had something to do with computers.

"You make good money?" she asked.

"Not bad."

Elena went on to talk about her daughter who worked in a hair salon. "It's a good job for a woman. She makes money, and knows how to stay nice for her husband, but she has no husband. She has solid bones. Are you married?"

Vit shook his head as he took another sip of *gira*. It was growing on him. "My grandmother asked me to visit your neighbor. I was hoping to talk with Jonas, but he isn't home. Have you seen him lately?"

"A few days ago, I brought him a plate of dumplings. He didn't eat. That man doesn't eat enough. Darius visited him that night. When I went to bed, his car was in the back, not that I looked. I just happened to see. A noise woke me up about midnight. When I got to the window to look, Darius's car was gone. I haven't seen either one since. Maybe they went off together. They're always going to Vilnius or into Utena."

"Did Jonas say he was going away?"

"He said nothing to me, but I'm not his mother. I'm just a friend. But Jonas doesn't like to go out at night. He has cataracts and doesn't see well. Maybe they went to Kaunas. Darius lives there. Or the cabin. Jonas has a cabin in the woods near Visaginas. I went with him a few times." Elena rubbed her chin. "I may have a map in my desk."

She got up and went into the other room, coming back with the item. "I like to know where I'm going, so Jonas marked it up for me." She handed it to Vit who took a picture of it with his phone, and handed it back.

"Is there any place that Jonas likes to go regularly? Say a bar or restaurant?" said Vit, hoping to find someone who knew where Jonas was. Vit wondered what would cause an elderly man to leave his comfortable house in the middle of the night and disappear for a few days.

"He likes Lukas's Bar, just beyond city center in Utena. Lukas's grandfather owned it during the war. He was an informant for the partisans. I'm surprised the Russians didn't find out about him and send him off to Siberia like my aunt. She was in a labor camp for twenty-five years. Thanks to God she survived. She lives in Cleveland now. Tsk."

Vit gulped down the last of the *gira*. He licked his lips, wondering if he could get some at the Lithuanian Club in South Boston. He thanked Elena and said goodbye.

From inside the car, Vit took out his phone. "Annie, check traffic cameras for any sign of Jonas."

A moment later, Annie responded. "A traffic camera on motorway 102 showed Darius in his car a little after midnight the night before last. Jonas wasn't with him. There's been no sign of Jonas on traffic cameras in the area since the day before last, but Darius has been caught on camera a number of times on different roads."

Jonas wasn't home, but he didn't leave. *What the hell is going on?* thought Vit.

"Annie, find Darius's mobile phone number and dial it for me, please."

She did. It went to voicemail.

# CHAPTER 25

## Puvociai, Lithuania—19 May

The village of Puvociai was sleepy and idyllic, the buildings looking like they had been carved out of the forest by wood nymphs. The homes were small and quaint. Many had sheds or barns. Well-kept fences surrounded some of the properties. Zuza stopped at the house Darius had told her about, where Jonas might be staying. Two vans were in the yard. When no one answered her knock, she went around back where the owner was digging worms from his garden. He told her that anglers often parked here and got last-minute supplies before fishing in the Merkys River. The owner hadn't seen Jonas in over a year, but he suggested a few other places the man might be. She stopped at every one, showing a picture of Jonas she had printed from a Baltic Watch newsletter. No one had seen him.

Zuza spent more time checking the nearby *sodyba*, or traditional guesthouse. A sodyba was usually out in the woods. It's appeal, especially to a man like Jonas, was in providing a quiet, simple, and restful place to stay. She talked to the owners, and even to people renting rooms. She checked cabins, but avoided the more primitive camp sites, as Jonas was old and stiff, and unlikely to unroll his sleeping bag on the ground. She found no trace of him. Either Jonas wasn't there or he had found a truly remote spot.

Fortunately, local law enforcement was on the lookout for his car, thanks to a phone call Officer Paulius Juras had made on her behalf to his counterparts in the area. She could have requested assistance from the local office herself, but asking Paulius to intercede made it clear she was running things, and that hers was a real investigation. Jonas's car was an older model that didn't have satellite tracking as most cars now did. So far, no one had seen Jonas or his vehicle.

"Damn," said Zuza as she turned onto the motorway, going faster than she should, trying to clear her head so she could think, just like she'd done when Leva was sick, and just like she did at the end of any particularly stressful day at ARAS. The day had been a waste, and Jonas's house in Utena was over two hours away.

It made sense that Jonas isolated himself from time to time. He was an intellectual and a loner. Zuza understood that behavior. Before Leva had taken a turn for the worse, Zuza often told friends she was going away for the weekend, only to stay home watching movies and reading books in blissful solitude. Darius had no reason she knew of to lead her astray, even though he had only speculated about Jonas's whereabouts, but had seemed quite nervous.

It was evening when Zuza arrived at Jonas's house. She parked the car on the side of a field and crossed the road to the house. The doors were locked, and no one appeared to be inside.

She went in the back, where she found a car. She assumed it belonged to Jonas, and made note of the license plate. She wondered why he hadn't taken it, unless a friend had picked him up and they had gone somewhere together. But that contradicted what Darius had told her, that Jonas had gone away alone to think. Darius hadn't mentioned taking Jonas anywhere, but perhaps a friend had. Jonas had never remarried, but maybe a woman was involved even this late in the game.

Frustrated that an arthritic old man was eluding her, she looked across the backyard to a woman at a neighboring house, picking plants from her garden. Zuza went over, showing her badge as she introduced herself.

"You're the second person who's been looking for Jonas today," said Elena, shaking her head. She told Zuza about Vit's visit.

Zuza raised an eyebrow upon hearing the familiar Partenkas name. She made a mental note to get background information on Vit tonight from her laptop. Elena went on to mention Lukas's Bar, and the cabin Jonas had spoken of, suggesting it might be another place to look for him. Zuza wondered why Darius hadn't mentioned the cabin. Elena showed Zuza the map. Zuza took a picture of it with her mobile phone.

Zuza desperately wanted to get inside Jonas's house to see if there were any clues as to where he might have gone. She couldn't break in, although expressing concern about Jonas's health might provide a reason. Instead, she put on her poker face. "Do you have a key to Jonas's house? He may need medical assistance."

Elena looked surprised. "You think he might be sick? *Dievas!* Let me get it for you." She went into her house and came back a moment later. "I keep it hanging on the wall by my door. It's only for emergencies."

Elena went to the back door of Jonas's house, unlocking and opening it. Zuza went past her into the kitchen.

"Stay here," said Zuza.

The air inside the house was musty. A dishrag was discarded in the sink on top of some dirty dishes. Zuza sniffed the rag and got a whiff of stale beer.

She went into the living room. Every flat surface held a jumbled mass of papers and books. Zuza poked through the top layer of debris, looking for a note, a ticket receipt, anything that might account for Jonas's recent whereabouts. From the floor near the front window, Zuza picked up a folded newspaper from two days ago. Its counterparts were stacked sequentially in a neat pile to the left of the front door, all folded back, and some with articles encircled in ink. There were no newspapers from yesterday or today. She noticed an old picture of a young woman hanging on the wall, and a security system that hadn't been activated. She wondered why Jonas would have left without turning it on. It didn't look like a high-crime area, but why would he have a security system and not use it?

Upon spotting a pair of glasses on the front windowsill, Zuza narrowed her eyes. She looked around the room again. A chair cushion was on the floor. The edge of the rug by the front door was folded back. Zuza wondered if there had been a scuffle, but it was hard to tell in the mess. One bedroom was very neat, with smooth bed linen, a few text books in the bookcase, and a dusty floor. The other was messy, like the rest of the house.

There was a toothbrush in the bathroom, but no prescription medications in the cabinet. She knew from his medical summary that Jonas was taking anti-inflammatories and pain relievers. That they were missing meant Jonas could've taken them with him, but the rest didn't add up. Zuza decided to go to the cabin in the morning to see if Jonas was there. If not, Darius would be her next visit, and he would have a few things to explain.

Zuza went back outside. She handed Elena the key and thanked her. She also gave the older woman a business card, and asked her to call if she saw Jonas. Elena nodded, tucking the card into a pocket of her pants.

Afterward, Zuza headed into Utena, and checked in at a hotel for the night. She ate at a local restaurant, ordering cabbage soup and thick slices of dark rye bread for dinner before going up to her room. She powered up her laptop and settled down at the desk to look for more information on Vit Partenkas.

There was a trove of it. He was a computer innovator who had started his own company. Occasionally, he was active in politics, and backed a number of causes, including a nationwide computer literacy program. A few of his op-ed pieces had been published in the *Boston Globe*. He seemed to be a bit of a Renaissance man and was only in his early forties, already well set financially. She stared at his picture on the Sagus website. He had nice eyes. Zuza leaned back in her chair, wondering what a man like that would want with Jonas Volkis and Baltic Watch.

Her last phone call of the day was to Otto, bringing him up to date. There wasn't a lot to tell him, other than vague speculation that something might have happened to Jonas. She caught her breath when he told her a representative of the president had called him, asking for information about Baltic Watch, as they'd seen Darius's video. Zuza asked which president. *The president of Lithuania*, he said. Otto went on to say he had been pleased to report that one of his agents was already on the case.

~~

It was dark as Elena stood in front of the stove, finishing the simmering soup by stirring in a large spoonful of cider vinegar. She was late with supper because of all her visitors. Often, she spent days without seeing anyone, except Jonas. She liked being alone, but with her husband dead for so many years, sometimes she missed the sound of another voice in the house. Today had been extraordinary.

As she chopped the dill she'd just picked from her garden to garnish the soup, there came a knock at the front door. *Dievas, another visitor!* Distracted, Elena put the knife down, but it fell to the floor. Superstition was that dropping a knife meant a visit from a man, but she was sure it was the ARAS agent returning to ask her something else. She didn't even bother to look out the window to see who it was.

She was startled to see a strange man standing on her doorstep. He was middle-aged, and had on a suit and tie. His was short, and thick through the shoulders. This man wasn't smiling like her other guests from today. Her skin prickled. "What do you want?"

The man spoke in her native tongue. Elena breathed in sharply. She recognized his accent: Russian. Very few Russians spoke Lithuanian. The only one she knew was Arkady, and he spoke it so badly it was funny.

Her face flushed. She remembered another large Russian who spoke Lithuanian perfectly, but he'd be dead by now. She told herself to stay calm. This wasn't him. She had just been a girl.

The man on her doorstep asked if she had seen Jonas Volkis.

"What do you want him for?" Seventy years ago, when she was just a girl, Elena had been awoken from a sound sleep by a man's voice speaking Lithuanian with a thick Russian accent. He spoke normally at first, but then shouted at Mama, who screamed.

*Elena had opened the door a crack and watched the man hit Mama. Elena's heart raced as Mama fell to the floor. She ran to the cabinet beside her bed and climbed in, closing the door slowly so no one would hear. Someone with a heavy step came into the room. Inside the cabinet, she held her breath. The footsteps stopped near her. She had never been so scared. She wanted to scream. The footsteps sounded again, and stopped. She didn't dare move, barely breathed.*

*When Elena had finally come out of the cabinet the next day, Mama was gone, and Elena never saw her again.*

All she had left of Mama's was an old pistol, a Russian Makarov, which she kept in the desk in the sitting room, along with her maps.

"Jonas Volkis." The man on her doorstep sounded angry. "It's very important I talk with him as soon as possible. Do you know where he is?"

Elena glanced at her desk under the window. The Makarov was in the center drawer. She kept it clean and loaded, for one never knew. She stepped back to slam the door shut, but the man gave it one quick shove. As it banged against the wall, she ran to the desk. She tried to scream, but his hands were already over her mouth.

~~

Ten minutes later, Bok went into the kitchen. He lifted the lid off the pot of soup and sniffed its aroma before turning off the heat. He took the heel from the loaf of bread on the table and dipped it into the hot liquid before biting off a piece. He smiled as he chewed, and dipped the remaining bit of bread into the soup again before stuffing it all in his mouth. As he went back into the sitting room to finish taking care of Elena, he was pleased she had told him about Darius Artis, her other visitors from today, and had even given him a map to Jonas's cabin outside Visaginas, all before she died.

# CHAPTER 26

## Utena, Lithuania—19 May

Darius headed toward Lukas's Bar, just down the road from the hotel where he was finishing his work on the bomb. It was pleasant outside, so he walked. He'd made good progress today, and even swang his arms casually as he made his way down the street. Upon reaching the bar, he went inside, nodding at Arkady, Jonas's drunken friend, who was in his usual spot.

"Where's Jonas?" said Arkady.

This was the perfect occasion to perpetuate the myth that Jonas was away. Arkady still suffered from the head injury that had ended his career on the oil rigs along the Caspian coast. The Russian had trouble remembering things, and was easily confused. Darius furrowed his brow. "Jonas left for a few days. He told you. He said he was going away with a friend. Don't you remember?"

Arkady rubbed his jaw. "I'm not sure. Which friend?"

"I remember him telling you. He'd be upset to learn you forgot already."

Arkady spoke slowly. "No, I remember, but where did he say he was going?"

"Maybe Puvociai. I thought he might've mentioned it to you."

"I don't think so." Arkady scratched his head. "Why didn't he go to the cabin?"

Darius shrugged, smiling at his ruse as he walked through a light haze of smoke to the corner table, the one he and Jonas always used. Lukas brought over a beer and left without saying a word, only a nod of greeting. Darius leaned back in the chair, his head against the wall, the beer's frothy head inviting him to take a sip. He yearned for a moment's rest as he waited for his guests to join him and arrange the last part of his plan.

Darius closed his eyes and the room faded into a dream. *A group of Red soldiers came in wearing drab olive uniforms. They went right to the bar. Everyone had a drink, even though Lukas was nowhere in sight. One of the soldiers came up to Darius. "I know what you're up to." Jonas was behind the man, laughing.*

Darius awoke with a start and fell off his chair, wincing as he hit the floor. He stood quickly and righted the chair, sitting back down. He flushed as he glanced at the bar. Arkady didn't appear to have noticed.

Now wide awake, Darius saw the door to the saloon open as two women came inside. One was taller than average, and had the energetic stride of an athlete. She had short white hair combed away from her sculpted cheekbones. Her muscular arms were visible under the black tank top. She had a tattoo of a burning tree on her left shoulder. Her companion had long, dark hair and was wearing a white T-shirt, the same tattoo on her shoulder. Her stained jeans had horizontal slits from the knees up her thighs.

They paused just inside the door, gazing at the other patrons, looking like they were ready to run. Both women wore too much makeup. The dark circles around their eyes told of late nights and little sleep. Both looked like they had already seen a great deal of life.

Darius didn't know if the tattoos were significant, other than demonstrating a bond between the sisters, but he really didn't give a damn. He didn't care if their tie was a pagan religious symbol, a cult, or a political ideology. All he cared about was their histories, because he wanted them for his plan.

Both women were smart, but they hadn't been able to afford an education, as their parents had passed away when the girls were just in their mid-teens. They ran away to avoid being split up and sent to live with different relatives. They got by at first on the proceeds from petty thievery. Eventually, they found a good business working in a car theft ring, driving to the Netherlands, stealing cars, and delivering them to buyers at various locations in Ukraine. They worked a side business selling things they found in the cars they stole, and had connections to get specialty items, but only for friends. Darius had known the women for years. They would do almost anything for the right price.

The women came to Darius's table and sat without waiting for an invitation. A moment later, Lukas appeared as if by magic. He had a reputation for minding his own business and spent most of his time in the back. Darius believed Lukas hid himself away because of the port-wine stain on his left cheek, and a fear that women found his appearance distasteful. Lukas had never married, and Darius didn't think he ever would.

Darius ordered beer for them all, and waited in silence until Lukas brought three bottles and glasses over, setting them on the table and leaving without a word.

Rina, the one with white hair, lifted the bottle of Ekstra and poured some into her glass, a beautifully creamy head forming over the amber brew. She took a long swallow and put the glass down. With a look of satisfaction, she stuck out her tongue and licked the residue clinging to her upper lip.

As Simona raised her glass to take a sip, Arkady came over to the table. His gait was unsteady. "Good evening, ladies," he slurred. "Can I buy you a drink?"

Rina glanced at Darius. She got up and took Arkady's arm. "Let me take you back to the bar. We have some business to discuss."

"You're pretty," he said, a wistful look in his eyes.

"I know." Rina returned Arkady to his seat. "Lukas," she called. The man with the port-wine stain came in from the back. "Give this man whatever he wants. Put it on Darius's bill."

Rina sat back down at the table. "I got some Semtex. You want to buy it?"

Darius gave her a seething look. "I told you never to mention the things I get from you."

"It's no big deal. So you like to blow things up once in a while. Who cares?"

Darius put his arms on the table and leaned forward. "I have an important package I need to deliver to an address in Ukraine."

"Where in Ukraine?" said Rina.

"You'll know soon enough."

"Try FedEx," said Simona.

Darius sneered at the sarcasm, but expected nothing less. "It's delicate and I want it to arrive unharmed. Besides, I'm going, too."

"We don't deliver drugs." Rina drank some more beer.

"You know me. There's none of that." Darius took a sip of brew, trying to think of a lie to defuse their curiosity. He remembered the drone with the broken props in his living room. "It's a drone I've modified for better control, and it's as quiet as a mouse."

"Who'd want anything like that?" said Simona, looking bored.

"I have a buyer."

"It's Ukraine," said Rina. "Somebody's going to use it to spy on somebody else. I don't give a shit what they do with it."

"If this drone is so important, why don't you drive yourself?" said Simona.

"I don't know the best places to cross."

"Take the damn train. We're not running a taxi service," said Simona, looking at her sister. "Let's get out of here."

"I'll pay you well." Darius opened his jacket and took out a bulging envelope from an inner pocket. He lay it on the table.

Rina smiled and put her hand on the other woman's arm. "Let's hear what he has to say."

Darius cleared his throat. "I don't want any record of our trip, or where we're going. I don't want us to show up on any traffic cameras. If we're stopped for speeding, you don't get paid. You're to tell no one where you're going, or that I'm traveling with you. I don't want to use a car with any type of GPS tracking or navigation. Can you find one?"

"We might have one available." Rina grinned at Simona.

"Besides that, I want to get through the border discreetly."

"You want us to drive you back?"

Darius nodded, staring into his glass. Yes, he needed a ride back home, but the women would be dead, tragic victims of the terrible explosion that would rock the world. Once in Kiev, he'd find an excuse to leave the women and have them go to the Russian embassy alone. He'd track their whereabouts by the GPS he'd installed in the bomb, detonate it remotely, and leave no witnesses, blowing up the only people who knew he was behind this. It made his plan all the better.

He would have to find his own way home, getting rides with delivery men and other strangers. It would take some strength and time, but he could do it. He had to. If only the ghost of Jonas would leave him alone so he could get some rest, for Christ's sake.

He pushed the envelope toward Rina, knowing it contained plenty for a down payment for the trip. "You get three times that once the job is done."

"Five times," said Simona.

"You don't even know how much is in there," said Darius. It was a moot point, anyway. He could promise them a million euros.

Rina opened the envelope and ran a finger over the bills. "Sounds simple enough. But we'll need a good portion of this to bribe the border guards." She handed it to Simona, who also looked at the money before putting it into the pocket of her jeans.

"If it goes well, there might be more trips. That could be good for you," lied Darius.

"Okay," said Rina.

"Simona, can I count on you, too?" Darius waited.

"Of course," said Simona.

Darius sat back, feeling like a burden had been lifted from his shoulders. "We leave tomorrow night."

"You expect us to waste a day?" If we leave tomorrow night, you have to pay more," said Simona.

# CHAPTER 27

## Utena, Lithuania—19 May

It was midafternoon when Vit left Elena's house. Annie guided him to Lukas's bar, but the place was closed. Exhausted and hungry, Vit made his way to the guest house just off the A6 motorway, where Annie had made a reservation. He had a large room, sparsely furnished, and scrupulously clean. He ate a late lunch of pork and cabbage at the restaurant next door, and went back to his room for a nap. He asked Annie to wake him, as he planned to go to Lukas's bar that night when it was open.

Sleep came easily, and Annie's voice woke him. Groggy, Vit sat on the edge of the bed, still in the clothes he had worn on the plane. He took a quick shower, dressed in clean clothes, and went out into a starry Lithuanian night. Lukas's Bar wasn't very far away, but he drove anyway. He parked out front.

As he went in through the door, the word *dive* came to mind. A party of three middle-aged women sat at a table along the back wall, huddled in conversation. The other tables were empty. No Jonas. Maybe he would come in later. Maybe he was at the cabin as Elena had suggested. Maybe somebody here knew where the hell he had gone.

Vit sat down a few seats away from a bleary-eyed fellow nursing a glass of dark brew.

While Vit waited for the barkeep, the man near him extended a hand and introduced himself as Arkady. He didn't give a last name.

"You look like a Lithuanian, but I can tell you're not from around here," said Arkady.

"Is the bartender around?" Vit glanced over his shoulder.

"Lukas!" shouted Arkady. The three women at the table across the room looked up.

A man came in from the back. Vit ordered a beer. The barkeep poured it and put it on the counter before returning wordlessly to the back.

"You speak Lithuanian even worse than I do," said Arkady.

"You don't happen to know a Jonas Volkis, do you?" said Vit. "I heard he comes in here."

"Who wants to know?"

Vit extended a hand as he said his name. Arkady asked if he was related to Tilda Partenkas. Vit nodded.

"They talk about her here," said Arkady. "They say she's a great lady. Personally, I never heard of her until I moved to Lithuania."

Vit returned the conversation to Jonas Volkis.

"Jonas is one of my oldest and dearest friends," said Arkady. "I'm from Dagestan, you know. I worked on the oil rigs along the Caspian coast. I used to be strong, but look at me now. Nothing but a weakling." He held up a scrawny arm. "I had to give up working years ago, because of an accident. I got hit in the head, and wasn't quite right after that. Got dizzy, and working became too dangerous. I'm Russian, so I came here because there are plenty of Russians nearby in Visaginas, and I could live well and be closer to nature. Besides, I like Lithuania's beauty, even though a lot of people here don't trust the Russians."

Arkady paused for another sip of beer before continuing. "I can't blame them for hating the Russians, but I was born three thousand kilometers away. When I first got here, no one even talked to me. I was miserable, but then I met Jonas. I was walking along the road, and he stopped to give me a ride. Just like that. He said I looked tired. He didn't care if I was Russian. He brought me to Lukas's and bought me a beer. We had a good talk and became friends. I was renting a room in a boarding house in town. I didn't like it. Very noisy. Jonas helped me find a nice apartment. He introduced me to a few people. They liked me. One day they hated me, and the next day they liked me, all because of Jonas. After I met him, I was never lonely again. He's good to me. I'm lucky to have such a friend."

136

"When did you last see Jonas?" said Vit.

"A few nights ago, I guess. I'm not sure. You know my mind isn't so good. Darius keeps telling me it's getting worse and worse. He said pretty soon I won't even know my own name." Arkady sighed into his beer.

Vit frowned. Darius had come up in two conversations: here with Arkady, and previously with Elena.

Arkady squelched a burp. "Darius reminded me that Jonas was going somewhere and wanted me to know, so I wouldn't worry about him."

"Where did Jonas go?"

"I think he went off with a friend. I don't know. Darius mentioned the name of a village, but I can't remember. You should talk to him. Jonas likes to fish and walk through the woods. Of course, he can't walk a lot anymore or fish very well, but he does what he can. Sometimes he goes to the cabin near Visaginas. He loves it there. I've gone with him a few times. We caught fish and had it for dinner. We stayed overnight. It's wonderful, surrounded by nature with no other people in sight."

That both Arkady and Elena had told him about Jonas's cabin was enough for Vit. He was going there in the morning.

Before he left, Vit bought Arkady another beer to thank him for the help. He went back to the guest house and up to his room. He got undressed, and went to bed. He fell asleep thinking about Tilda.

In the morning, Vit had breakfast downstairs in a small dining room with a rustic fireplace. It wasn't particularly early, but he was the only one there. On a buffet table, there were eggs, kielbasa, herring, soft cheeses, bread, jams, and honey. It had been a long time since he'd eaten so richly, and he looked forward to the meal as he filled a plate. There was no packaged food, and probably no preservatives. The honey had a hand-written label on the jar, the kielbasa was in a natural casing, and the bread had a wonderful crust. Tilda had put together breakfasts like this occasionally when he was a boy, but over the years, the old-world favorites had been replaced by granola, fruit, and yogurt. As Vit chewed a piece of cheese sweetened with honey, he decided granola was a step backwards.

After breakfast, Vit got in the car, heading east. He followed the directions on Elena's map, and found the dirt road that snaked into the woods. A Toyota was parked on the side of the road. He drove a short distance to the end, and what he surmised was the general area of Jonas's cabin.

Vit got out of the car. The scent of the trees reminded him of the times Tilda and Senelis had taken him into the woods for picnics when he was little. They'd drive to central Massachusetts, with its stunning forests and walking trails. Often, they stopped at the state forest outside of Paxton. Vit remembered holding Tilda's hand as they walked between the trees that were lined up in beautifully straight rows. They'd stop somewhere for a picnic of bologna on fresh rolls. Every time it was the same lunch in the same forest, but Vit had loved it.

He felt sure he'd find Jonas today. After a conversation, he'd be able to report to Tilda that all was well, and she had nothing to worry about. There was no bomb. There couldn't be. She was his *grandmother*, for Christ's sake!

Vit looked at the map on his phone's screen and got his bearings before walking across the meadow toward the trees and the path. An owl's hoot reminded him of a legend Senelis had told him of *Giltine*, the bearer of death. In her white robes and scythe, Giltine killed by stinging her victims with her tongue, strangling them, or slashing them with the scythe. Sounds would tell that she was in the area; a barking dog, an owl's hoot in the forest. After hearing the story for the first time when he was about six, Vit was so disturbed he wouldn't go into a forest. It had taken several visits to bucolic Paxton and a little aging to get past his fear of Giltine.

His phone rang and he jumped, amazed he had service out here, even though the stewardess on the plane had told him Lithuania had excellent internet and phone coverage. He glanced at the screen and accepted the call. "Hi, Ma."

"You're too busy to call me and tell me you're safe?"

"Annie should have called you. She's programmed to contact you when I'm traveling, telling you when I arrived and when I'll be home."

"She did, but I want to hear from my own son, not some stupid machine. Everything's okay?"

"Sure."

"What's wrong?"

"I'm just tired."

"Pick up a piece of amber for me, okay? There's plenty there. I'd rather have a necklace than a bracelet. A pendant might be nice, too."

"Okay, Ma."

"How do you like the country?"

"The woods are nice."

"Make sure you go to Trakai Castle. It's supposed to be fabulous."

"I gotta go. Bye, Ma."

After hanging up, Vit told Annie to screen his calls.

He followed the path for a short distance before noticing the roofline of a small cabin. It seemed idyllic through the trees, but up close, it looked old and worn. A window was cracked. The logs were gray from the weather. Weeds and tall grasses surrounded it. He looked in through a window. It had one room with a fireplace. A table, a few chairs, and a cot were the only furniture.

The cabin was as Tilda had described, right down to the fishing poles leaning against a wall. She must have been here, but her award had been presented in Vilnius, almost two hours away by car. She had to have had good reason for coming here. Maybe Jonas had wanted to show her the place.

He went to the door. The padlock securing the wooden latch was unlocked and hanging to the side. The door was ajar. He pushed it open. Even though he hadn't seen anyone through the windows, he called out, "Jonas?" No answer. Vit stepped over the threshold and went inside.

The first thing he noticed was that there was no bag or personal items; no razor, clothes, boots, or even a jacket hanging from a peg in the wall. The floor was dusty, although he could see a pair of footprints. He wondered if they belonged to Jonas. The cot was covered by an old blanket. He couldn't tell if someone had slept there recently. The charred wood in the fireplace was stone cold. Vit went to a closet in the back of the cabin, but the dark space held nothing of consequence. There was no food, just a few plates, a few cups, and a rusted pair of wire cutters with a small piece of blue wire insulation caught in the handle. He picked up the wire cutters and as he was examining them, a female voice said, "Show me your hands."

Startled, he turned to find a woman standing in the middle of the room. She was stunning; tall, lean, with golden-brown hair. She was wearing dark slacks and a suit jacket. Vit smiled as she raised her hand. He noticed the gun. He didn't know whether she meant to rob him or shoot him.

Instinctively, Vit raised both arms. "I won't say no to a woman with a gun, but I don't speak Lithuanian very well."

The woman flashed a badge. Her next words, spoken in perfect English, were as distinct as a bell. "Agent Zuza Bartus. ARAS. Lithuanian Police. Now who the hell are you?"

# CHAPTER 28

## The Woods near Visaginas, Lithuania—20 May

Even before he told her his name, Zuza recognized Vit Partenkas from one of the pictures she'd found online. *So this is the Renaissance man.* He had indicators tagging him as an American; a great haircut, and clothing that looked relatively new, except for work boots that were scruffy and well worn.

"Put down the wire cutters," said Zuza.

Vit laid the tool on the floor. She ordered him to turn around, then checked him for a concealed weapon.

"You're trespassing," said Zuza as she lowered the gun alongside her leg.

"The door was open."

"What are you doing here?"

"I'm looking for Jonas Volkis."

"What do you want with him?"

"My grandmother asked me to call on him. He wasn't home, so I came here."

Zuza gazed at him. Tilda Partenkas's grandson had visited Elena just before she had, and now he was here at Jonas's cabin, apparently as anxious to find Jonas Volkis as she was.

It felt like there was something going on she didn't know about. It would be best to talk to him on her own ground and her own terms, rather than chatting in this dilapidated cabin. He might balk if she demanded he come with her to police headquarters, though. Zuza took a gamble on his gullibility. "ARAS is interested in Jonas Volkis in regards to an open case. Based on its importance, I'll need you to accompany me to Vilnius to answer a few questions."

"I'd prefer it if you took me out to lunch."

She holstered her gun and crossed her arms. "Are you refusing to cooperate?"

Renaissance man looked uncomfortable. "Not at all."

On the walk to the end of the dirt road where her car was parked, Vit asked what ARAS was. She explained it was the anti-terrorism organization of the Lithuanian Police. Vit blanched. He got in the car while Zuza made a quick phone call to Otto, telling him she was coming in, and who she had found at Jonas's cabin.

As they drove, Vit asked what this was all about. Zuza didn't answer, so they settled into a lengthy silence. Before long, the forest gave way to massive tracts of cultivated land. Homesteads bordered the road and tractors were out on the fields, some pulling plows, others planting crops. They slowed down behind a large John Deere and waited as a semi sped by in the opposite lane. When the way was clear, Zuza put on her blinkers and poured on the speed, passing the tractor while Vit held onto the door handle.

"I bet Lithuania feeds a lot of people with all this land," said Vit.

Zuza ignored him. She wasn't in the mood for small talk. Besides, he looked too relaxed. She kept up the speed.

Soon, the word *Vilnius* appeared in sculpture on the side of the road, and city traffic slowed them down. At police headquarters, Zuza pulled into a driveway and followed it to the back where she usually parked. They got out of the car, and she escorted Vit past the small blue booth, greeting her friend inside with a nod. They climbed a set of steps and she swiped her card in the reader. The door clicked open. They went down a long corridor. She stopped by a door and motioned Vit inside. The room looked placid for what it was. The three chairs, a table, and two-way mirror showed no evidence of the sensational interrogations that had been held here, or the uneventful ones held more frequently. Zuza noticed Vit glancing at the video camera mounted in a corner near the ceiling.

She asked Vit for his phone and passport. He began to protest, but she gave him a hard stare and he handed them over. She told him to sit down, then left.

~~

Alone, Vit crossed his hands and stared into the large mirror. He felt paralyzed without Annie. He was alone in a foreign country and the police were about to interrogate him.

*Oh shit.*

The lights were bright, just like interrogation rooms on TV. He assumed the door was locked, but didn't bother to check. He didn't know his rights here, but he hadn't broken any laws. He doubted trespassing warranted questioning. He felt sick from the possibility that an anti-terrorism organization might know about Tilda and the bomb, but that was ridiculous. If they asked him about it though, he'd know Tilda's story was true, and he'd have to tell them everything. He would be marked as having terrorist connections. It would mean the end of a deal with Homeland Security. It would probably mean the end of his company, his livelihood, and his lifestyle. It would tarnish the people who worked for him. It would destroy any dignity Tilda had left.

He forced himself to take a breath. *I'll tell them if I have to.*

If ARAS didn't ask about a bomb, he'd know Tilda's story was fabricated, and just a product of her deteriorating mind. This made Vit calm down. At least in a few hours, he'd know.

He would tell ARAS everything he knew to be factual, but he wouldn't implicate his grandmother in a fantasy. Besides, if ARAS acted on Tilda's made-up story, they'd be wasting their time.

He glanced at the door again, wondering if he could simply walk out. Should he contact the US Embassy? He wanted to call Max, but he had no phone. He missed Annie. As he waited for Zuza Bartus to return, it felt like he was waiting for Giltine to come in with her white robes and scythe.

Twenty minutes later, Zuza came back with a man she introduced as Agent Rokas Klem. He was of medium height, wiry, and fair skinned. She opened her mouth to speak, but Rokas cut her off. "I have some questions for you."

Although her glare was aimed at Rokas, Vit caught it too, and felt even more distress.

Turning to Rokas, who was already pulling out the chair directly across from Vit, Zuza said, "A word."

They both left.

~~

When the door clicked shut and they were alone in the corridor, Zuza poked Rokas hard in the chest. He grimaced. "Otto's office," she said.

"You go. I'm going inside to question this man. When I'm done, you can drive him back to Utena to get his car."

"I'm not driving anyone anywhere. And I don't need your help here."

"Otto thought you did. He sent me over after you called."

"I found this guy. He's mine. Back off."

Rokas chuckled. "You think you know what you're doing, but you don't. You spend your time catering to Otto. It must be nice working for a man who treats you like a relative but gives you no real responsibility. Watch me. You'll learn something."

"How can that be possible when your mind is as empty as your soul?"

"Lithuanian women are gentle and kind. I don't know what you are. Living in America has spoiled you. Learn your place!"

"*You* learn my place." Zuza took a step toward him.

"What's going on here?" Otto came up behind them, carrying a file that he handed to Zuza.

"We're discussing the case, as much as there is one," said Zuza.

"I'm going in," said Rokas.

"You're both going in. Zuza's in the lead. She knows more about this than you. Plain and simple. I'll be watching," said Otto.

Zuza recognized a glimmer of the old Otto: tough, and always watching out for his rookies. Zuza cast Rokas a withering look before opening the door and going in. Rokas followed her.

She sat down directly across from Vit, leaving Rokas the chair to her side. She opened the file Otto had given her, skimmed a few pages, folded her hands, and stared at Vit. From the corner of her eye, she noticed Rokas glaring at her.

She kept her gaze on Vit, and her expression as neutral as possible. She tried to ignore Rokas and her anger. A few moments of silence appeared to be too much for Renaissance man. He spoke without being prompted, just as she had hoped.

# CHAPTER 29

## Vilnius, Lithuania—20 May

"Look. I want to do the right thing and cooperate as much as possible," said Vit. "But I don't know what you want from me. I've never even been in Lithuania before. So why are you questioning me?"

Zuza looked down at the papers again. "Your company is called Sagus. In Latin, that means prophetic."

"That's right." He pointed at the company logo, prominent on a sheet of paper in front of Zuza. "I see you've already downloaded some information."

She closed the file. "Tell me more."

Vit took a breath. "The Annie program, Sagus's product, is a high-speed algorithm that learns about people. It creates information profiles using online data, and timelines of what a person has been doing and where they've been, based on social media activity and other things."

Zuza raised an eyebrow. "I know all that from your website. Tell me something I don't know."

Vit cleared his throat. "There are already massive databases about most people in developed countries. Besides, people willingly, although perhaps unknowingly, tell more about themselves every day through social media. Annie discovers new data sources regularly and puts all the information together into comprehensive profiles. She can even use this information to predict a person's behavior. We can't use any of the data for personal gain, and privacy organizations watch us like hawks, but I have no problem with that. It's likely a branch of the US government will buy us out."

"To find terrorists?"

Vit was surprised she came to that conclusion so quickly, but he guessed it was her job. Nothing seemed to get past her. It made him even more nervous. He tried not to show it. "I suppose. And cybercriminals, thieves, scammers. Are you talking to me because of what we do at Sagus? Or do you need my help in finding someone?"

Zuza opened the file again and looked at the papers inside. "Tilda Partenkas is your grandmother?"

"I'm surprised that so many people here know the Partenkas name." A bead of sweat ran down Vit's back.

"Who knows the name?"

"You seem to."

"And how is your grandmother?" Zuza smiled like the frigging Mona Lisa.

Vit couldn't believe this. If Jonas Volkis was a terrorist, or even a suspected one, Vit had nothing to add to the equation. He ran a hand through his hair. "Tilda's not doing well. She's in the hospital. The doctors say she doesn't have long to live."

"I'm sorry to hear that," said Zuza. "So why are you here when your grandmother is so sick at home?"

*This woman doesn't let up!* "Tilda always spoke of Lithuania fondly, and she wanted me to see it so we could share the visit from her hospital bed. I think she wanted to hear about my trip as a way to return here one last time before she died."

"How do you know Jonas Volkis?"

"I don't. My grandmother mentioned him once or twice. She said he heads a group called Baltic Watch." *Do they think Jonas is a terrorist?*

"But you seem anxious to find him."

"Tilda asked me to look him up. I went to his house and he wasn't home. So I talked to his neighbor, who mentioned the cabin. I also went to Lukas's Bar in Utena and a man there, I think his name is Arkady, talked about the cabin, too."

"When did she meet Jonas?"

"I don't know exactly. I think it was when she got her medal. Sometime in the 1990s?"

"Are you asking me or telling me, Mr. Partenkas?"

"Why are you asking me about Jonas? Is he a terrorist?" Vit's throat was dry.

"You tell me."

"How would I know?" *If they think Jonas is a terrorist, and I've just linked him to Tilda, it could be a disaster. But she hasn't been here for thirty years. Focus, Vit.*

"Are you going to arrest me?" Vit held his breath.

"Should I?"

"Hell, no. What's this all about?"

"Do you know Darius Artis?"

"My grandmother mentioned him. I think he's also in Baltic Watch." Vit remembered the video. Did they think Darius was a terrorist?

Zuza continued, asking the old questions in new ways, and finding new things to ask. They continued on for what seemed to be hours. Vit's head pounded. *Just tell them what you know to be true. Don't even mention Tilda's fairytale.*

Rokas left. Zuza kept at it. Finally, a knock sounded at the door.

Zuza watched Vit, saying nothing. She stood, picked up the file, and left the room.

~~

Otto was waiting outside the door. He held out Vit's passport and phone. Zuza took them.

"Rokas checked out his story," said Otto. "Vit arrived in the country yesterday morning. He's never been here before. We confirmed his story about Lukas's Bar, but haven't been able to get in touch with Elena, the neighbor. She isn't home and local police haven't been able to find her. We checked Vit's background through Interpol, who got in touch with the FBI. They've already done an extensive background check on him. There's been no contact they know of with Jonas or Darius. Aside from a few parking violations, there's nothing. In fact, his company is doing some business with the US government."

"So it's just a coincidence that he happened to be at Jonas's cabin this morning? I don't believe in coincidences."

"There's no crime here. He's done nothing illegal. You're done questioning him."

"There's something he's not telling me. I can feel it," said Zuza. "I need more time."

"We're not the damn Soviets! I've already let you go too far. Release him. He hasn't done anything."

Zuza scratched her head, desperate for a new angle. "You can't object if I offer him a ride to his car, can you? Since we've taken up most of his day, it's the only decent thing ARAS can do to thank him for his time and cooperation. Please, Otto. I'll be the perfectly behaved agent."

Otto frowned. "All right. Just get back here right away."

Zuza took a deep breath and prepared to be nice. She hoped she could pull it off.

# CHAPTER 30

## Vilnius, Lithuania—20 May

Vit started when the interrogation room door opened and Zuza walked in again. He braced himself for another round. *Just tell them what you know to be true.*

"Thank you for your time, Mr. Partenkas, you're free to go," she said, handing him his passport and phone.

Vit stood, stuffing the items into his pocket, feeling incredible relief at having Annie back again. He wanted to get out of the room, out of the building, and out of goddamn Lithuania.

Vit followed Zuza down the hallway, through the outside door and down the steps, wondering how the hell he was going to get to the woods to retrieve his rental. She hadn't offered him a lift, which he would've refused, and he wasn't about to go back inside to ask anyone else to give him a ride. It simply felt too good to be free of Zuza's talons. A cab would probably cost more money than he had in his wallet. He wondered if they took credit cards.

As he followed Zuza past the blue booth, a wave of warm air hit him, bringing the welcome feeling of freedom. He wanted to run, but knew she would chase him down and haul his ass back inside.

"One more thing, Mr. Partenkas," said Zuza. "Let me take you to your car. I promise, no more questions." Her smile seemed natural and spontaneous. It surprised Vit. He felt like slapping himself on the side of the head for even considering her help.

"Please. It's the least I can do." She smiled again, and like an idiot, he agreed. Within minutes, they were in her car, weaving through the city streets. She was damned attractive, and clearly enjoyed being behind the wheel. But his anxiety from the interrogation room stayed with him. Zuza hadn't questioned him about any bomb, so that was good.

It meant Tilda's story was a fantasy.

Vit was worried he might inadvertently say something that would bring Tilda back into the conversation. He wanted to keep her out of it. There was no need to cause her more pain. He glanced at Zuza. She wasn't at all like his old girlfriend, Gina. Under her uniform, Gina was soft and supple. Zuza was lean and hard as a rock, both physically and mentally. It was better if he controlled the inevitable conversation they would have during the drive to Visaginas.

"You speak English well. Where did you learn?" asked Vit, already thinking ahead to more questions to keep her occupied.

"I was born here, but raised in New York and California. My father relocated to the US for his job, and we spent a few years in the city. When my father got an offer from his firm to relocate to LA, we jumped at the opportunity."

"What did he do for a living?"

"He worked for a company that made lasers. It's a big industry here in Lithuania."

"Where did you go to college?" *So far, so good.*

"Claremont McKenna, in southern California. Most people from the East Coast don't know the place."

"I've heard of it. It's a damn good school. It has excellent economics, government, and poly sci programs. It's a leap from there to ARAS agent, though."

"I was in college on 9/11 during the attack on the World Trade Center. The train bombings in Madrid in '04 showed me that terrorism was going global. My father was killed in London a year later, in the July 7 bombing." Zuza stepped on the gas.

"I'm sorry," said Vit.

"There was a push for international cooperation among security organizations, so I joined Europol. I lived in Holland for a few years, but spent all my time working on a computer. I learned a lot, but wanted to do more, so when a position came up in ARAS, I took it. The job is challenging in many ways."

"Like the other guy in the room today? It looked like he had a problem with your authority."

Zuza didn't even flinch. "ARAS has a vital role and adapts to the needs of the country. In Lithuania, women have fought alongside men for a long time. Just in the 1940s and 1950s, women were partisans, members of the resistance fighting the Soviets. That tradition continues, but today, we're fighting terrorists and organized crime."

"But some men want you to stay home, have babies, and cook dinner for them."

The car went even faster. Vit swallowed hard. "A lot of women are in law enforcement in the US. Why didn't you stay?"

"I thought about becoming a US citizen after college, but the job at Europol came up. I thought there would be more opportunities in the EU. And it got me back to my European roots. My mother was from Poland, my father from Lithuania. I speak both languages, as well as Russian, German, and French. I'm learning Farsi, although I find it hard to read. I love the US, but thought I could make more of a difference working abroad."

Vit held onto the dashboard as Zuza swerved around a car, passing it.

She continued. "Over the past few years, many people my age have left for the UK and better jobs. But I find something almost innocent about this place, despite everything that happened with the Soviets. I want to keep it safe for the people who stay."

"How much can one woman do?"

"As much as she can imagine."

Vit nodded. She certainly *sounded* genuine. "Any regrets?"

"I never second-guess my decisions. I never look back."

"I don't either. Don't believe in it. You deal with the problem facing you, make your decisions, and move on. As long as you know your reasons, you'll sleep well at night."

Zuza glanced at him.

"Any brothers or sisters?" said Vit.

"One brother. He's a doctor in New York. Has a wife and two kids. My mother lives in San Diego. Both are US citizens. I'm the only renegade."

"No siblings for me. My mother has her heart set on a little bungalow in Florida. At least that's what she calls a twenty-five hundred square foot condo with a pool, health club, and beach access."

Zuza's face softened. "What got you into computers?"

Just because Zuza was giving him a lift didn't mean she wasn't probing him for information, but the question seemed innocent enough. "I always had an interest in computers and politics. But I didn't think I could make a living as a politician, at least not right away. I went to the Rensselaer Polytechnic Institute in New York, and got a degree in computer engineering. I worked for years before coming up with an idea for my own company."

Vit looked out the side window, waiting for the usual attack. Many people objected to even the premise of Sagus, claiming their privacy was being eroded. But good guys *needed* Sagus, because terrorists and criminals were getting smarter at hiding their tracks. Right now, Vit wasn't interested in defending his company. He was too tired. If she didn't see the value, fine. She was just a cop and didn't know any better.

"If I gave you a name, what kind of information would you be able to find?" said Zuza.

Surprised, he answered. "We can get addresses, phone numbers, education, parents, siblings, and even recent whereabouts for most people. Do you have someone in mind?"

"Darius Artis."

*That name again.* Vit took out his phone. "Annie."

"I've missed you, Vit," said Annie.

He smiled at Zuza. "Annie's my computer."

"I see."

"Annie, do a level one search on Darius Artis. Display the results on my phone. And kick off a level two."

"I'd love to."

"Let me know as soon as you have something."

"This will take a while, won't it?" said Zuza.

"The data is ready, Vit," said Annie.

Reading from his phone's display, Vit rattled off some of Darius's information: personal code number or *asmens kodas* in Lithuania, date of birth, educational history, parents, number of credit cards, banks where he did business, favorite places for online purchases, and recent travel.

"That's remarkable," said Zuza.

They continued to talk about Sagus, and the data Annie could retrieve. Before long, the sun set, darkness fell, and they were at the meadow where his car was parked. Zuza pulled up next to it.

"When had you planned on going home?" she said.

"I have an open ticket, so I think I'll take a few days to get a feel for the old country. I don't want to leave with bad memories."

"Sorry about that." Another smile.

As he opened the door to get out, she handed him her card.

"I know what it's like to be in over your head," said Zuza. "Call me if you want to talk."

For a second, it felt like she had read his mind. Vit considered assuring her he was fine and that she was mistaken, but decided against it. It would have sounded hollow, and she would've noticed. He put the card in his shirt pocket. Zuza stayed until he got inside the Mercedes and started the engine.

He followed Zuza along the dirt road. At the motorway, she turned right. He went left, in the direction of his hotel. Relieved as he was that ARAS hadn't mentioned any bomb, he began to wonder whether the organization just didn't know about it. But fatigue and jet lag were preventing him from putting his thoughts together. Everything would become clear after a good night's rest.

He was so distracted that when he turned onto 102 north toward the turnoff to Utena, he didn't notice the car behind him until it was close, coming on fast, and flashing its headlights.

*Zuza must have forgotten something.*

# CHAPTER 31

## The Woods near Visaginas, Lithuania—20 May

Vit put on his blinkers as he moved to the side of the motorway. Instead of stopping behind him, the car behind passed, then screeched to a halt in front of him, blocking his way. It looked like a BMW.

This wasn't Zuza's car.

Unsettled from the day's ration of surprises, Vit's instincts kicked in. He slammed on the brakes to avoid hitting the car. He put the Mercedes into reverse and backed up, going as fast as he dared. He had heard of robbers forcing cars to stop, but never expected anything like this to happen here. He remembered the road was straight in this stretch, and hoped that would save him. Without streetlights, it was hard to see well enough going forward, let alone backward.

A short distance from his pursuers, Vit turned the car around, but so had the other car. It was already on his tail. "Chase me, assholes. I'm from Boston!"

Vit gripped the wheel and got down to business. Built for the *Autobahn*, the Mercedes performed beautifully, holding the road well around the first curve. Vit sped up. The trees a few feet back from the road reminded him that any mistake would lead to a crash. The car behind stuck to him.

The gray pavement folded into the tall grasses and trees lining the road in one smooth blanket of dark. His left hand cramped, but he didn't dare take it off the wheel.

"Annie, get a picture of those plates."

"Computers don't have eyes, Vit. Mount your phone on the dashboard."

He did.

Vit hoped that as soon as the people behind him realized he wasn't going to be an easy target, they'd leave him alone. But his pursuers continued to follow him. They turned their headlights on high. The car came closer. Vit braced for a hit as he demanded more of the Mercedes. The hit didn't come.

Another car flew by, going in the opposite direction. He gasped, relieved they hadn't collided.

The car chasing him hit his rear fender. Vit's body slammed against the shoulder harness. He almost went off the road, but managed a last-minute correction. He pressed the gas pedal down to the floor. He noticed a second set of headlights in the rearview mirror. *Fuck. Two cars?*

A loud bang sounded, like a car backfiring. He poured on the speed, glad that he had indulged himself with a high-performance vehicle. He focused on the road.

Another loud bang to his fender. His steering wheel jerked to the side. For a crazy second, he thought he was losing control. The car behind was so close, Vit couldn't see the grill. Another boom.

When Vit passed a side road, the car behind him broke off the chase. It was so sudden that Vit wondered if it was a trick, and the car was using a side road to cut him off. A pair of headlights followed him. He kept up the speed. Sweat stung his eyes. He brushed it away. He wasn't out of this yet.

The rear car kept pace, but didn't seem to be trying to overtake him. The dome light went on. It took several quick glances from the road to the mirror before he recognized Zuza Bartus behind the wheel. He felt a wave of relief, astonished at how glad he was to see her.

He slowed the car. Zuza closed the gap, keeping the interior lights on. When he came to a stop, she pulled up behind him. He kept the engine running.

She got out and ran to him. He lowered the window.

"Are you all right?" she said.

"Who was that?"

"I don't know yet, but I have my suspicions. You'd better come with me."

"No, thanks. I'm going to the police station in Utena and report this. After that, I'm going to my hotel, having a shot of whiskey or three, and trying to get some sleep."

"What do you think the police are going to do? Tuck you into bed and kiss you good night? That man was after you. He knows your car. He's probably been following you. And it's likely he'll come after you again."

Vit shook his head. "He was trying to rob me. What else could he possibly want?"

"To get you to stop! He either followed us from Vilnius or knew about the cabin. How else could he have found you out here?"

"That means you were following me, too."

"I noticed a car off the dirt road when we got here. It was there when we left, so I stayed back, just in case. When he started following you, I followed *him*. And it's a good thing I did. Now get out of your car and come with me!"

"I'll follow you."

"That man knows your car. Leave it here, and come with me. You'll be safer."

Reluctantly, Vit closed the window, cut the engine, and got out. As he paused at the shattered rear light and dented bumper, the relief at being rescued by this woman was replaced by a heavy dose of dread.

He followed Zuza to her vehicle and got in. "Why did that guy break off?"

"Because I was shooting at him."

"Remind me never to tick you off," choked Vit.

Zuza turned the car around again and headed in the opposite direction. "Does Annie know who that man was?"

He was surprised that Zuza would think of Annie right away. "Annie, do you have anything yet?"

"There was one man inside the vehicle. The car was rented at the Vilnius airport yesterday. Facial recognition confirms he came in on a flight from Istanbul. His name is Alexy Bok, a metalworker from Brest Oblast."

"Get me the level two data," said Vit. "And see if there have been any large payments to his accounts lately."

A moment later, Annie spoke. "He's married, has a son, likes to gamble. No unusual payments to any accounts."

"The Russians hide payments in foreign accounts all the time. They're almost impossible to trace," said Zuza.

"Why the hell was he chasing me?" said Vit.

"There are several possibilities," said Annie. "He might know about Sagus, and is interested in kidnapping you and holding you for ransom. Another possibility is industrial espionage. He may have been hired to force you to tell him proprietary information about your company."

Bok's picture flashed up on the phone. Vit looked at it for a minute, memorizing every blemish and wrinkle. He held the camera up so Zuza could see the picture as she drove.

"I have another theory," Zuza said. "He may want to know why Dr. Partenkas's grandson is here, and why he was snooping around Jonas Volkis's cabin just after Darius Artis made threats against NATO. This Bok won't be obliged to put up with your bullshit like I am. The next time you may not be so lucky. You know something that this Bok wants to learn, or he would've just killed you. Honestly, you Americans are naïve. You don't look beyond your vicious capitalism. The guy chasing you is Russian. You call yourself a Lithuanian, but you know nothing."

"What's there to know about his backwater country? Your ideas are wacked. You think every Russian is with the KGB and out to get you."

"The KGB is dead. He could be with the SVR, or was hired by them to do a job."

Vit crossed his arms. "I don't believe you. Annie, what's SVR?"

"*Sluzhba Vneshney Razvedki*. International spies."

At first, Vit thought Zuza was being ridiculous, and that Bok couldn't possibly want anything from him. Even though Vit was in the business of finding data that could identify potential terrorists and criminals, there had was always been an abstraction to his work. He had never met a spy or even a criminal. He dealt with data, not people. But spies dealt with data, just like he did.

Even if Bok wanted details on how Annie worked, it would take years for Vit to reproduce the program. If Bok wanted money for a ransom, Vit was well off, but far from wealthy, at least not yet. If Bok wanted to steal Annie, her duress codes were extensive. She could pick up on nuances in Vit's voice indicating stress factors that would prevent her from following Vit's commands.

Bok might be a Russian agent, but what was he doing here? Lithuania was merely a footnote to the rest of the world. No one cared about what happened during the war or what was happening now. There was nothing here except for farmland and trees; nothing that was a matter for spies and intrigue.

Except if what Tilda had told him was true. It was inconceivable to Vit that the Russians suspected he had knowledge of a nuclear bomb here, but why else would Bok be chasing him? Vit was the link between Tilda and Jonas, and even a link to Darius.

"You forget your history," said Zuza. "The Baltic countries have access to the sea through a corridor that goes straight to Saint Petersburg. That's why the Soviets came here during the war. They had to block that path from the Germans. After the war, the Russians stayed to protect their interests. They watched many of us, using both spies and equipment. The level of surveillance here was unprecedented. You think that changed after the breakup of the Soviet Union? Countries spy on each other. There are plenty of Russians here and in Latvia and Estonia, and they're watching. Stalin's legacy lives on. Russian intelligence organizations are alive and well. And don't ever doubt that when they want something, they're going to get it."

Annie's voice. "Level two data. Alexy Bok began his career in the Russian army, became an explosives expert and a hand-to-hand combat instructor. After leaving the military, he traveled extensively. He has been here twice in the last eight months. Over the past year, we identified him through facial recognition at an airport in Kiev three times, and four times at the Tehran Imam Khomeini Airport."

"An ex-military man from Russia who spends significant time abroad," said Zuza. "I'd be scared if I were you."

Vit leaned back into the seat as the information sank in, his head swimming in a sea of improbable truths.

# CHAPTER 32

## The Kremlin, Moscow—20 May

From behind the desk, Vera smiled at the latest addition to the decor, a Remington bronze of a cowboy on a horse, a gift from the president of the United States, commemorating her recent rise to power. Before long, he too, would be eating out of her hands. Nina sat across from her, looking troubled, but whatever it was would have to wait.

The TV was on, the bottom of the screen below her smiling face displayed the caption *Vera Koslova, President of Russia*. It was the first broadcast of the taping two days ago. Vera was pleased with the way she looked. She used the remote control to turn up the sound. The interviewer, an American man with a square face and straight teeth that looked unnaturally white, smiled at the camera before introducing her and saying a few words about her stunning rise to power.

"How is Russia adapting to a woman president?" said the interviewer.

*Instead of asking about economics or domestic policy, he asks if the people like a girl running things*. Vera smiled, remembering she had answered in Russian, thinking at the time that the delay for the translation would put the interviewer off his game. "Russians are noble and intelligent people who recognize good leadership. Popular opinion is tremendously favorable toward me and the Kremlin. I'm moving forward with new security, economic, and human rights programs such as the world has never seen before. As Catherine the Great advanced the condition of women through educational reforms, improved the economy through trade agreements, and created great institutions like the Bolshoi and the Hermitage Museum, I will enact reforms to improve the intellectual and economic situation of every citizen, and once again make Russia the greatest country in the world."

"Do you think this is a honeymoon period, and how long do you think it will last?"

*If only I had my old PSM automatic, I would've shot this idiot in the head.* "Sometimes, good leadership is measured in seconds. When really well done, it's measured in years."

The interviewer nodded thoughtfully. "The bombs detonated at the recent riots in Novosibirsk killed fifteen people in one of the most horrendous acts of terrorism in Russian history. What are you doing to make sure something like this never happens again? And are you worried that it will?"

"We regret the passing of our beloved citizens, and will mourn them for many years to come. One of my priorities is ensuring that Russian people living in Eastern Europe and Asia are safe and secure. I will see to it that terrorism has no place in Russia or in any country bound to us diplomatically. The Russian military is the finest in the world. For now, our troops will secure our safety, while other teams determine the parties responsible for those horrible explosions."

"Do you know who was behind the bombing?"

"We are ruling out no organization, and no person. We're even looking into outside influence."

"Outside influence?"

"I'd rather not say anything more until our investigation is concluded. We're just considering all possibilities."

The interview continued for thirty minutes, enough to air on channels abroad as a news special event. Vera was pleased. She picked up the remote and turned off the TV. She took out the Khortytsa from the bottom drawer of her desk and poured some into glasses. Overall, it had been an excellent show. She had carried it off with grace and cool composure.

Nina took a glass and held it in her hand without drinking. She wasn't smiling.

"What's on your mind?" said Vera.

"Bok."

That Nina even mentioned Bok's name meant something was wrong.

Nina put the glass down. "He didn't find Jonas Volkis. He's disappeared. Volkis's neighbor told Bok that Vit Partenkas was also looking for Volkis. Partenkas is the grandson of the radiation specialist Tilda Partenkas, who's living in the US. Bok tracked him to the woods in eastern Lithuania. There, Partenkas met with ARAS agent, Zuza Bartus, who escorted him to the police station in Vilnius. When Partenkas was released, Bok tried to stop him, but the ARAS agent interfered, and the American got away."

"Remind me. What did Tilda Partenkas do?"

"She created Z-109, an anti-radiation drug. Despite excellent early test results, the long-term effects proved fatal. It never made it to mass markets. She is apparently dying from side effects. Even so, she got a medal from those Lithuanians. A national award."

"Who is that other fellow from Baltic Watch?"

"Darius Artis. It seems we can't find him, either. But Bok found something interesting in his apartment: trace amounts of beta and gamma radiation."

"So right after Darius Artis made that video, Bok finds traces of radioactive material in his apartment, the head of Baltic Watch disappears, and the grandson of the woman who created an anti-radiation drug flies all the way from the US looking for him. Besides that, ARAS is involved." Vera settled back in her chair to do what she had done best as Director of the FSB, to follow the threads in the spider's web and make the associations no one else could.

"When was Dr. Partenkas last in Lithuania?" said Vera.

"Nineteen-ninety-two. When she got her medal."

"Where did she stay?"

"Vilnius, at the Nerutis Hotel. But she flew in several days prior. She didn't check into a hotel. Perhaps she stayed with friends."

"A radiation specialist flies in just before the breakup of the Soviet Union. There were thefts of radioactive material about that time in Lithuania, weren't there? I remember reading about it. They caught some of the people who did it, didn't they?" Vera pressed her fingertips together.

"A guard at the nuclear power plant was convicted of the theft, but they didn't recover all the missing material."

"If Darius Artis has a nuclear device at his disposal and detonates it, it could be a disaster. But he wouldn't be foolish enough to use it in any major city in Russia. Radiation detectors are in place in important buildings, and we have patrol vehicles constantly checking for radiation. But those devices aren't located everywhere."

Vera leaned in. "Get more people in there and find Darius Artis! If you have to, activate every agent we have. Tell Bok to assume Vit Partenkas knows where Artis is. Have him learn what Partenkas knows, in particular where Artis is headed with that bomb. Find Darius Artis and stop him. I don't care how they do it, just as long as it's done once and for all. And I want no trace back to the Kremlin."

Nina stood.

"Put the borders and the military on high alert."

"Yes, Madame President."

"Keep the reasons to yourself for now."

Vera stared up at the ceiling, barely noticing Nina going out the door.

# CHAPTER 33

## Utena, Lithuania—20 May

Driving along the E272 with Vit in the car next to her, Zuza felt the adrenaline wane from shooting at Alexy Bok. Vit seemed like a decent fellow, but she was through being nice. Her words came out like heat from a blast furnace. "I know you think I'm a hard-ass. But we don't have time to develop understanding and mutual trust, which are overrated concepts anyway. You need me to protect you from the Russians right now, and I need to know why they're after you."

Vit looked down at his hands.

"After Bok finished talking to you, he would've . . . well, maybe I should put a bullet in your head myself and save the Russians the trouble," said Zuza.

"Isn't your killing me a little harsh?"

Zuza frowned.

"Maybe you're right. Maybe I'm stupid. I've never been in danger before. I've never even been in a real fight. Sure, there were a few near misses with a drunk here and there after a Red Sox game, but nothing serious. Once somebody sideswiped me during a blizzard and said he was going to punch my lights out. But nothing happened. They were just words." He looked at her. "Things are just getting started, aren't they?"

Zuza gestured to the dashboard with a nod of her head. "Open the glove compartment. There are two chocolate bars inside. Have one. You must be starving."

Vit reached in and took out the chocolate, folding down the wrapping on one of the bars and handing it to her. She took it and had a bite.

"Where do you think Bok is now?" said Vit.

"Out looking for you!"

Vit put the chocolate down on the dashboard.

"Eat. Maybe a little food will help. I'm on your side, Vit. I wish you believed that."

"After Bok drove off, you could've chased him. Instead, you stopped to see if I was all right."

"What else would I do? We need to find Darius. Can Annie find out where he is right now?"

"Vit, is that what you'd like me to do?" Annie's voice sounded from Vit's phone.

"Is she always listening?" said Zuza.

Vit nodded. "Pretty much."

"And she takes orders from only one person?" said Zuza.

"Annie uses a proprietary eavesdrop-proof application to get her instructions, and yes, I'm the only one who can give her orders. But I, on the other hand, have been known to take orders from many women."

Several seconds later, Annie's voice came out over the phone's speaker again. "A security camera across the street picked up Darius waiting outside Lukas's Bar."

"Can you show me the video?" said Zuza, pulling off to the side and stopping the car.

"Do it, Annie."

"Of course." Annie displayed the video on Vit's phone. Darius was barely visible in the dim light, leaning against the wall near the bar's front window, a suitcase on the ground next to him. Annie adjusted the resolution and his face displayed clearly. There was no doubt it was him.

Zuza got back on the road, turning the car toward Utena. "He's got some explaining to do, and I want to know what's in that suitcase." She glanced at Vit. "You get a pass for now, my friend. But the next time I ask you a question, I want an answer, or I'm going to throw you to the wolves. And out here, they speak Russian."

# CHAPTER 34

## Utena, Lithuania—20 May

Darius stood outside Lukas's Bar, the suitcase containing the carefully packed refurbished bomb on the ground next to him, and the small overnight bag hanging from his shoulder. He glanced at his watch. Rina and Simona were supposed to pick him up. They hadn't wanted to wait the extra day, but in the end, he had convinced them by promising a bonus of a thousand euros. Simona had actually shaken his hand. It was too bad they wouldn't be alive to collect. *And now they're late!*

The walk from the hotel had calmed him a little, and had given him the chance to dispose of the equipment he no longer needed in a trash receptacle a few streets down. But he was so anxious and excited he could barely feel the cool night air. He watched the road for Rina and Simona. A car passed. It wasn't them.

As he leaned against the side of the building, the sense that he was about to change life for millions of people made him tremble.

It had taken yesterday afternoon and most of today to carefully complete the job. When it was done, he had a few hours to spare before meeting Rina and Simona to begin their journey. The bomb was packed inside the dark green suitcase with wheels and zippered pouches in the front. He had put Jonas's gun inside one of the pouches before settling into the upholstered chair in his room, the suitcase on the floor next to him, and closed his eyes.

*Jonas entered the room through the fog of a dream, going straight to the suitcase and extracting the deadly device.*

*"I'll detonate it for you," said Jonas. The old man pulled a mobile phone from his pocket and punched out a number. Darius tried to stop him, tried to scream, but he was like a bug encased in amber. He whimpered at the pain he was about to experience.*

When Darius woke up, he was so relieved it had only been a dream that he cried.

As Darius waited outside Lukas's Bar, shivering at the memory of Jonas's last ghostly visit, another car drove down the road. *It's still not them, dammit!* He cursed himself for trusting those girls. His ire grew with every passing second. Another car went by, and another. *Not them.* The first signs of panic came in the feeling of heat in his chest, and overall weakness. The mission wouldn't succeed without those two bitches. If they didn't arrive, all of this would've been for nothing. What he did to Jonas would have been for nothing. He had to think of another plan. Maybe Lukas would let him sleep in the back room for the night. No, that would be too strange. He would stand out, be remembered. He should've thought of another plan long ago. How stupid he was! One could never trust thieves.

Another car passed by. He barely looked at it, but this one stopped about ten meters away. A woman got out of the passenger side and walked toward him. Darius exhaled upon recognizing Simona. She stopped in the light cast by the fixture over Lukas's front door, and glanced down at the suitcase. "That must be a big drone."

"What took you so long?"

Simona shrugged.

Darius looked at his watch, not even registering the time. He followed her to a black Saab. Rina waited inside, her skin glowing from the instrument lights on the dashboard. Darius leaned over and spoke to her through the passenger side window.

"What's this? We can't use this car! It's almost new. It has a GPS device. I'm sure of it," he said. "I told you. I want an old car, with no possibility of being tracked."

Rina laughed. "If there's one thing we know, it's how to find and disable navigation and tracking devices."

"How can you be sure?"

Rina looked him straight in the eye. "Darius, we steal cars for a living. The Americans call it jacking. We jack cars." She giggled. "American English is so funny."

"Can we get back to business, please?" said Darius.

"We're absolutely sure all tracking devices and navigation systems are gone from this car. Our lives depend on it. I guarantee it. It is safe. It cannot be traced in any way by anyone. And the plates are stolen," said Rina.

Darius would only have to tolerate them for a relatively short time, a few days at most. He could stand it. He had to. He had no choice. "All right. Remember. Stick to back roads. Stay away from traffic cameras, no speeding, and I want to go into Ukraine through Poland so we don't have to worry about Belarus guards."

"We always go in through Poland," mumbled Rina.

Simona had straightened, obviously unaware of what her sister had said. "It's longer that way. It will cost you more."

Darius forced a cough to hide his smile.

# CHAPTER 35

## Utena, Lithuania—20 May

Zuza opened the door as the Toyota came to a stop in front of Lukas's Bar. She got out and canvassed the area, Vit following her. With a man like Bok after them, she didn't blame him for staying close.

She went up to a man smoking a cigarette outside, holding out her badge before speaking to him. The man said he had just arrived, and had seen no one. Her search of the alleyway on the side of the building yielded nothing except a relatively new car that probably belonged to either the owner or someone working there. Vit had Annie run the plates. It was Lukas's car. Zuza went around to the back. Darius was nowhere in sight.

Zuza walked back to the front and went inside. A lone man sitting at the bar stared into an empty glass. A couple sat at a table in the back with a bottle and two glasses. The bartender wasn't in the room.

She went around behind the bar and into the back room. Vit followed. Zuza was about to tell him to wait in the car, but thought better of it. She didn't want to be too far away from Annie because she might need more information. Besides, Vit was safer with her and she could keep an eye on him.

The room was lined in dark paneling that looked like it hadn't been updated in years. The banker's lamp on top of the filing cabinet provided the only lighting. Cases of beer were stacked along a wall, next to a leather couch and a TV.

Zuza knocked on the door to a private toilet, waited a second, and opened it; no one. She opened the door to the outside, thinking the bartender might have just gone out for a smoke. Again, no one. She returned to the back room, wondering why anyone would abandon the bar with customers inside, and whether their decision to leave was due to the unexpected arrival of an ARAS agent who was now looking for them.

A sheet of paneling moved in the far corner of the room. Zuza reached for the gun in her shoulder holster, motioning Vit to get behind her. He did so without a word. A man emerged from a passageway inside the wall. Zuza identified herself. He froze. She quickly patted him down and put the gun back in its holster. She asked his name and he identified himself as Lukas, the owner.

"What do you want?" he said.

Zuza showed him her badge. Lukas gazed at it. She went into interrogation mode. During her rapid-fire questioning, the barkeep confirmed he hadn't seen Darius all evening.

"I haven't seen Jonas, either," said Lukas. "I have nothing against ARAS. I think they do good work. We have to get a handle on those car theft rings, and keep watch on the terrorists. It's only a matter of time before something happens here, too. Something big. Now, if you were KGB, I'd want to stick a knife between your ribs."

"KGB is extinct," said Zuza.

"The change of a few letters means nothing. Russians cling to their past—most of them anyway. Not Arkady there, though." Lukas gestured at the door leading to the bar. "He's my best customer. Russian and apolitical as they come. Not a bad man. He's welcomed here. Not everyone is."

"Is Darius Artis welcomed here?"

"Yes, even though he's a hothead, just like his father. I knew Ignas. He was a fanatic. He refused to accept that the Soviets were here for good. So he abandoned his son to live in the woods. He wasted his life. My grandfather was different. He bought this place before the war, to do something useful. My grandfather was a good man, but a half-assed carpenter. He reconfigured the room."

Lukas looked askance at Vit. "Is he ARAS, too?"

Zuza introduced Vit.

"Tilda Partenkas's grandson?" Lukas shook Vit's hand. "Very good to meet you. How is she?"

Before Vit could answer, Zuza spoke. "I want to see what's behind that opening." She pointed to the wall from which Lukas had emerged moments before.

Lukas crossed his arms. "I *have* to trust that you'll keep your mouth shut, but I don't know him, even if he is related to Dr. Partenkas."

"Stay," said Zuza. Vit sat down on a stool.

Lukas led Zuza to the opening in the wall. The narrow piece of paneling was hinged from the inside, allowing it to open like a door to what looked like a narrow hallway. Inside, holes drilled into the wall at eye height every few meters allowed light from the bar to brighten the claustrophobic hallway in a pattern of dull cones. Going sideways, Lukas entered. Zuza followed him. At the end of the narrow room, a slightly wider space held a single stool and an empty beer glass.

"What is this?" said Zuza.

Lukas put his finger to his lips, gesturing for quiet. He pointed at the stool and held the glass's bottom against the wood. She sat and put her ear to it. "I can hear people talking," she whispered.

"That's the farthest table back," whispered Lukas. He pointed to one of the small holes in the wall. Zuza moved to look through the makeshift peep hole.

They returned to the storage room. Zuza sat on a stool, brushing a cobweb from her face. Vit went to her side. He seemed relieved that she was back, even though she had only been gone a minute.

"How did your grandfather get away with building that?" said Zuza.

"It was different those days. A lot of people took risks. Back then, people would rather die than talk, Russians and Lithuanians both, so you had to spy on them to learn anything. My grandfather reconfigured the room so he could listen in on the Communists and soldiers. He learned a lot from people sitting at the farthest table in the back where no one could hear them—or so they thought. If they said anything important, Grandfather reported it to the partisans."

"And now you spy on your customers?"

"It's not spying. I'm upholding a family tradition. Jonas knew what it was like in the old days. His parents were partisans. Freedom Fighters. People who resisted the Soviets. I remember them all, even though I was just a child. They used to work with Ludmelia Kudirka, the one they called Amber Wolf."

Zuza nodded. "I met her at a political speech. I was just a girl. Ludmelia must have been in her eighties. My father said we're related to the Kudirka family, through Ludmelia's father."

Lukas gazed at her. "There might be a resemblance. It's hard to say. My grandfather talked about Ludmelia often. Her exploits were legendary. He said that just after the war, she made friends with a woman who worked as administrator in the Communist Party here in Utena. Ludmelia said she was getting married, and that she'd supply the food and drink if the administrator would organize a celebration. The administrator told her coworkers about the party, and sure enough, all of the Communists in the office showed up at the administrator's apartment on the appointed night to celebrate the happy couple's pending nuptials. But they really came to eat and drink for free. Who wouldn't? After a while, people were feeling good. Ludmelia and her pretend fiancé, Dana Ravas, another partisan, came in. There was a round of toasts. Before too long, Dana and Ludmelia were on the couch kissing. Ludmelia got up and went into the kitchen. He followed her. There was some noise, as if they were clearing plates from the table. People were laughing, assuming that the couple was practicing for their wedding night. Three men dressed in suits come in from the outside. One was Marius Partenkas."

Lukas turned to Vit. "He was your great-grandfather, wasn't he?"

Vit nodded.

"They opened fire, killing everyone in the room, except for the administrator. Men had balls in those days, and women, too," Lukas chuckled.

"Why did they let the administrator go?" said Vit.

"She was already dead. The party was in her apartment, and she'd invited everyone. The Soviets would assume she knew what was going to happen. As the story goes, the Soviets carted her off. No one knows what happened to her, but we can guess she suffered. That was the kind of thing the partisans did all the time; take advantage of the Soviets whenever they could. My grandfather was a registered party member, but he wasn't one of them. He made a point of joining the party so the Communists would come to the bar. He sided with the Freedom Fighters, and was proud of it. Today, there's some criticism about what the partisans did, and how brutal they were. But that's what the Soviets were. Brutal. Some say the partisans made conditions worse by inciting the Soviets to even more violence. I say, fuck it. They thought they were doing the right thing for their country and risked their lives. That's good enough for me."

"And did you learn anything from Jonas and Darius all the times they were here?" said Zuza.

Lukas shrugged. "Usually, they argued about politics. What the Russians were doing, what they were planning. Things like that. Recently, Darius was angrier than usual, acting more like his father. Darius is worried about Vera Koslova. He's convinced the Russians are going to invade and is trying to think of ways to stop them. But what can one man do?"

"What was Darius planning?"

Lukas watched her for a moment. "I don't know."

"Did he recently mention wanting to go anywhere? A trip perhaps?"

Lukas crossed his arms. "No, but he talked about Kiev a few times. He asked Jonas if he'd been there."

"Could Darius possibly have been here tonight without you seeing him?"

"I like to keep an eye on all my customers, even when I'm in the wall, but I'm only one man."

They went to the front where Vit introduced Zuza to Arkady. Vit sat on one side of him, Zuza on the other. Lukas poured out two beers and brought them over. He poured Zuza a tumbler of *krupnikas*, a sweet honey-flavored liqueur. She took a sip. Lukas returned to the back.

"Did you see Darius tonight, Arkady?" Zuza asked.

Arkady shrugged and shook his head.

"Think. It's important."

"No. I don't know." He looked anxious. The growth of beard on his face made him look old.

Zuza ran a hand through her hair before turning to Vit. "Maybe Annie has some more information by now."

"Who's Annie?" said Arkady.

"A friend."

"Jonas is *my* friend and he's a good one."

"Do you know where he is?"

"I'm not sure. Maybe he's home or at the cabin. Maybe he's off with some friend, although I don't know who. Usually, Jonas and I stay right here. We have drinks at the bar. Sometimes Lukas brings us food. He makes wonderful *cepelini*—potato and meat dumplings to you Americans," he said to Vit. "The best I ever ate." He turned to Zuza. "You don't look Lithuanian. But he does," Arkady gestured at Vit with his thumb. "He looks like he's minding his own business, but you can tell nothing gets by him."

"Did Darius and Jonas get along?" said Zuza.

"They fought all the time. They were like oil and water. Separate, even when they were together. Darius was like a son to Jonas. Nobody else was as close to him, not even me. But Jonas always talked about politics, and that's not a subject that makes people happy."

"What did they fight about?"

"Everything. They would huddle in the corner table over there and argue. They thought I was too drunk to notice, but I can hear like a bat. Darius has ideas that Jonas doesn't agree with."

"What kind of ideas?"

Arkady glanced over his shoulder. "I forget."

"Please try to remember."

"I shouldn't say. I don't want to get anyone into trouble. I can't be sure. Besides, Darius says only half of what I say is true. He says I remember what I want to and make the rest up. One time, Darius talked about making the Russians pay for what they did. But it was just words."

"Did Darius always come here with Jonas, or was he ever with other people?"

"Usually he was with Jonas even though Darius lives in Kaunas. Even so, they were together a lot. Darius helps Jonas with his bills and makes sure there is food in the house. But the other night, Darius was here with two women. I don't think I've ever seen him with women, let alone without Jonas, but I can't be sure." He winked at Zuza. "Those girls weren't as pretty as you."

"Do you know who they were?" said Zuza.

"I don't know them, but they were young, and each one had a tattoo of a burning tree on their shoulder. The taller one bought me a drink."

Ten minutes later, back in Zuza's car, Annie displayed on Vit's phone screen the security camera's tapes from the cheese store across the street from the bar. They watched a few cars pass by with Lukas's front door clearly in view. Then Darius came into the picture. He stood near the door, a suitcase at his feet, clearly waiting for someone. More cars went by. Darius glanced at his watch a few times before he was joined by a woman. They exchanged a few words, and he followed her beyond the scope of the camera.

Zuza spoke. "We can't see a tattoo under that jacket, so we don't know if she's one of the women who spoke to Darius the other night."

"Annie," said Vit. "Run facial recognition on the woman with Darius, and see if you can resolve the license plate on the last car that went by." He turned to Zuza. "What now?"

"Have Annie get me everything she can on that woman. If Annie can identify the car, can she track it?"

"She can get into security videos stored online and recordings from the speed cameras. I suppose she could identify ones from this general area, and go through them to see what road they're on."

"Good. Have her tell us as soon as she finds something. If we know where they've been, maybe we can figure out where they're going. In the meantime, we're getting off the road. I don't want Bok coming after us again." She checked her watch. Otto would be expecting her call in another hour or so, and she had a lot of details to get straight in her head before speaking to him.

# CHAPTER 36

## Utena, Lithuania—20 May

"Can Annie find Bok?" said Zuza.

Vit nodded as he passed on the command, and Zuza steered the car though Utena's streets and alleyways in an effort to spot anyone who might be following them.

A moment later, Annie spoke. "The car Bok was in earlier is parked outside the Queen of Martyrs Chapel in Utena. A security camera from a coffee shop across the street caught him leaving the car. There's been no trace of him since."

"I bet he changed vehicles." Zuza was even more worried about Bok than before, sure he was out there looking for them. But after twenty minutes of deft driving, she couldn't spot anyone following them.

She headed toward to a sodyba. The one she had in mind was next to a pond, about fifteen kilometers outside the city. Zuza had been to a wedding there a year ago. The guesthouse was on a rise with a view of the surrounding area, as well as a view of the road. Standing on pilings in the pond and connected to the shore by a narrow pier was a large gazebo where the wedding ceremony had taken place.

Zuza stopped the car across from the inn's small gravel parking area, behind a pine tree with its branches hanging down as if laden with ornaments. The car was hidden as well as she could manage.

They knocked on the front door. An older woman in a lime-green bathrobe brandishing a tennis racket opened it. Zuza showed her credentials. The woman lowered the racket and led them in to a foyer with a tiny writing table next to a stairway. The walls and ceiling were paneled with pine boards. The woman introduced herself as the innkeeper, putting the tennis racket down on the writing table. "This late at night, an old woman doesn't know what to expect."

Zuza asked for one room for the two of them and signed her name on the registration form. Vit showed his passport. Zuza asked for something to eat.

"You're hungry, my dear? Of course. I'll heat up some cabbage and kielbasa for you. Look at you both. You're just skin and bones. Why don't you meet me in the dining room?" said the innkeeper.

"I don't want you going to all that trouble," said Zuza.

"What, you don't like kielbasa?"

"I love kielbasa."

"So, what's the problem?"

"We're very tired and want to rest. How about some sandwiches and coffee?"

"But the coffee will keep you awake. Of course, you don't need any sleep. You're young. I'll bring up a tray." The innkeeper winked.

Zuza and Vit went up to a room with white curtains, a yellow crocheted afghan on the bed, and a red tablecloth on the corner table. She opened the window and took a deep breath of the fresh night air. Then she moved a chair to the side of the window, where she had a view of the road and the small parking area in front of the house. Vit sat on the bed, looking exhausted.

Zuza answered a knock on the door, and took a tray of food from the innkeeper, placing it on the table. Vit put two sandwiches on a plate, kicked his shoes off, and lay on the bed with his head propped up by pillows. He took a bite. Zuza devoured one sandwich, then reached for another.

Zuza set her coffee cup on the sill. She needed a theory for Otto, but all she had was a jumble of details. It was too bad Annie couldn't just tell her what was really going on. Maybe if she took her mind off things for a few minutes, it would help. "Why did you name her Annie?"

Vit looked startled.

"I'm not trying to trick you. It's just a question, but if you'd rather not tell me, that's fine. It's no big deal." Zuza glanced out the window. She felt tired, and even though she was an ARAS agent, she was also a little scared.

"No, it's just that you might think it silly. When people ask me that, I usually say I like the name. But in truth, Annie's the name of my first real girlfriend. She was smart, beautiful, and had a great voice."

"She sounds perfect."

"She was, but she left me for someone else."

"I'm sorry."

"Joey Blaze. He could rollerblade, had all of the *Metallica* albums, and had two piercings in his left ear. We were in high school. I never forgot her. She's the only person I ever met who could skip a stone four times before it sank."

"Talented, too. Anyone since?"

Vit put the remains of the sandwich down on the plate. "I didn't have time for much besides studying in college. None of my friends did. It was too demanding. After I started working, I dated, but nothing serious. I thought I was going to be a bachelor for the rest of my life. When I met Gina, I thought she was beautiful, accomplished, smart. I thought she was the one. After two years, she broke it off. She told me she had waited long enough, and she was right. I liked her, but I didn't love her. I tried, but I'm a man who doesn't have the good sense to fall in love with the perfect woman."

"If you didn't feel that way about her, there's nothing you could do. Your heart wasn't ready. You slept with her though, didn't you?"

Vit looked annoyed. "Well, you may have insights into human behavior, but I don't see a wedding ring on your finger."

"I was with someone for a year. It didn't work out. I always thought that if you loved a person, you'd find a way to be together. But he left me."

"Ah."

Zuza gave him a dirty look. "We met at Europol. I think some of the men there didn't believe that a woman could do well, but I did. One tried to make it even tougher for me. Others, like David, were different. They encouraged me. David and I dated for a while, and he asked me to marry him. I thought he understood that I was committed to my career, but after a while, he started talking about babies, and my staying home to take care of them. I told him that wasn't for me, so he broke it off. We wanted different things, that's all. He lives in Brussels with his wife. He quit Europol and got a job with a private security firm. They just had their second child. He sends me a Christmas card every year." Zuza shrugged. "He got what he wanted. He's happy and I'm glad for him."

"And did you get what you wanted?"

Zuza nodded, but her heart wasn't in it. She rarely talked about David, even with Leva. Somehow Vit had gotten her to say more than she had in a long time. It was she who was supposed to get *him* to talk, not the other way around. Frowning, she got back to business.

"Bok is probably a Russian intelligence operative. If I had to guess, he's after you because of Darius's video, because you're Tilda Partenkas's grandson, and for a reason you haven't told me yet. But there's one thing I'm reasonably sure of. If the Russians were interested in Sagus, they'd have gone about things differently."

"What do you mean?"

"They would have tried to turn you and use you as an asset. That means gaining your trust, and finding some leverage to use against you. They'd try to get you to tell them things voluntarily, but once they had leverage, you would talk. The Russians think you know something. My money is on some tie you have with Jonas that you're not telling me. You can bet Bok is looking for us. And once he's done talking with you, do you know what he'll do? Have you thought about your grandmother? Russian agents are all over the world. If you don't care about what happens to yourself, at least think about what could happen to her."

Vit swung his legs around so he was sitting on the side of the bed. He put his elbows on his knees and glanced at Zuza. He looked like he was in agony. "I never thought about Tilda's safety. She told me a story that's too bizarre to be true. That's why I didn't tell you. I didn't want to mislead you."

He told Zuza about Tilda's trip in 1992, and her visit to the cabin where she built the nuclear device with Darius's help. He talked about his last visit with Tilda in the hospital, and his promise to go to Lithuania, find Jonas and Darius, and make sure they weren't going to use the weapon.

"I *knew* you were hiding something. And you didn't think this was important enough to tell me?"

Vit looked down at the floor. "I thought it was a fantasy."

"You think Bok's a fantasy?"

As Zuza pondered what Vit had told her, he spoke. "It was ironic that the cabin where they built the bomb was so close to Ignalina. It's like they were challenging the authorities to find the missing nuclear material hidden right under their noses. Tilda told me about the bomb just a few days ago, but she had talked about Ignalina many times, calling it Amber Widow. Amber because it's a symbol of Lithuania, and Widow because she thought the nuclear power plant would eventually be the cause of many deaths. After Chernobyl, I thought she was talking about a possible meltdown."

"But Ignalina was shut down in 2009," said Zuza. "The EU didn't want a member country running a Chernobyl-style nuclear power plant."

Vit nodded. "Tilda hadn't been thinking about a meltdown. She was talking about using the nuclear material in a weapon. If you expose Tilda, you'll be making her the world's most wanted terrorist. At her age, I don't know if people will be appalled or amused. But I don't think many will believe the story. Even I don't believe it, at least not all of it. You'll be spending your time chasing down an old woman's fairytale."

"You misunderstand me, Vit. I would happily track down the mere whisper of a nuclear threat, no matter how unlikely, even if it meant the end of my career."

"I know. You have to assume the threat is real. It's your job. I also know I can't protect Tilda anymore."

"Don't think that I won't see this through to the end. It's too important." Zuza pointed at Vit's phone. "It would help if Annie got us some information on Darius's current location as soon as possible."

"Do it," said Vit.

Annie answered. "We know the name of Darius's visitor. Simona Kleptys. She has a sister, Rina. They both have records for petty theft. Right now, authorities suspect that they're part of a car theft ring that operates in the Netherlands."

"Annie, what about that last car we saw in the video in front of Lukas's just before Simona arrived?"

"The plates were stolen. There's no trace of the car before it arrived at Lukas's. We haven't picked it up anywhere since. Would you like me to keep tracking the car?"

"Yes, Annie." Vit turned to Zuza. "What's Darius doing with *them*?"

Annie spoke. "The Kleptys sisters are suspected of delivering stolen cars to Ukraine. Darius may be going with them in order to get through the border undetected. Bribing border guards is one possibility."

"Maybe Darius is doing what he talked about in the video. Maybe he's trying to fulfill his own prophecy," said Vit.

"A dirty bomb exploding at a strategic location in Ukraine, made to look like the rebels are behind it. Russian military might invade. NATO could respond by sending troops into the Baltic countries and Poland," said Zuza.

Vit nodded. "That's just what Darius wants."

"Problem is, Ukraine's a big place, and we need to find out where he's going."

"Western Ukraine is pro-West for the most part, and the east is pro-Russian. A high value target in the west makes sense to me."

"Like a factory or a government building." Zuza checked her watch. "You better get some sleep."

Vit stretched out on the bed. She turned the light out, and went to the chair by the window, looking out into the night, thinking it was stupid of Vit to have hidden Tilda's story, but sweet that he wanted to protect his grandmother.

# CHAPTER 37

## Eastern Lithuania—20 May

While sitting in the backseat of the Saab, Darius draped his arm over the suitcase belted into the seat next to him. When his arm felt numb and heavy, he rubbed and shook it until the little spikes of pain brought fresh blood to his fingers.

They hadn't seen another car in over an hour, although it wasn't unexpected this time of night in the Lithuanian countryside. Rina was driving more slowly than usual, as the secondary roads weren't built for speed. Most roads were one lane in each direction, and street lamps were nonexistent. The one they were on wound through tall trees that made the night look even blacker. The road itself was dark. It was impossible to see where the shoulder began, and often there *was* no shoulder. The only markers were the trees, often set several meters back behind a gulley. Rina was doing well, though. She probably had plenty of practice on roads like this. His gaze met hers in the rearview mirror.

"Tell me where we're going in Ukraine. I have to know. It's a big place," said Rina.

Darius closed his eyes and pretended to be asleep. He was hoping to be near the border with Poland by daybreak. Poland and Lithuania were members of the Schengen Agreement that abolished border checks among member countries. The demarcation between countries was noted only by road signs, or in certain locations by abandoned guard houses. Darius thought of all those people who had risked their lives to get out of Lithuania during the occupation. They must have seen the border as impenetrable. It was patrolled day and night. People caught crossing into Poland were shot; few escaped. It was a far cry from today. The Saab would cross into Poland without even slowing down. Not too many years ago, lives had been lost trying to cross the border. It was something people didn't even think about any more.

The darkness was interrupted occasionally by homesteads connected by wires strung along old-fashioned telephone poles. It could have been a scene from fifty years ago or more. Darius doubted much had changed in these sleepy old villages since the war.

Relieved that they were finally well on their way, Darius relaxed into the comfortable seat. The air was warm. He felt more peaceful than he had in days. The most difficult part of the journey was behind him. All he had to do now was get across the border and into Ukraine, which unfortunately was not a Schengen-member country. Rina and Simona had crossed through the border many times, and he was confident they could go to a spot where border guards looked the other way in exchange for currency. They knew where and when to cross so that it was easy, quick, and above all, unrecorded. After that, another day traveling and it would be all over. He took a deep breath and fell asleep.

At his next moment of awareness, Darius started. *Jonas was sitting next to him in the backseat.*

"*I told you not to do this,*" *said Jonas.*

"Go to hell," said Darius.

"*You* go to hell." Simona's voice. "His eyes are closed. He must be dreaming. He's so strange. I can't wait for this to be over." It sounded like she was talking through a tunnel.

"All we have to do is drive. The money's good. Just concentrate on that." Rina's voice.

Darius shifted in his seat, wanting to say something, but he couldn't take his eyes off Jonas. He wanted the women to shut up and leave him alone. He wanted Jonas to go away, but the ghost continued to speak. "*I believe that people should behave with compassion and hope for the next generation. But the last time I told you this, you killed me. Where are you taking the bomb?*"

"Kiev."

"Kiev?" Simona's voice again. "I was hoping for Lvov because it's closer and we could get this over with sooner. It's going to take at least another day to get to Kiev, especially if we keep avoiding motorways and speed cameras. And then there's the trip home."

*"You're insane," said Jonas.*

"No, you're insane," mumbled Darius.

"Fuck you," said Simona.

"Leave him be," said Rina.

"He's making me crazy. This is our first and last trip with him."

"He's paying us. You can take it."

*"I loved you like a son." Jonas put his hands around Darius's neck and squeezed. Darius thrashed, struggling with the ghost, gasping for air. In a moment, Jonas was gone.*

Darius was awake and alone in the rear seat. He reached out for the suitcase. It was there. He leaned back and breathed a sigh of relief.

"Bad dream?" said Simona.

# CHAPTER 38

## Utena County, Lithuania—20 May

Vit's breathing was deep and slow as he lay on the bed, holding a partially eaten sandwich. Zuza took it out of his hand and put it on the plate. She drew the afghan up, laying it gently over him, watching him smile as he shifted on the bed. Despite everything, Vit was sleeping like a baby. She found his feelings for his family endearing, but in light of the threat the bomb presented, she was angry at him as well, for not confessing his secret sooner.

She turned off the light and went into the hallway, keeping to the side to avoid creaks in the floor. At the bottom of the stairs, she unlocked the front door and went outside. She crossed the pier to the gazebo in the middle of the pond, and sat on a bench. The water was glossy all around her. The night was quiet. She had a partial view of her car and could see the road. More importantly, she was positive no one would overhear her, especially Vit. Otto was sure to ask about him. She looked up at the room where he slept, picturing him on the bed. The house was quiet, the innkeeper undoubtedly in bed. A gentle breeze rustled the leaves.

She took a deep breath. Zuza found it comforting that nights felt familiar, no matter where she was. In the dark, she felt invisible, and she liked it. A car drove by. She watched its lights fade through the trees.

Zuza took the phone out of her pocket. She couldn't avoid the conversation she was about to have with Otto, and shouldn't feel guilty that she didn't have any proof for what she was about to tell him. He needed to know regardless. He was probably waiting for her call. She dialed his number. He answered on the first ring.

She brought him up to date on their encounter with the Russian Alexy Bok.

"How do you know he's with the SVR?" said Otto.

Zuza mentioned the facial recognition trace Annie had run on airport security tapes.

"Who the hell is Annie?" said Otto.

"A sophisticated computer program."

"Get back to Vilnius, and bring Vit Partenkas with you. You're not his personal bodyguard, and I want to know what's going on."

"What are you going to do, lock him up? Vit isn't under arrest." Zuza clenched her jaw. Otto wouldn't say those things to any other agent. If anyone broke protocol, they were disciplined. If anyone made a decision that paid off, they were rewarded. She had made the decision to work with Vit, and that was well within her authority. Vit was a source of information. That's all.

She was about to mention Vit's conversation about Tilda, but Otto interrupted. As he explained Rokas had searched Darius's apartment, Zuza noticed a dark figure entering the sodyba. Her heart skipped a beat, realizing it was probably Bok. One hand went to the gun in her shoulder holster as the other pressed the button terminating the call. As the figure entered the building, Zuza darted down the pier. She pictured Vit asleep in the bed, desperately hoping to get to him before Bok did any damage.

~~

As Vit stirred from the bed, the first thing he noticed was that Zuza wasn't in the room. He was glad to have taken a nap, but the mess about Bok, Tilda, and the bomb returned in a groggy mix. He watched the white curtain move in the breeze, wondering how a partisan would act in his situation, and remembered a story Tilda had told him about Ludmelia.

It was winter, during WWII. The Soviets had deported many Lithuanian families, leaving their homesteads abandoned. Russian supporters had permission from the Communists to take over the property as their own, but Ludmelia and her band of partisans didn't agree. In the middle of the night, wearing camouflage suits made from white tablecloths, Ludmelia and her men entered a house occupied by squatters. Ludmelia, rifle in hand, broke through the door of the bedroom. A Russian couple were in bed. The woman yelled, "Giltine!" The Russians jumped out of bed, grabbed their boots and coats, and ran out into the snow.

If Giltine came into his room right now, he wouldn't even bother with his boots. He'd just dive out the window. He pulled the afghan up around his shoulders and tried to go back to sleep.

A creak sounded from the hallway. At the sound of a soft click, the door opened and someone came inside. He was glad Zuza was back.

Before he could even switch on the light, the figure was on him, with a hand pressed hard over Vit's mouth, a gun pointed at his head.

"You be very quiet when I move my hand, or you die," said a rough voice.

*Bok!*

"The woman. Where is she?" said Bok.

"Her room's down the hall," lied Vit. He almost panicked, thinking Bok had gotten to her. But if Bok had, he wouldn't have asked about her.

Bok glanced at the door. "We'll be quiet so we don't wake her. Why did you come to Lithuania?"

"Visiting."

Bok hit Vit in the face with the back of his hand. Something sharp cut into Vit's lip. He tasted blood.

"Just tell me the truth. It will go much easier for you," said Bok.

Vit scanned the room for anything he could use as a weapon, anything he could grab, but nothing could match a gun.

"Why have you been following me? What do you want? Is it money? I have money. Take all of it. Just get out of here," said Vit, groping for his wallet on the nightstand.

"Stay where you are. Where is Darius Artis going?"

"I don't even know him."

Bok hit Vit in the face again. Vit winced. More blood.

"Tell me," hissed Bok.

If this was how he was going to die, he wasn't about to make it easy on the Russian thug. "Go fuck yourself."

The door slammed against the wall. Bok turned and fired. As Zuza shot back, Bok leaped from beside the bed and pitched himself head-first through the open window. Zuza ran to it as Bok stumbled toward the road. She tried to aim, but the range and darkness made the attempt useless.

She dashed down the steps. Bok was already at the road, his figure dark like a shadow. A bullet whizzed by her ear. She threw herself to the ground, responding with more gunshot. She rolled, and got to her feet, running after him. A car came at her fast, the headlights blinding her. She fired into the glare, then jumped away. Bok was gone.

She ran back to the room. Vit was on his feet, although wobbly.

"Are you all right?" said Zuza, holstering her gun. She put Vit's arm around her shoulder and helped him sit. He smelled faintly of sandalwood.

"Shaken," said Vit. "And stirred."

The inn keeper ran at them, swinging the tennis racket. "What's going on?"

"Somebody tried to rob us," Zuza lied. "I'm calling the police. Go to your room and lock the door until they arrive." She touched a smear of red on the windowsill. Blood. At least she had wounded Bok. "We have to go."

From the edge of the bed, Vit put on his shoes.

The old woman straightened. "You go. I'll be all right. I can take care of things."

"Thank you," said Zuza.

Zuza and Vit hurried down the steps and out the front. Zuza dialed a number on her phone and spoke, identifying herself and giving a quick summary of what had happened, ending with the sodyba's address. They got into the car. Zuza started the engine and threw the car into gear, heading back to the road.

"You still think Bok wants to rob you?" she said.

"I thought he was going to kill me."

"What did you tell him?" said Zuza.

"Nothing. How did he find us?" said Vit.

"He had to have followed us here. But how did I miss him? I should have spotted him in Utena. I saw a car pass the inn before all hell broke out. I should have known it was him. I should have expected the worst." She slammed the palms of her hands into the steering wheel.

"What are the police going to do?"

"Keep the innkeeper safe for a while. Otherwise, nothing. File a report."

Vit let out a long, slow breath. "He's going to come after us again, isn't he?"

"You can count on it."

They drove in silence. *Vit did well, surviving Bok*, thought Zuza. She spoke. "Otto searched Darius's apartment. They found a trove of electrical equipment, wires, specialized tools, that sort of thing. Oddly enough, the apartment was unlocked and the security system disabled. I think Bok beat us there."

"What are we going to do now?"

Zuza pressed her lips together in a frown. The idea of going back to Vilnius and letting Otto handle this would be the smart thing. But taking an easy way out would meant that Rokas would think she ran back to Otto when things got rough. He'd lose what little respect he had for her, and the others would, too. She'd be finished. Perhaps she already was. By disregarding Otto's order to return to Vilnius right away, she might save her career. Or ruin it.

Thankfully, Annie spoke. "We spotted Darius, Simona, and Rina in a car outside of Jonava as they passed a traffic camera."

"That's near Kaunas." Zuza reached for her phone.

"If word gets out that my grandmother's behind this, it'll destroy her. But we have no choice, do we?"

Zuza shook her head as she pressed a button on her mobile phone. Otto answered right away. "You're on your way in, aren't you?"

"The Russian national I told you about, whom I believe to be a foreign agent, tried to kill us a few minutes ago. We're all right, though," said Zuza.

"What the hell is going on out there?"

"Inform the government of a credible threat of the highest level."

"What are you talking about?"

"A nuclear device."

"What the hell, Zuza?"

"We believe Darius reconfigured a nuclear device and is going to detonate it in Kiev."

"Where did he get a nuclear bomb?"

"I got a tip that he may have had an expert from the US help him assemble it back in the '90s, using nuclear waste from Ignalina that's been hidden in the woods," said Zuza.

"You want me to alert the president of Lithuania in the middle of the night about a nuclear threat from Lithuania, targeting Ukraine, and expect her to take it seriously? What proof do you have?"

"I'm not *sure* of anything, Otto."

"Well, when you have something concrete, let me know."

"Vit said Dr. Partenkas built the bomb."

"Then get me some proof. In the meantime, I'll alert local police to be on the lookout for Darius Artis, on suspicion that he is involved in the disappearance of Jonas Volkis, based on evidence I don't have. In fact, I'll have them set up roadblocks. I'm going to have to do a song and dance to pull this off, dammit. But keep that theory to yourself."

"Otto, please. The threat is enormous. And real. I know it is."

"Then get me some enormous fucking proof!"

Zuza's knuckles were white, clasped around the steering column. She was ready to explode.

Vit spoke. "I never knew how brave my great-grandfather was until tonight, when Lukas told us that story. Tilda said her father was a courier who carried messages into partisan camps. I thought he was a meek old man who had never done a dangerous thing in his life. I never knew he had actually fought the Russians. He stayed in Utena when Tilda and her mother escaped, so the Russians wouldn't notice they were gone. The family never saw him again. Can you imagine what the Soviets did when they realized they'd been fooled? It must've been horrible. He sacrificed his life for his family.

The West didn't want to believe what the Soviets did here during and after the war. Some people say it was genocide. But the people here kept fighting, because they knew they had to for their children's sake. If we know what Darius is up to, we have to stop him. We have to keep fighting. Quiet heroes are all around us. We don't know they're there until we need them, and they come out of hiding, and do whatever's necessary."

"Do you actually have a point with this story?"

"You're one of those heroes, Zuza."

# CHAPTER 39

## The Kremlin, Moscow—21 May

Vera had been working in her office for over an hour when Nina arrived. It was early, and Nina had said the meeting was urgent. The office smelled of coffee. The scent reminded Vera of Paris.

The women greeted each other as usual before going into the private sitting room. Vera helped herself to a serving of cottage cheese dumplings. Nina just took coffee. Vera poured herself a fresh cup.

"Vit Partenkas is still in Lithuania with that ARAS agent," said Nina. "Bok tracked them to a guesthouse outside Utena, but he was shot and barely got away."

"Is he all right?"

"They got him in the arm, but he's alive. He extracted the bullet by himself." She shuddered. "I believe Vit Partenkas is also trying to find Darius Artis. Since Jonas Volkis has gone missing, it's logical to assume he would want to find the next best person."

"And everybody's in Lithuania."

"That's the issue. If Darius is headed to Russia, he should be out of the country by now. He's either driving, or he went by sea. In any case, if Vit Partenkas is following him, he shouldn't be in Lithuania."

"We have nuclear detection in our major cities and at the border crossings. It would be extremely difficult to get a bomb into Russia. Even if Darius did, we'd find it long before he could do any damage."

"That's the point. He's going someplace else."

Vera put down her plate. "Where?"

"I think Ukraine."

"How sure are you?"

"Very." Nina's coffee sloshed into the saucer as she set it down.

"Explain."

"As you said, he wouldn't try to set it off in Russia because of the security measures we have in place, unless he's stupid. I don't think Darius is stupid. There'd be a certain irony to setting if off at the construction site for the nuclear reactor in Belarus, but he couldn't even get close. Ukraine is the logical alternative. Political groups didn't stop fighting in 2014 after the ceasefire between the Ukrainian government and the pro-Russian rebels. They continue to kill each other, millions of people have been displaced, and there's a movement against government corruption. The country is in turmoil. Any spectacular show of terrorism, such as detonating a nuclear device, will destabilize the country even further. It's conceivable that NATO will respond by sending troops into Poland and the Baltic countries in fear of Russian troop action, just as Darius Artis wants."

Vera put her plate down. "Good."

"I'm sorry?"

"Have Bok and the other agents come home. We don't need them there anymore."

"But how are we going to stop Darius Artis? He may be perpetrating the most devastating act of terrorism ever attempted."

Vera helped herself to another piece of syrniki. "That a nuclear disaster may be imminent in a neighboring country could present an interesting opportunity to achieve one of my territorial goals and show the world how great Russia is."

"We can send someone else in if you think Bok is too badly injured to finish the job."

"Keep our border guards and military on high alert."

"It's Ukraine, Vera. The bomb is headed into Ukraine. Think of all the Russians living there. What are we doing to find it and stop it from being detonated?"

"Nothing. As far as anyone knows, we were never in Lithuania. And Bok isn't going into Ukraine."

"What?" The color drained from Nina's cheeks. She grasped the armrests. It looked like she was going to stand, but didn't.

Vera took another bite. "Our troops are already outside Ukraine. Once this horrible act is perpetrated, our military will cross the border, ready to assist in any way possible. I want our national broadcast services to send in reporters to film our soldiers risking their lives to rescue the good citizens of Ukraine. I want film of injured children and bodies crawling out from under the rubble. I want eyewitness accounts of our military doctors and nurses trying to save people scarred with radiation blisters. We'll do all we can to assist. Once the world sees what terrorists have done, and how we are helping our neighbor, we will be supported like at no other time in history."

"And what if the world assumes it was Russia who detonated that bomb?"

"The world will assume no such thing. We had nothing to do with this, and investigations will find nothing. The world will think us brave and fearless, and no one will object, including those meddling fools from NATO, who wouldn't go near radiation if their lives depended on it. While the West holds its breath in shock at this blatant act of terrorism, we'll behave as good neighbors. When it's over and things have quieted down, our soldiers will already be in Ukraine . . . and there they'll stay."

# CHAPTER 40

## Vilkaviskis, Lithuania—21 May

In the Saab's passenger seat, Rina stretched her arms while Simona drove. Their late start last night had slowed their progress even farther, despite the short stretch on the motorway that they couldn't avoid because of a detour. But they had traveled this route a few times already this year, delivering cars to their customers, sticking to backwoods roads that ultimately led south. It felt familiar.

Overall, it would be one of their better months financially, but Rina was looking forward to the end of this trip. She had hoped for more opportunities with Darius because it seemed easy money. But he was a strange one. Maybe Simona was right in not wanting to do anything more with him. He talked in his sleep like a madman, and it bothered Rina. She was sure he was bad luck.

She looked over her shoulder. "He's asleep again. When he's awake, I want him to be asleep; when he's asleep, I wish he would just shut up."

"I'd like to know if he's really got a drone in that suitcase. I think he's hiding something," said Simona. "Do you think we should open it?"

"Forget about it. We're not far from Poland. Once we cross the border into Ukraine, it's just another day's drive to Kiev, and the trip back home. Darius will pay us, and we'll be on our way."

"That's two, maybe three more days. It's a long time with that one."

"Shut up, fool." Darius's voice was strident, and the words clear.

"That's one thing I won't miss," said Simona.

"I killed you once; I can do it again." Darius's voice was even clearer this time.

"What the hell is he talking about?" said Simona.

"The idiot's asleep. He's dreaming," said Rina.

"Come with me to Kiev and I'll blow us both up." Darius shifted in the seat, obviously in distress.

The women exchanged a glance. "We don't even carry guns," said Rina. "We've stayed out of jail by being careful. No violence. We may sell a gun now and again, but we don't use them. It's how we survived. Stealing cars is one thing, but he's up to something. Normal people don't talk like that, even in their sleep. He's crazy. I don't trust him."

"We should get away from him. This job feels risky," said Simona.

"Stop at the next petrol station."

Simona nodded. "Gladly. We're low on gas anyway."

The sun was up when they pulled into a Circle K gas station. A green Opal came in behind them, stopping next to a black car parked alongside the building. A man wearing a red polo shirt and light pants got out and went inside. A moment later, a different man came out wearing the same color polo shirt, and got into the black vehicle. Before driving off, he glanced at the Saab.

"Be ready to leave quickly," said Rina. She got out of the car, pulling out her wallet as she went inside. She put forty euros on the counter. The man in the polo shirt nodded and Rina went back to the car. Simona was already pumping gas. Rina got in behind the wheel. When Simona finished, Rina turned around and touched Darius's knee. He started awake.

"Want some coffee?" asked Rina.

Darius nodded. He looked disoriented.

"Why don't you go in to use the toilet, and get something to eat. It'll be a while before we stop again."

Darius shook his head. Like an obedient child, he unclasped the seatbelt around his chest and the one around the suitcase before getting out of the car. He looked a little unsteady as he lifted the suitcase out and headed inside. Rina watched him go into the building. When he was out of sight, she started the car. "Get in."

Simona ran around to the passenger side and got in.

Rina gunned the engine and sped onto the road.

"What about Darius?" said Simona. "He hasn't finished paying us."

"Forget about him. He's one crazy fuck. He can deliver his own packages."

"No complaints here."

~~

After the call to Otto, Zuza and Vit drove in silence until Annie spoke. "The Kleptys sisters and Darius were seen on a security camera at a petrol station in Vilkaviskis, Lithuania." The address of the Circle K flashed on the phone's display screen.

"They haven't left the country? Maybe their target isn't what we thought it was." Vit had a glint of optimism in his voice.

"Don't get your hopes up. They're headed for Poland. It's a lot harder to get through border control into Belarus, and again into Ukraine, even though the road to Kiev is more direct through Belarus. Going through Poland is simpler, easier, and because the border checks can take hours, they might save time, even though it's a roundabout route."

She punched a number into her phone and spoke through clenched teeth. "Otto?"

A moment passed. Her face softened a fraction. "We believe he's in Vilkaviskis. Can you get a team there?"

A pause. "One agent is better than none."

Another pause. "Local police would be great. We could use the assistance."

In a moment Zuza said, "I can't do that. We don't have the time. Besides, he's been useful."

Another pause. "Yes, Otto." She hung up.

"What can't you do?" said Vit.

"Drop you off."

Vit tried to hide his smile. He didn't *want* to be left anywhere. Staying with Zuza was fine with him.

With both hands on the steering wheel, Zuza looked as focused as a race car driver. The speed was nerve-wracking, but he knew she could handle it. Vit held onto the door handle as Zuza wove through traffic, going into the soft shoulder occasionally to maintain the pace while kicking up a cloud of dust.

Finally, she spoke. "If Darius crosses into Poland, this becomes an international incident. You better hope we find him and that damned bomb before anything happens, because if we don't, it will mean my ass, your ass, and even Tilda's ass. That is, if Bok doesn't get to us first."

Vit felt like all the air had been sucked out of the car. His phone rang. He almost jumped out of the seat. He answered.

"Hi, Ma," said Vit.

"What are you doing today?"

"Nothing much."

"How do you like it there so far?"

"I've had a unique experience."

"That's good, right? Listen, your grandmother's been asking for you. She wants to know why you haven't visited her lately. Didn't you tell her you were going away?"

"Maybe she forgot."

"Even without that damned drug, the mind is the first thing to go. I should know."

"You're as sharp as a steak knife, Ma."

"Stop buttering me up. When are you coming home?"

"Not sure yet."

"Get some amber for Tilda, too."

"Gotta go. Bye, Ma."

Vit hung up the phone.

"It's nice to see a man get along well with his mother," said Zuza.

# CHAPTER 41

## Vilkaviskis, Lithuania—21 May

Standing next to the sink in the men's toilet at the Circle K station, Darius watched the water drip from his face. He felt stubble on his chin, and realized he had left his overnight bag containing a razor and toothbrush in the Saab. He considered going back for it, but he was too tired. No matter. He wasn't here for a beauty contest. The mirror was cracked near the bottom, making his neck look like it wasn't quite attached to his head. *It'll be over soon,* he thought.

He took another glance at himself and cried out loud at the reflection, the initial shock quickly turning into anger. "Can't you leave me alone, old man?"

*Jonas laughed. "You are alone."*

"You could never have done what I'm doing. You're too soft. Too timid. You have no vision, not like me and my father."

*"Your father's dead. I'm dead. And soon you will be."*

"I'm about to change the world."

*"I'm glad you think so."*

"Leave me alone!"

Darius rolled the suitcase outside. The Saab wasn't at the pumps. Frantic, he scanned the area. No Saab in sight. He felt the cold hand of impending failure as the impact of the betrayal slowly set in. The women were gone. The Saab was gone. The place was deserted, except for a green Opal.

*"Good luck getting to Kiev," said Jonas.*

"Shut up!" Darius hadn't planned for this. His eyes wouldn't focus. He couldn't move. His head was spinning.

*"So much for your friends,"* said Jonas.

He lunged at Jonas, but instead of hitting the old man, Darius crashed to the ground. The blacktop was hard. His hands stung. His knees throbbed. As he picked himself up, he looked around, hoping that no one saw. He rubbed his bruised knee; his pants were ripped. A truck sped by with a roar. He reached for the container of medication in his pocket, not knowing if he had taken his morning dose, or even last night's for that matter. He swallowed some and waited for his racing heart to slow.

The door to the station opened. The man from before came out carrying containers of windshield wiper fluid that he stacked in front.

Darius followed the man inside. He smelled coffee. Darius went to the dispensers and tried to make the right selections on the screen for coffee with milk, but he was too preoccupied with his dilemma to focus. The machine beeped. No coffee came out. Darius hit the side of the dispenser with his hand, and glanced over his shoulder. The red-shirted man was watching him.

"This machine isn't working," said Darius.

"I'll get it for you," said the man. He placed a paper cup under the spigot. "Cream and sugar?" he said. Darius nodded.

The man looked to be Darius's age, more or less, but much shorter. The man picked up the cup filled with steaming coffee and carried it to one of the tables in the center of the room. Darius followed him, placing the suitcase next to his chair and sitting down. The man went behind the counter.

Darius's heart continued to race as he waited for the prying questions asking why he had been abandoned, what he was carrying in the suitcase, why he was there. He didn't want to look nervous and raise any suspicions. "My friends had an emergency and had to leave." His voice sounded raspy and high as he blurted out the words.

The man looked surprised. "Oh. I just thought you were waiting for someone to pick you up. A lot of people come through here."

"I need to get to Kiev," said Darius.

"You could take the bus. It connects through Vilnius about noontime. If you leave now, you can make it. Or you can wait for the nighttime bus and wake up in Kiev. Both are good options."

"How do you know so much about Kiev?"

"My sister's husband is from a little village outside the city. I've taken the bus there many times. It's a long trip, but all you have to do is sit back and enjoy the scenery. It's much easier than driving."

Darius gazed out the window at the lone Opal. The bus wouldn't do at all, especially since it meant traveling back to Vilnius, through Belarus, and into Ukraine. It meant two border checks and two opportunities for guards to look inside the suitcase. He couldn't possibly take the bus. There might be radiation sensors along the border. Such devices were small and relatively cheap. The guards probably used them, but Darius didn't know for certain. His heart beat like a hammer in his chest. He sipped some coffee. His plan was falling apart. And so was he.

*Jonas was sitting on the chair next to Darius with a leg draped over the suitcase.*

"Leave that alone," said Darius.

The man looked at him. "Sorry?"

Darius didn't answer, but focused on his coffee, pretending he hadn't heard. Several trucks passed by the gas station, none stopping. A man in a small brown car pulled up to a pump and began filling his tank. His hat was pulled down low and Darius couldn't see his face. Maybe he could get a ride with someone. He touched the suitcase, fingering the zippered compartment holding Jonas's Mauser. *So small; so deadly.* The man in the brown car drove off. Darius sipped some more coffee. He gazed out the window at the Opal.

"Can I rent your car?" said Darius to the red-shirted man behind the counter. The idea had come to him out of the thin air. Already, he felt a little better. Perhaps there was a way after all.

"Oh no. I need it. I have to pick up my son at school later today. His mother and I divorced, and he lives with me. It's just us men at home. I miss her cooking the most." He laughed nervously. Another vehicle pulled up to a pump. This time it was a white van.

"I'll pay you well. I have an appointment that I must make in Kiev. It's very important I get there," said Darius. Even if he took the Opal, he couldn't possibly drive all that distance by himself. The car was useless to him without a driver. Besides, he didn't know the best place to cross from Poland into Ukraine. Those bitches were supposed to have handled that. He should have them arrested.

The man stared at him suspiciously. "I can get you a taxi to the bus station. It's not far and won't cost much. I'll phone them for you."

"No. Give me a moment. I have to think." Darius stood, his legs weak. From behind the counter, the store manager slashed open a box of pastries, and began setting them on trays in the display counter.

Darius started as the door opened and a young man who didn't look a day over twenty years walked in. He was wearing a vest, white shirt, and jeans. The man behind the counter spoke. "Filip. This man's looking for a ride. Where are you going today?"

"To Marijampole to pick up some used tires that I'm delivering to a mechanic in Suwalki. He'll give me a good price if I get them there by noon. He's waiting for me." Filip glanced at his watch.

"That's wonderful news." The man behind the counter called to Darius. "You're in luck. You can get a bus from Suwalki—that's in Poland—right to Kiev. Maybe you'll even find someone to give you a lift. Probably all the way. There you are. Problem solved."

*That might work,* thought Darius. He remembered the gun in the suitcase's front pouch. It brought him confidence, strength, and clarity of mind. If he didn't catch the bus, the Mauser could persuade Filip to take him to Kiev.

"Filip, you mind giving this man a lift?"

"Sure." Filip got some coffee and paid for it as Darius watched. He followed Filip outside to the white van, carefully placing the suitcase beside him on the front seat and then climbing in.

# CHAPTER 42

## Vilkaviskis, Lithuania—21 May

Rokas was talking to a nervous looking man in a red polo shirt when Zuza and Vit pulled into the Circle K. Rokas went over to Zuza, nodding at Vit.

"I want to talk to you alone," said Rokas.

"Vit stays."

Rokas frowned, but continued. In a moment, he had brought them up to date. "Otto told me your theory. That's one helluva bedtime story you came up with."

"It's not a fairytale," said Zuza.

"Well, you convinced Otto to send me, so I'll make sure things are resolved. The store manager verified Darius Artis has been here. He got a ride with a Filip Lemski, who does odd jobs and some hauling in his van."

"Does he have a mobile phone?"

"The manager said Filip just got one and was showing it off the other day, but he doesn't have the number. Our IT people in Vilnius are trying to find it, but nothing yet. Filip and Darius left about an hour ago for Marijampole before heading into Poland. Otto already made a few calls. Local police are setting up road blocks to intercept Filip's van."

"That's not going to work." Zuza put a hand on her hip. "If Darius is as nervous as he was when I met with him in Kaunas, he'll explode. They have to slow him down until I can catch up to him. If

Darius crosses the border, this becomes an international incident," said Zuza.

Rokas chuckled. "There's no bomb. All you have is a theory, and it's a bad one. As far as we know, Darius hasn't broken any laws. I'm surprised Otto was willing to involve local police, but they're going to take care of it. It's already arranged." Rokas cocked his head toward Vit. "And he stays here."

"He's with me. He's useful."

"Aw shucks," said Vit. His words were light, but his expression dead serious.

"Shut up," said Zuza. She turned to Rokas. "You can come with me, you can follow me, or you can go to hell. Your choice."

Zuza got back into her car. She had the engine running by the time Vit got in and closed the door. They turned onto the road, tires squealing. As Vit watched the countryside pass by at its usual fast-forward pace when Zuza was driving, she spoke. "I need Annie to find Filip's mobile phone number."

Vit passed the order on. In a moment, a phone number flashed on Vit's screen. He passed the phone to Zuza.

"God, I love Annie," Zuza said and dialed the number. "Filip? How are you?"

"Fine. Who is this?"

"This is ARAS Agent Zuza Bartus. I need you to listen to me. Pretend I'm your mother. Say 'Hi, Mom' if you understand."

He did. She explained that his companion was a wanted man. "Say 'Okay, Mom.'"

Again, Filip did what he was told.

She asked if Darius had a suitcase with him.

"Yes."

"Have you left Marijampole yet?" She put the phone on speaker, gesturing Vit to remain silent.

"Yes, Mom."

"Has he threatened you?"

"No, Mom."

"Stay within the speed limit. If he wants you to go to the border and cross it, do it. Do whatever he says. We're on the way."

"Okay, Mom."

"Don't hang up the phone. Just put it in your shirt pocket so we can listen."

Muffled sounds, then a dial tone that echoed through the car.

"Damn," murmured Zuza.

"Why didn't he stay connected so we could hear what they were saying?" asked Vit.

"Either he didn't mean to hang up, or he had to," said Zuza.

"He was forced? Darius doesn't have a gun, does he?"

"We should assume he does."

~~

Darius felt a pang of jealousy as he listened to Filip talk to his mother. Darius's mother had never cared for him; had never called. He had never even known her. Filip, a mere delivery man who traded junk tires for cash, had a mother who loved him and called him on the phone, even during the day when a capable man should be working. Darius, brilliant architect of a plan that would save his country from ruin, had no mother and no phone calls. He had no one, not even Jonas. He wiped his nose on his sleeve and turned to the window, watching the trees go by and trying not to cry.

Had he made the right decision in catching a ride with a stranger rather than taking the green Opal and forcing the store manager to drive? Perhaps not. The manager was a stranger, too. Darius decided he had made the best choice possible. Customers at the Circle K would've found it odd that the manager was gone and the store deserted. They would have reported it. Besides, he would've had to watch the manager all the way to Kiev. At least with Filip, Darius was just another traveler catching a ride because his friends had let him down. He could rest for a few hours before pulling out the Mauser. He desperately needed to rest.

He felt his face twitch as he thought of Rina and Simona again, feeling the sting from their abandoning him. He would punish them somehow. Maybe when he got back to Utena, he'd make an anonymous call to the police and expose them as car thieves. Prison would be their reward for what they'd done to him. But if they described him to the authorities, he'd go to jail, too. They would know he was behind the bombing. He would've failed to save Lithuania.

Panic set in. He felt weak. No, the women had no idea what he was doing or even where he was going—at least he didn't think he had told them. It was hard to remember. *Damn that Jonas!* They had no reason to suspect he was the grand architect to the terror that was about to strike Ukraine . . . did they?

An hour and a half had passed since they left the Circle K petrol station. They had just left Marijampole, the back loaded with tires. Darius had even managed a brief nap without the pleasure of Jonas's company. He could take a bus from Suwalki, but it would be better overall if he made Filip drive all the way. After dropping off the tires, Filip wouldn't be missed, at least not right away. That gave Darius time to get into Ukraine. He didn't think anyone would be looking for them there.

Using the gun wasn't necessarily the best solution, forcing Filip to take him into Ukraine, but it was possible. They could be in Kiev by nightfall. If Filip refused, well, Darius had the gun. Killing wasn't that hard. He had done it before. He'd be no worse off, and he'd have a vehicle. The rest would be up to him.

It occurred to him that he had no plan for getting the suitcase to the Russian Embassy, and that Filip would only deliver it at gunpoint. That meant they both would die. But Darius would think of something. At least he hoped he would.

# CHAPTER 43

## Western Lithuania—21 May

Vit couldn't believe he was in a car driven by an ARAS agent, chasing a suspected terrorist through Eastern Europe. Never in his wildest dreams had he imagined a scenario like this. He was excited and energized. Not fearful, he wondered if that confirmed he was stupid. He should be terrified, but he felt safe with Zuza.

"When's the last time you qualified for the Indy 500?" he said.

Zuza ignored him as she calmly negotiated the next curve in the road. Vit counted the seconds, forcing himself not to look at his watch. Ever helpful, Annie mentioned points where the van was caught on speed trap cameras and the changing coordinates as she followed the track of Filip's mobile phone. The last sighting came from the town of Kalvarija, Lithuania.

"How far to the border, Annie?" said Vit.

"Twenty-eight point three-two-five kilometers."

Zuza went even faster. Vit glanced back at Rokas in the black SUV. He thought of the night Bok had chased him, and the cold feel of the Russian's gun pressed against his temple in the sodyba. Then he looked at Zuza, and felt better.

Filip's white van came into view. Zuza touched Vit's arm as she slowed the car. Punching a number in her mobile phone, she spoke. "I've got the subject in sight." They passed a church behind a row of birch trees lining the narrow road.

Zuza punched another number into her phone, and put it on speaker. A man answered. Zuza spoke. "Filip? Say 'Hi Mom.'"

"Hi, Mom."

"Are you all right?"

"Sure."

"Keep your eyes on the road. We're close."

"That's great."

"When you get to those trees up ahead, pull over. Tell him you have to take a piss."

"Sure."

"If he asks, tell him I asked you to pick up some milk on the way home tonight. Don't be nervous. You're doing great. Say 'Goodbye, Mom.'"

Another dial tone sounded on the speakers as the right-side turn indicators flashed on the van, but the vehicle kept moving down the road.

"Damn. Darius isn't letting him stop," said Zuza.

There were no cars between them and the van. The road behind them was clear except for Rokas. *No Bok, thank God,* thought Vit.

A moment later, the van came to a stop behind a blue tractor trailer truck with pictures of fresh vegetables on the outside, blocking the lane. A police car was parked ahead of them, off to the side.

"What the hell?" said Vit.

Zuza pulled up behind the van, and slid down in the seat. "Darius knows me."

~~

Darius rubbed the palms of his hands against his forehead. As close as the border was, it felt like it was unreachable. Earlier, when Filip had slowed the van near some birch trees, Darius had insisted they keep going. Now, Filip was slowing down again! Darius felt his heart throbbing through the veins his neck. He put the window down for some air.

"I told you I'm in a hurry to get to Poland. No stops until we get there," said Darius.

"I had to," said Filip. "It looks like they're checking the contents of that semi." As he came to a halt, he gestured to the trailer truck's driver climbing down from the cab and the two police officers waiting to speak to him.

"It's an open border. What're they doing?" said Darius.

Filip's hands hung onto the steering wheel. "They do spot checks once in a while. It's completely random."

"How long is this going to take?"

"I don't know. It shouldn't be long. Probably a few minutes."

"Get us out of here."

"I can't. We're blocked in."

"Go around them."

"There's a police car there. Do you want them to chase us?"

Darius stuck his head out the window and looked back at the vehicles waiting behind them in line. At least they weren't being singled out. *It wasn't supposed to happen this way.* He wiped the sweat stinging his eyes. *After all this planning, all the inprovisations, I'm trapped.*

The police officers and driver of the blue semi opened the truck's back door.

~~

Filip looked nervous. Darius knew that feeling well. He also knew that the police were only minutes away from looking inside the van. They might even ask to inspect his suitcase. He might fail unless he took some action. The future of his country depended on him.

The clarity of what to do next reminded Darius that he was brilliant, and his plan would succeed, for no one matched him in sheer brain power. He patted the suitcase.

"You didn't see two women back there, did you?" Darius said.

"Huh?"

"They gave me this suitcase. They wanted me to deliver it to Kiev. They paid me to do it." Darius leaned toward Filip. "I think they're Russians."

"What? I don't see anyone." Filip looked scared. *Even he is frightened of the Russians,* thought Darius.

"They wanted me to deliver it by a certain hour. With this delay, I know I'm not going to make it." Darius blinked away the sweat dropping into his eyes. *Only I can do this.*

"Call your mother and tell her you'll be late. Tell her that you have a passenger who needs to deliver a package to Kiev that two Russian women gave him. Go ahead. We don't want her to worry."

"Why should she care about your package?"

"Do it!" Darius fumbled with the suitcase's front zipper and pulled out the gun.

"Sure." Filip's hands shook as he punched in the number of the last person who had phoned him.

"Mom?"

While missing the mother who didn't care about him, Darius hung onto Filip's every word. *Two Russian women, probably from Ukraine. Paid to deliver a package.* After Filip finished the call, Darius let out a long, slow breath. Filip's mother would tell the police. The explosion would be blamed on the Russians. NATO would react by sending troops into the Baltic countries. Darius's plan would work exactly as he had intended. No more waiting. He wouldn't even have to go to Kiev. He wouldn't have to suffer more days and nights of visits from Jonas, for he would atone for the old man's death. He would save his country. His job would be finished in seconds. Mere seconds.

Darius took a deep breath through the open window, relishing the air's sweetness. His heart slowed. He didn't feel dizzy anymore. How clever he was. In mere seconds, the world will think that he was a tragic victim of terrorism. By this time tomorrow, his country would be safe. His life would have meaning. His work was done. *Are you proud of me, Ignas?*

*"I give you credit for persistence," said Jonas.* He was standing outside the van, leaning in through the open window, inches away from Darius. The swelling on his neck had turned black.

"Are you with me? Do you understand what I'm doing? Why I'm doing it?" said Darius.

"Of course I'm with you," said Filip.

Darius exhaled. "Thank you." He had always dreamed that somehow, people all over the world would learn what he had done for his country and reward him by remembering his sacrifice. It would be hard to piece together the full story, but someone would. Someone always did.

Even if that never happened, his reward would be joining the proud millions who had died for their country over the centuries. Even if no one knew his sacrifice, or shed tears over his greatness cut short by death, he, like Ignas, would be a celebrated albiet anonymous hero.

"Do you forgive me, Jonas?" said Darius.

*"I'll see you in hell!" said Jonas.*

In death, Jonas would forgive him and learn to love him again. He had to. Darius was sure of it. Ignas would finally be with him. The mother he never knew would wait with open arms to greet him. It didn't matter that he didn't know whether she was dead or alive, or even what she looked like.

Darius leaned back against the seat. Yes, in death he would finally know love.

"Good bye, Filip." Darius took out the phone from his pocket, laid the gun on his lap, and began punching out a number. He paused to glance at the woman behind them getting out of her car. He thought she looked familiar as he turned his attention back to the phone.

# CHAPTER 44

## Kalvarija, Lithuania—21 May

Filip's last call and his ramblings about a package Darius was trying to deliver had raised the hairs on the back of Zuza's neck. She had asked Filip if he was in danger. He had responded simply: *yes*. She had asked if Darius had a gun: *yes*. When the connection went dead, she knew this was it. She was convinced Darius was about to detonate the bomb. There was no time left; no intervention possible. There was no hope of talking Darius down and convincing him to act like a rational human being. She had to act and pray that what she was about to do would be enough.

Zuza jumped out of the car and raced toward the passenger side of the van, knowing Rokas would be steps behind. Her gaze met Darius's in the side window, he looking back and she looking to the side as if some hand of fate had brought them together. He seemed oddly at peace. He didn't appear to care that she was there.

She pointed her service revolver at him through the open passenger side window. Darius continued to enter numbers into the mobile phone.

"Put the phone down, Darius," shouted Zuza.

He didn't react. It was as if he hadn't even heard her. Zuza stepped back and simply took the shot; a single bullet into the side of Darius's head, just an inch above his right ear, leaving a small red spot. He stopped, almost turning to her but not quite, almost reacting to the shot, but not quite. Then he collapsed.

With her gun still pointed at Darius, Zuza opened the door. The driver's side was awash in blood and gore. Desperately, she looked inside for the gun, praying she would find it. It was on the floor between Darius's legs. She picked it up.

Filip's face was covered in blood and pieces of gray matter, his eyes wide, the white color vivid against the red.

"Are you all right?" said Zuza.

Filip's answer was a scream.

Rokas opened the driver's side door, pulling Filip out of the van before guiding him away. She avoided the agent's gaze, unsure whether she would react with anger, triumph, or tears.

A chill seized her. She could almost taste the blood.

The phone lay on Darius's lap, his arm resting languidly to the side. She picked it up and examined the screen. He had entered five numbers. She cleared them out, guessing it was a detonation sequence. She felt his neck, and couldn't find a pulse, but she hadn't expected one.

She went around to the driver's side and put the gun down on the ground, knowing that the old weapon was probably unsafe. She holstered her gun and stepped up on the bumper. She reached in through the door, gently unzipping the bloody suitcase, stopping once to look at the red on her fingertips. She wondered if it would ever wash off. She hesitated before opening the lid, dreading that she would find only men's clothing inside. But there it was, clearly a bomb, replete with wiring in bright red and blue colors that looked almost cheerful, like something that belonged on a child's toy.

Zuza stepped down. Her ears were ringing.

Vit ran to her. "Are you all right?"

"All right. I'm all right," she said, the adrenaline that had driven her to take care of the crisis already beginning to fade.

Then Vit's arms were around her. He kissed her full on the mouth. All she knew was that they were safe and alive. Although she didn't really know this strange man who was kissing her, and it didn't make sense, she was drawn to him and it felt good.

As she stepped away from Vit, Rokas ran to them.

Zuza swallowed. "Take a look in the suitcase."

Rokas looked pale as he gazed into the van. "Well, lick a donkey's ass."

~~

Soon, several police vans arrived, along with two men in protective suits. Everyone moved a good distance away as the bomb disposal unit began their work by placing a containment unit over Darius's suitcase.

While this was going on, Zuza tried blocking the images of the blood-washed interior of the van, telling herself it had to be done. It was enough for a while, but eventually, the images of Darius's dead face came back. She took out her phone, pretending to make a call as she walked down the road behind one of the police cars parked near the trees. Alone for the first time since the shooting, the reality of what had happened hit her like a jab to the gut. She bent over and vomited into the weeds. As she spat out the bile, she remembered vomiting at the news of her father's death, and the little pieces of his body scattered on a London street. It felt like death was her constant companion. She wiped her lips with a tissue and put a breath mint in her mouth before going back to Rokas and Vit.

"Even Otto didn't believe you. How were you so sure?" said Rokas.

"I put a lot of pieces together," said Zuza.

"You couldn't have been certain."

"But I was."

"Well, you were right."

Rokas held out his hand. Zuza held up her palms, showing him Darius's dried blood on her fingers.

"I don't care," he said.

Zuza clasped his hand and looked him in the eye.

"Good damn job," he said. He got into his car, and before pulling away, rolled down his window. "See you back in Vilnius."

Zuza's phone rang: Otto. She brought him up to date.

"I know, Zuza. Rokas already told me. The president of Lithuania sends her congratulations."

"Wow."

"I'm sorry for not listening to you."

"Apology accepted. Thanks for setting up that roadblock. It did the trick. I didn't think it would, but you were right."

Zuza's next words came in an uncensored flood too powerful to stop. "Listen. It's about time you learned to trust the people who work for you. I'm sick of being challenged in simple decisions like keeping Vit with me. I'm sick of being told to make coffee. I'm sick of being the ARAS ambassador to every damned law enforcement officer in the country. I'm sick of being called back to base to do deskwork once my investigations start getting hot, while you send out the boys to chase down real leads. I'm going on strike. You're giving those jobs to someone else from now on. Try Rokas. I'm sure he'll appreciate the attention."

Zuza heard a smile in Otto's voice when he spoke. "I'll think about it. Good job, Zuza. Come on home. You got reports to fill out. By the way, how does it feel to have just saved your country?"

"Damned good." At that, Zuza's smile broke into a toothy grin.

# CHAPTER 45

## Moscow—21 May

Inside her Kremlin office, Vera stood under the massive chandelier, gazing at the room's distorted reflection in her grandmother's samovar. It had come from the bowels of Russia, as she had, and both had managed the journey strong and intact.

She felt a little sad recalling Nina's latest update on the crisis in Lithuania, and the dirty bomb found in a van occupied by Darius Artis near the Polish border. Of course, news of the incident had been recast as a robbery gone bad between two traveling companions, and the death of the perpetrator. There had been no mention of a bomb. Vera grinned at the similarities between Russian media and the free press of the western world; both organizations manipulated the news.

It was unfortunate, though, that her plan to expand Russia by occupying the land of neighboring Ukraine had failed, but there would be other opportunities. Besides, the Lithuanians had given her a fabulous idea: detonate a homemade nuclear device somewhere in Ukraine, then send in troops to help the survivors. Of course, it might take more than one bomb for the plan to work, but it was genius. All she needed to do was decide when. Perhaps those pesky Lithuanians were good for something after all.

A knock sounded on the door. She glanced at her watch. The last meeting of the day; Grinsky, a man whose legacy would be as enduring as the mark a pitchfork made in water. She sat down behind her desk. "Come."

Grinsky looked more smug than usual as he strode into her office.

"Just in time." Vera opened the bottom drawer of her desk and drew out the bottle of Khortytsa and two small glasses.

He sat across from her. She poured and handed him a glass. He downed it, exclaiming his satisfaction with a smack of his lips. *No civility at all, this one,* thought Vera. *Nyekulturi!*

"I wanted to tell you about our investigation into the riot at Novosibirsk," said Vera.

Grinsky put his glass down. "You know the instigators?"

"Not yet. But we know the plastic explosive was made in the US."

"We should have suspected the Americans from the start. There's plenty of chatter online about how the US government is trying to influence our citizens and government policies."

"The Americans love their internet."

"But this is wonderful news, Madame President. I suggest we use this information to force the Americans and the EU to lift their sanctions against us, or at least modify them. Unfortunately, I don't expect them to offer an apology or to even be embarrassed by this. There's so little that embarrasses people these days."

*You're right about that, Grinsky.*

Smiling, he continued. "If we're sure the Americans are behind the riot in Novosibirsk, there's no need to continue any investigation. It's done. We know what happened. And we can focus on making them pay for what they did. This horrible embarrassment is over for you, Madame President."

*Impudent bastard.* Why was he so happy about dropping the investigation? There had to be a reason. She remembered Grinsky's advice not to run for the presidency when her term ran out, his look of envy when he had touched her chair at the first meeting of her inner circle, his comments about keeping the status quo, and now this. It came to her like a splash of water to the face. She should have put things together before, but she had been too distracted by those damned Lithuanians to connect the threads in the web.

*Grinsky had a role in the riots.* She didn't know what role, or how significant, but she knew he was involved. Somehow. *He had to be.*

"I suspect the Kremlin will issue a statement condemning the West for this blatant act of aggression," said Grinsky.

Vera took in a sharp breath. "No. Not yet. I want to keep this a secret for now."

Grinsky waited, as if expecting Vera to say something more. He looked uncomfortable. When she didn't speak, he continued. "It's all for the best. Our businessmen were happy with the way things were under Fedov. Our companies are doing well. All you have to do is send our troops back to their barracks. You'll be scaling back the military, won't you? I've heard complaints that workers are nervous now that armed soldiers are protecting their facilities, especially those involved with the Nord Stream 2 pipeline."

"I think we'll leave our soldiers where they are for a while. Your businessmen will get used to having them around, eventually. Of course, you must keep everything I've told you this evening confidential. For now." She put the bottle of vodka away.

"Of course. It would be treasonous to go against your orders, Madame President."

"I'm glad we understand each other."

~~

The elegant dining room was empty as it was late for dinner, but Nina had reserved the room anyway. Anyone trying to enter would be turned away until she'd left. Rank had its privileges. Crisp white tablecloths and gleaming china enhanced the softly polished mahogany walls in an elegant touch of Old Russia. Nina chose a table that seated four and sat down, the waiter rushing to help her with her chair. Orlov sat down across from her. The waiter removed the other two place settings, and a moment later returned with a decanter of red wine. He poured out two glasses and left. He came back carrying a platter on a tray. He lifted the lid and dished out the *golubtsi*, meat-filled cabbage rolls in a sauce of tomato puree, laced with sour cream.

Orlov ate with gusto. Nina picked at her food. She put down her fork after a few bites. "I want an update on the riots in Novosibirsk."

He stopped chewing. "I thought we were blaming it on the Americans—a plot to sway the people against Vera Koslova."

Nina gave him a cold stare.

"Nonetheless," he continued, dabbing his mouth with a napkin, "we're still working to find out who was behind the attacks. Our investigation has to be done discreetly, and it's taking time."

"So you have nothing."

"As far as we know, Grinsky had nothing to do with it. At least we have no clear indication that he gave the order. Not yet."

"Who do you suspect?"

"We're investigating Rozoff, the oil billionaire from Siberia. He's behind Nord Stream 2. More than that, we think he's behind the protests against the planned nuclear power plant in Belarus."

"Rozoff is backing the demonstrators?"

"We believe he's funding the protests, yes. The Lithuanians are the most vocal opponents to the power plant, as it's so close to their border. They're calling it evil, saying if there's an explosion similar to what happened at Chernobyl, the Exclusion Zone would extend well into Lithuania, virtually making their country unlivable. Rozoff doesn't want that plant to be built because nuclear power would drastically reduce Belarus dependence on Russian gas, which would directly affect Rozoff's bottom line as well as Russia's economy, of course."

Orlov took another bite. "But Vera Koslova supports the power plant in Belarus. Maybe she just wants to irritate the Lithuanians."

"Let's not assume we know what Vera Koslova is thinking. Do you have anyone in the Rozoff camp?"

"Yes, a woman who is finessing an asset. Once she turns him, we'll know more. It may take months, though."

"We don't have that much time. Have her turn him now." Nina sat back and crossed her legs, watching Orlov eat. He seemed calmer than usual, and a bit detached. For a fleeting moment, she wondered if he were involved in the riots. She took a sip of wine. Soon it would be time for her to look into this herself, find the conspirators, and put a noose around the devil's neck. But uncovering a conspiracy against Vera Koslova, if there was one, was work for another day.

# CHAPTER 46

## Vilnius, Lithuania—22 May

Twenty-four hours after Darius Artis was killed in a van near the Polish border, Vit was in bed, pulling the sheet up over his bare chest. He was tired, but aside from that, he felt damn good. The air smelled of linen. The shades were drawn, and the gray light that remained made it feel peaceful. At the special ring identifying his mother's phone call which Annie had just selected as Brunnhilde's "War Cry," Vit sighed. His trousers lay crumpled on the floor, his phone in a pocket. He let it go to voicemail and clicked on the lamp over the night stand.

The soft light showed details of the room. The bedding looked relatively new, definitely modern, but the nightstands were worn, the uneven finish presenting an invitation for coffee cups or tumblers of vodka to be set down without concern to the rings and spots left behind. A wall of books to the left, and a painting of Zuma beach in Malibu to the right. Four pillows in an exotic print were scattered over the floor, among other pieces of his clothing, and Zuza's.

She came in carrying a tray, and wearing Vit's button-down shirt, the muscles in her legs flexing as she walked. He felt a rush of warmth. She put the tray on the nightstand and filled two small glasses halfway with *suktinis*, a spicy and potent mead liqueur. She handed him one.

Smiling, Zuza passed him a plate of rye bread and thin slices of smoked ham. She got into bed and pulled the sheet up. She held up her glass in a toast. *"Į sveikatą!"* They clicked their tumblers together and sipped. Vit made them both an open-face sandwich and set the plate down between them on the bed.

"After all that happened, I've forgotten about poor Jonas. Did you ever find out what happened to him?" said Vit.

"We haven't found him, but in all likelihood, he's dead."

"Do you think Darius killed him?"

"The protégée killed the master? I don't know. Anything's possible."

"I'm going to have nightmares for a long time about Bok."

"Don't worry, Vit. He was spotted at the airport, leaving the country. If he comes back and you're still here, I'll protect you. I don't think Bok is going to Boston to find you. Did you know that the maintenance team at Police Headquarters found a tracking device on my car?"

"It explains how he found us at the sodyba. I find all this unbelievable."

"Believe it."

"What's going to happen to my grandmother?"

"Tilda's old and sick. She doesn't have much time left. Extradition alone would take a good deal of time and effort. We're not going to pursue any action against her."

"She made a hard choice in assisting with that bomb. I never considered how difficult her life had been growing up here. I wonder if I would've done the same thing in her situation. At one point, I thought she was crazy. Now, I think all of her decisions were deliberate, and she simply came to regret what she had done even though at the time, she thought it was the right thing to do. I wish she were well enough to know that her bomb isn't a threat anymore."

"And you can't tell her. We're putting the lid on this. We have to. Even the thought of how close Darius came to detonating that bomb would bring a panic. The public knowing how close we came to a nuclear disaster would be a disaster in itself. As far as the world knows, Darius died while robbing a man who was giving him a ride. Besides, if what you told me is accurate, Tilda may not even remember the bomb, let alone why she asked you to come here. Let's hope so, anyway. Word of the near incident can never get out. You're sworn to silence. If we hear anything about this, you're the first person I'm going interrogate." Zuza's expression was playful, but her tone dead serious.

"Yes, ma'am."

"Let's just hope we're never confronted with nuclear terrorism again." Zuza took another sip of *suktinis*.

Vit shook his head. "What's going to happen to Baltic Watch?"

"Technically, there is no Baltic Watch without Jonas. He did a real service to the country, offering political analysis and fresh perspective. The organization needs someone like that; sharp, smart. Someone who can find bits of data and tie them together into a comprehensive picture. Someone unafraid to speak up. Someone who can build an organization from the ground up. Only time will tell if anyone steps in."

"Are you implying I should take over for Jonas?"

Zuza shrugged. "But you're going back home to sell your company and become rich."

"Well, I have to get back and hash through agreements until the sale is final. But I'd like to come back—I haven't seen much of the country yet, except for inside the police station here in Vilnius."

"You're leaving right away?" She raised an eyebrow.

"After I go back to Utena for my things and the rental car."

"I took the liberty of asking Rokas to take care of that for you. He owed me a favor. In fact, he owes me a lot of favors to make up for how badly he's been treating me. Your car and belongings should be here tomorrow."

Vit cocked his head. "Here?"

"Yes, at my apartment." She clicked her glass against his again. "If you stayed a few days, I could show you the city: Old Town, the cathedral, the cafes and shops. There's even a church the Soviets made into a basketball court. Of course, the hoops have been taken down and the church made beautiful again. I know you'll love it. Everyone does."

"I have a lot to do at home." He picked up another slice of ham. "But maybe another day here wouldn't hurt. I have found Lithuania to be full of surprises. Besides, I know Sagus is in good hands with Max."

"Once you sell the company, what happens to Annie?"

"She comes with me. She's mine forever."

"You'll have enough money to live well for the rest of your life. What if you get bored? Maybe you should consider something new.

You're too young to retire." She put down her glass and moved the plate of food to a nightstand.

"Like what? Taking over at Baltic Watch?"

"Baltic Watch could use someone with your creativity, and your computer skills. You said you liked politics. You might like living here for a while. You could at least try it."

"I'll have to brush up on my Lithuanian."

"I'm good with languages."

Vit grinned. "Are you sure it's not Annie you really want?"

Annie's voice sounded through the phone's speaker. "Yes, Vit, is there something you need?"

He reached down for his trousers, found his phone, and turned it off. Zuza leaned toward him and draped her arms around his neck.

"So, are you offering to show me around Vilnius?" said Vit, drawing her close.

Zuza put her lips against his. He didn't get an answer.

THE END

# ABOUT THE AUTHOR

Ursula Wong writes gripping stories about strong women struggling against impossible odds to achieve their dreams. Her work has appeared in *Everyday Fiction, Spinetingler Magazine, Mystery Reader's Journal,* and the *Insanity Tales* anthologies. She is a professional speaker appearing regularly on TV and radio.

Wong's debut novel, *Purple Trees,* and the enchanting Peruvian folk tale, *The Baby Who Fell From the Sky,* are available on Amazon and other online retailers.

Her World War II thriller *Amber Wolf,* the first in the Amber War series, is about a young Lithuanian woman who joins resistance fighters. *Amber War,* the second in the series, tells a little-known story of post-World War II Eastern Europe and the continuing fight against the Soviet occupation. *Amber Widow,* third book in the series, matches Eastern European radicals against Russia in a vicious game of nuclear chess.

Connect Online:
Website: http://ursulawong.wordpress.com
Email: urslwng@gmail.com

## *Other works by Ursula Wong*

*Amber Wolf (The Amber War Series Book 1)*

*Amber War (The Amber War Series Book 2)*

*Purple Trees*

*The Baby Who Fell From the Sky*

### With other Authors

*Insanity Tales*

*Insanity Tales II: The Sense of Fear*

*Insanity Tales III: Seasons of Shadow: A Collection of Dark Fiction*

Ursula is available for speaking events and lectures on writing and publishing. For more information, contact her at urslwng@gmail.com and sign up for her popular Reaching Readers newsletter at http://ursulawong.wordpress.com.

# LIST OF CHARACTERS

Annie – Sagus computer program and Vit's personal assistant.

Arkady – Jonas's Russian friend.

Darius Artis – Second in command at Baltic Watch.

Ignas Artis – Partisan. Darius's father.

Zuza Bartus – ARAS agent assigned to investigate Baltic Watch.

Alexy Bok – Contract killer for the Russian SVR.

Boris – Russian guard at the Ignalina Nuclear Power Plant. Steals nuclear material and sells it to the partisans.

Mrs. Brown – IT Manager from Homeland Security.

Elena – Jonas Volkis's neighbor in Utena.

David – Zuza's ex-boyfriend.

Nina Ditlova – Special assistant to Vera Koslova, and her friend.

Ivan Ditlov – Nina Ditlova's grandfather, advisor to President Putin.

Galina – The name of Babushka's cow.

Urte Gatus – Old woman from the camp in Irkutsk.

Grinsky – Prime Minister of Russia.

Paulius Juras – Police officer in Kaunas.

Rokas Klem – ARAS agent.

Rina Kleptys – Simona's sister. Car thief.

Simona Kleptys – Rina's sister. Car thief.

Michael Koslov – Vera Koslova's husband.

Vera Yaroslavna Koslova – President of Russia.

Leva Krukas – Otto Krukas's daughter. Zuza's friend.

Otto Krukas – Zuza Bartus's boss at ARAS. Leva's father.

Filip Lemski – Darius's hostage.

Lukas – Owner of Lukas's bar.

Max – Second in charge at Sagus. Reports to Vit Partenkas.

Misha – Guard at the Ignalina Nuclear Power Plant.

Tomas – Worker at the Ignalina Nuclear Power Plant. Boris's friend.

Orlov – Deputy Director of the FSB.

Vit Partenkas – Tilda Partenkas's grandson. IT expert. Owner of Sagus Corporation.

Tilda Partenkas – Nuclear physicist, co-inventor of the anti-radiation drug Z-109.

Yuri Rozoff – Russian oligarch and oil billionaire.

Senelis – Vit's grandfather, Tilda's husband.

Smirnov – Vera's secretary.

Jonas Volkis – Head of Baltic Watch.

# READING LIST

*In Wartime: Stories from Ukraine,* Tim Judah, Tim Duggan Books, New York, 2015.

*"Nuclear Smuggling and Threats to Lithuanian Security,"* Egle Nuraukaite, Lithuanian Annual Strategic Review 2015-2016, University of Maryland.

*Poland,* James Michener, Ballantine Books, NY, NY, 1983.

*Putin's Russia,* Lilia Shevtsova, Carnegie Endowment for International Peace, Washington DC, 2003.

*Red Sparrow,* Jason Matthews, Thorndike Press, Detroit, MI, 2013.

*Secondhand Time,* Svetlana Alexievich, Random House, NY, NY, 2016.

*The New Tsar: The Rise and Reign of Vladimir Putin,* Steven Lee Myers, Alfred A. Knopf, 2015.

*The Putin Mystique,* Anna Arutunyan, Olive Branch Press, Northhampton, MA, 2014.

48987765R00137

Made in the USA
Middletown, DE
17 June 2019